THE RELENTLESS DEAD

More tales of the Astra Militarum from Black Library

KRIEG
A novel by Steve Lyons

SIEGE OF VRAKS
A novel by Steve Lyons

DEAD MEN WALKING
A novel by Steve Lyons

MINKA LESK: THE LAST WHITESHIELD
An omnibus edition of the novels *Cadia Stands, Cadian Honour, Traitor Rock* and several short stories
by Justin D Hill

SHADOW OF THE EIGHTH
A novel by Justin D Hill

HELL'S LAST
A novel by Justin D Hill

THE FALL OF CADIA
A novel by Robert Rath

CREED: ASHES OF CADIA
A novel by Jude Reid

DEATHWORLDER
A novel by Victoria Hayward

LONGSHOT
A novel by Rob Young

KASRKIN
A novel by Edoardo Albert

CATACHAN DEVIL
A novel by Justin Woolley

STEEL TREAD
A novel by Andy Clark

VOLPONE GLORY
A novel by Nick Kyme

WITCHBRINGER
A novel by Steven B Fischer

VAINGLORIOUS
A novel by Sandy Mitchell

WARHAMMER 40,000

THE RELENTLESS DEAD

STEVE LYONS

BLACK LIBRARY

A BLACK LIBRARY PUBLICATION

First published in 2025.
This edition published in Great Britain in 2026 by
Black Library, Games Workshop Ltd., Willow Road,
Nottingham, NG7 2WS, UK.

Represented by: Games Workshop Limited – Irish branch,
Unit 3, Lower Liffey Street, Dublin 1,
D01 K199, Ireland.

10 9 8 7 6 5 4 3 2 1

Produced by Games Workshop in Nottingham.
Cover illustration by Igor Kieryluk.

A CIP record for this book is available from the British Library.

ISBN 13: 978-1-83609-396-1

Printed and bound in the UK.

For more than a hundred centuries the Emperor has sat immobile on the Golden Throne of Earth. He is the Master of Mankind. By the might of his inexhaustible armies a million worlds stand against the dark.

Yet, he is a rotting carcass, the Carrion Lord of the Imperium held in life by marvels from the Dark Age of Technology and the thousand souls sacrificed each day so his may continue to burn.

To be a man in such times is to be one amongst untold billions. It is to live in the cruelest and most bloody regime imaginable. It is to suffer an eternity of carnage and slaughter. It is to have cries of anguish and sorrow drowned by the thirsting laughter of dark gods.

This is a dark and terrible era where you will find little comfort or hope. Forget the power of technology and science. Forget the promise of progress and advancement. Forget any notion of common humanity or compassion.

There is no peace amongst the stars, for in the grim darkness of the far future, there is only war.

I

The prisoner was held deep underground.

The witch hunter tightened his satin-lined cloak as he made the winding descent down worn stone steps into the foetid cold.

His duties had taken him to many such dungeons, on many backwater worlds, but something about this one was different. He felt the weight of the place's damp black soil pressing on his chest – the weight of its dry, dead bones.

The jailer, a hunchbacked servitor whose parchment skin had surely never been exposed to daylight, unlocked a cell for him. The light of sconce-mounted torches in the passageway spilled over the crumpled form therein.

Though manacled, bloodied, soaked in her own filth, the prisoner glared up at her visitors defiantly. 'At last,' she huffed, 'somebody in authority! Do you know who I am, and how long I have been kept waiting here?'

The witch hunter's most thuggish acolyte sprang forward,

stopping her mouth with a meaty fist. 'Speak only when Inquisitor Idelax demands an answer from you!'

The prisoner spluttered indignantly, but heeded the caution.

She was wrapped in a lady's robes, but they were torn, dirty, stripped of their fine accoutrements. She had lived a pampered life, so the witch hunter was given to believe, and thus he had expected to find her spirit broken. Ideally, his acolytes would have had a few days with her, to wrench a confession from her throat, but time was of the essence, so he chose another tack.

Inquisitor Idelax crouched before the chained dignitary. Defiance melted into a desperate appeal as her red-rimmed eyes found his. Blood trickled from her swollen lip. The witch hunter knew his smile looked like a trap, but also that his prey had no way to avoid it. With honey in his voice, he laid the bait.

'My lady, I hear there has been a terrible misunderstanding.'

Lady Emelian recalled her first impressions of Oleris III.

She had wrinkled her nose and complained as her shoe squelched into its mud, but a wet foot had become her least concern.

An overcast sky had cast a grey pall over churned-up fields and simple tracks. Though a serf had hefted a parasol over her head, still a mean wind had whipped her powdered face with shards of rain. Modest headstones had stretched beyond her sight. This entire world had felt oppressive to her.

Though she had travelled here in search of life, now she had felt keenly that this was a place of death – perhaps, she thought fleetingly, her own.

Her titled husband had expressed the same foreboding. Had he only held his tongue, she might have mustered the strength to turn back. Instead, she had despised him for his weakness and marched on to their damnation.

'Tell me what brought you to this world,' the inquisitor demanded.

'To pay our respects to the sainted Josefina, why else?'

He showed no reaction to the lie. The lady had no doubt that he had discerned it, all the same. Her guilty silence hung between them until she felt compelled to add, 'And in hope that her spirit might bestow a great blessing upon us.'

Inquisitor Idelax nodded. That was more like it.

'You may be aware that my... our son is interred here.'

'I am aware that you went to great lengths to arrange it.'

'The invitation was extended,' said the lady. 'We were perfectly entitled to accept it.'

'Of that, I am also aware,' he said.

'My son was a soldier of the Emperor, proud and true. A captain in His Astra Militarum, decorated for his valour. Torn from us by some filthy xenos bomb on a foreign battlefield.' Her voice trembled with her deepest grief exhumed. 'They couldn't even piece him back together.'

A thousand Guardsmen had perished that fateful day, too brave and loyal to withdraw from a hopeless battle. Her son had ordered them to stand their ground. At punitive expense, Lady Emelian had chartered a necrofreighter to gather their remains and ship them to a better resting place. She refused to abandon him to rot where he had fallen, in eternal anonymity, not the merest scrap of him.

'You came to Oleris for him,' said Idelax.

'Yes, we did, only for him. I wished to see the monument we had commissioned for him. We wished to be close to him, pray for him.'

Idelax's eyes flashed as he leaned closer to her. 'And?'

Naivety was not one of the lady's flaws. Despite his handsome face and gracious manner, she knew whom she faced.

She knew that, no matter where they looked, few witch hunters ever failed to find a witch. But this was her chance, her first and last, to plead her case, her one slim hope if she could make him understand.

She met his gaze unflinchingly. 'And speak with him,' she said.

She remembered:

Everything about the monument was wrong. The sculptor had entirely failed to capture her son's likeness, despite the holo-pict she had provided. His stance lacked nobility. He was cast in too dark a shade of bronze, and his eternal flame burnt neither highly nor brightly enough.

Enumerating these defects at length, she tuned out the whispering behind her. She assumed it was only a serf requesting her attention. The lord and lady had brought just a skeleton staff, wishing this to be a discreet visit, and they had been instructed to stand back for this intensely private moment.

The voice intruded again, and the lady whipped around with a piece of her mind ready, but nobody was behind her.

She turned to her husband. 'Did you hear that?' she demanded, but as usual he only looked bewildered. She rounded on their guide, a plain young girl with plain, straight hair in plain hessian robes. 'I heard a voice. Tell me you heard it too.'

'It may have been meant for your ears alone, milady.'

'Then... it is indeed true, what they say?'

Lady Emelian swallowed dryly. Her husband tried to speak, but impatiently she shushed him. She listened as hard as she could, wishing her heart would quiet its pounding, and at first there was only the mournful wailing of the wind, but then she fancied she heard soft words carried upon it.

'Father, mother, I am here, can you not hear me?'

She threw a hand up to her mouth, stifling a racking sob.

She looked at her husband again and he returned her glare with haunted eyes, his gaunt face pale. This time, there was no doubt about it.

This time, the lady knew the voice was real.

'Sorcery!' hissed Idelax.

'No! I mean, we did not know,' the prisoner protested.

'Is that not what brought you to Oleris III? The true reason? Is that not why you had your son's remains shipped here?'

'We only wished to speak with him again. Just one more time. I had to know that he... that he was at peace.'

'Your son fought for the Emperor, died for Him, died with honour.'

The lady agreed vehemently: 'Yes. With honour.'

'But you would not accept his noble fate.'

'I heard... Certain rumours reached our ears. It is said that, on Oleris, the veil between life and death is stretched thin and can be parted, but I swear not by such means as you suggest.'

'How else?' the witch hunter accused her. 'How else but by consort with the vilest, darkest powers could you hope to raise the dead?'

'By the grace of a saint!' the lady wailed.

Idelax straightened and paced the cramped confines of the cell, clasping his hands behind his back. He let the prisoner believe that she had given him pause for thought, judging this to be the most expedient way to keep her talking.

She continued, 'On my world, on Vostroya, it is custom that the firstborn child of every family is given into service.'

'More than custom,' Idelax snapped. 'It is a duty shouldered gladly by your people in atonement for your sins.'

The lady inclined her head in meek acknowledgement. 'But, inquisitor, what of we who...? What if, through no fault of our own, one child is all we have and there is no other to further our bloodlines, our titles and our lands?'

'You do your duty as well and accept that it has been thus ordained.'

'Of course,' the prisoner agreed, 'of course we do. Of course we did. But when that child, our only child, is sent to fight and...' She choked back the rest of the sentence, taking several shuddering breaths before speaking again.

'Is it really so wrong of us to pray that our duty, our loyalty, might be recognised, at least? That the Emperor might bestow a fraction of His great mercy upon us? Tell me, inquisitor, is it such a sin for the likes of us to have faith in a miracle?'

The truth was, in her heart, she had known everything was wrong.

She had felt it, perching on a dirty wooden pew inside a dirty wooden hut that, though its walls were chalked with holy symbols and though candles burnt atop a simple altar, resembled no chapel she had seen before.

She had found it incongruous for such a ritual as this to be staged in such grubby surroundings – and by such grubby congregants and clergy members, gravediggers with stooped backs and filth beneath their fingernails.

She had silenced her husband as he tried to voice similar concerns. They had reached out formally to Oleris' priests, she reminded him, impressing the force of their many titles upon them, but had not been so much as acknowledged. What choice had they been left with?

As wrong as their being here felt, it could only be right. It had to be. So, Lady Emelian had bitten her tongue and borne her great discomfort.

She remembered:

Red fingers of the setting sun probing between the wall slats, shadows lengthening beyond their reach. The heady scent of incense, almost blotting out the odour of their hosts. The lady joined in prayers to the Master of Mankind, feeling that this made it better, the words forming a shield of faith around her. Faith that deserved its reward.

Her heart sang as she heard the voice again. It was stronger and clearer than it had been outside. The speaker could almost have been seated in the pew behind her, but this time she knew better than to look.

'Father. Mother.'

'We hear you, son.' The words emerged from her throat as a deathly whisper.

'Thank the Emperor. I have been so lost, so alone.'

'We are here now. You have no need to fear.'

'So cold. Why? Why am I so cold? Where am I? What happened to me?'

The music in Lady Emelian's heart died.

She searched the other faces in the chapel for inspiration, but her husband's face was frozen, his damp hand leaching strength from hers, while the others' eyes were closed, their lips still forming incantations. 'You did your duty, son. You made us proud, and you can rest now.'

'I cannot,' the disembodied voice insisted. His voice, exactly as she remembered it, perhaps a little younger than when last she had heard it. *'Mother, there are things here. Screaming, clawing, biting things.'*

'Then you must do as we always instructed you. Fight. Fight for Him as you did in life. Fight your way to His side. He will protect you.'

'There are so many of them, too many, tearing, gnawing at my soul. I am so weak, so tired of fighting and so very, very cold. I need you, mother!'

A savage gust of wind rattled the wooden walls and snuffed out the altar candles. The lady heard shocked gasps around her – and emitted a small squeal herself – as the hut was plunged into darkness.

She called out to her son, but he was gone. Instead she heard a female voice. The voice of the plain young congregant, she thought.

'The veil has once more closed around him. For now, he is beyond our reach.'

'No. You must get him back. I insist you bring him back. I will pay any price. Anything you ask.' A whimper of protest from her husband raised her ire. 'You heard him. You heard our son. He is in torment.' She turned back to where she thought the girl was. 'Please. There must be something you can do, a way to save him?'

She heard a striking match. A candle was relit and, in its glow, a wizened figure came to sit beside her. The woman who had led the ceremony. The others had deferred to her as if she held some rank, although no one had said as much and her vestments were as plain as theirs. Close up to her now, the lady saw that she was younger than she had looked, her face prematurely lined and worn. Wisps of white hair escaped from her hood – or were they blonde?

The wizened woman laid a gnarled hand on the lady's knee. 'Perhaps,' she said. 'One thing alone.'

The prisoner sighed. 'I see it now. I see it clearly, though I couldn't in the moment. I see how we were drawn into...' She met the witch hunter's steely glare and couldn't quite make the confession. 'But surely you too understand why we did what we did?'

Idelax growled, 'I see that you were weak of faith.'

'No! Our faith was strong, as it has always been, even when

most sorely tested. But must faith not also necessarily be blind? Is that not how our priests instruct us? We were blind, my husband and I, and our blind faith was used against us.'

He was tiring of her self-justifications. 'Faith that drove you to take a life!'

'Not take. Our intention was to exchange one life for another. A worthless soul for the soul of a nobleman, a soldier. A far better servant for the Emperor.'

The witch hunter's voice was like a breaking storm. 'Your faith, I believe, was only in yourself and your own selfish desires!'

His prisoner burst into tears as she let go of her final shred of hope. He had seen it happen many times before.

'We wanted… I needed to believe,' she sobbed. 'That was my only crime. I only acted out of love – you must believe me, only ever out of love. Have mercy upon me!'

She remembered:

Another fitful night in a stifling cabin aboard a merchant ship. Whenever the lady closed her eyes, behind them she saw her son's face, frozen at an age before his moustache had grown out. He was screaming.

Trudging through the planet's mud again as twilight glimmered. Asking why the ritual must be conducted in the dark, she was told the veil was thinnest then. Back to the ramshackle hut that it helped her to think of as the chapel. They had left most of their staff in orbit, bringing only one serf with them today. She had picked out the strongest, healthiest of them. The young-old woman, whom she chose to call the pastor, examined him as a butcher might a slab of meat. 'Yes, he will do nicely,' she said.

The lord and lady took their seats.

The lady had not prepared herself for her serf's sudden panic. She avoided his beseeching eyes as he was hauled up onto the altar. He started to struggle against his robed captors, too late, as ropes secured his wrists and ankles. 'Milord, milady,' he howled, 'haven't I been loyal to you?'

Squeezing her husband's hand tightly, she kept him in his pew.

The ceremony itself was interminable, as the pastor led her followers in endless murmured chants around the altar. Unable to make out the words, instead the lady bowed her head and mouthed her own silent prayers. At some point, it occurred to her that she had been praying for forgiveness.

The realisation made her blood run cold. It flushed the haze of sweet incense from her mind, and with it the lies she had been telling herself.

Lady Emelian leapt to her feet, startling her husband, and drew breath to speak up in protest at this terrible transgression. The words never came, because at that second the chanting swelled to its triumphant climax and the pastor plunged a black-bladed dagger into the bound serf's heart.

He screamed.

The altar candles flared fiercely and died.

Despite this, somehow there was light to see as the congregants dropped to their knees in awe. Only the lady, and now her husband beside her, were left standing as the body on the altar stirred. Ropes fell away from it, unwinding into slender threads, as it swung its legs over the side and levered itself to its feet.

For a moment there it stood, swaying slightly as if testing its balance, and the lady realised that the dim light was coming from its green-glowing eyes.

Eyes that now turned upon her.

The serf's body, or whatever controlled it, took a jerky step towards her. Its torn tunic exposed the glistening wound in its chest, from which miraculously no blood flowed. Lifting an arm like a dead weight, it reached for her. A guttural snarl welled from its throat, resolving itself into a slurred word: 'Mother!'

The lady couldn't help herself. Despite everything her heart and mind were screaming at her, in a tremulous voice she spoke her dead son's name. 'Eoric? Is that... you?'

'You... did it... saved me from that... torture.'

'No, don't come any closer!'

He halted as she bade him, as she warded him off with raised hands, but she saw the same look of confusion and fear in the serf's face that had been there before. That same look of betrayal.

'How do I know it's really you?' she asked.

His speech was already clearer. 'I knew you'd find me, mother. It was my faith in you that strengthened me in that thrice-damned place. I knew you would come for me and take me home. May we go home now, mother?'

She said, 'A ship is waiting for us.'

'I long to see my home again. I miss the salty taste of ohx and the gritty smell of industry. I long to reunite with cousin Laena as I promised her we would when we parted. She must have ascended to the ruling council now?'

Tears stung the lady's eyes. She couldn't speak. All she could do was open her heart and her arms to the unkempt, shambling figure before her, the only one who had ever truly found a place in either. Drawing together, they embraced, and she clung to the still-cold body that wasn't her son's body, but it didn't matter now. Nothing in this world or any other mattered but this, but the two of them together.

She said, 'I'll never let you leave my sight again. If they come for you again, then I shall fight them to my final breath.'

'Take me home, please,' he begged her.

'I will,' the lady swore. 'I will, my son.'

She turned to her husband.

She saw the knife in his hand.

She couldn't stop him. Never had she seen such resolve in Lord Emelian before. She howled as he plunged his blade into her son's fresh wound. Almost gleefully, he worked it to draw out the blood that had been stopped there. Perhaps he ought to have paused to ask himself, if one knife blow had not severed this body's life thread, then why would another?

His victim groaned in pain but didn't fold. He lashed out with his knuckles to the noble lord's face, sending him sprawling. One hand clamped to his gushing chest, he raised the other. His eyes flashed, and that same green energy coalesced around his outstretched fingertip. Crackling, it flared to strike the prone and trembling lord.

The serf's face had contorted into a mask of purest malice, and when the thing inside him spoke again, its rasping voice pained the lady's ears. Her son's tongue could certainly never have shaped the profanities it spewed.

Her husband writhed and whimpered in green fire. She smelled his burning hair and skin. Turning to the altar, she saw no salvation there. The congregants cowered around it, most gaping at the scene in abject horror. Contrary to her later assertions, she believed that they had genuinely not expected this.

Then, locking gazes with the young-old pastor, she saw satisfaction in her eyes and a smile tugging at her dry, cracked lips.

She did the only thing she could possibly have done. She turned and bolted.

The lady knocked her shin on the corner of a pew. Her impractical shoes, already soiled and split, turned under her and she crashed into the hut's door, splintering its wood. A bright green flash dazzled her, and she felt her lacquered hair bristling. Only her fall, she realised, had saved her from a blast that had passed above her head.

She couldn't think about that now, else she would lose her mind. Blindly, she fumbled for a latch and found it. She tumbled through the door into the cold, wet night. As she scrambled to her feet in the mud, the lady's head turned and she caught a last glimpse of the thing behind her, in the chapel. The daemon – how could she have mistaken it for anything but? Its green-burning eyes were fixed upon her, casting the face of her old serf into shadow.

Its fingertip was poised to strike again, but then, with a grunt, it doubled over, clutching at its wound. The lady felt an unfamiliar sensation. She was grateful for her husband's actions. Her husband, whose blackened, twisted body lay on the chapel floor. She couldn't think about that either.

In its slow, thick, rasping voice, the daemon-thing commanded, ***'Stop her!'***

So, the lady ran.

'Evidently, you made your escape,' said Inquisitor Idelax.

'I know not how, if not by the Emperor's grace.'

He scowled at her presumption. 'I find that doubtful, unless He wished only that I find you. Did the entity in your servant's body pursue you?'

The prisoner shook her head. 'No. I mean, not that I saw, but perhaps I… I did not wish to see, so I…'

'Did not look back,' he concluded.

'In the dark, I knew not to where I ran, nor for how long before my straining heart and lungs arrested me. I only ran.'

'Leaving your husband to his fate.'

She left the accusation unaddressed. 'I came upon another hut, a shed. I broke it open with a rock and, though it shames me to admit it, sheltered in there beneath a pile of rags. Throughout the night, I heard footsteps and voices without, and presumed the members of that blasphemous church to be seeking me out.'

'And once daylight returned?'

'I fortified myself with prayer and set off to find a priest, anybody in authority, to tell of the horrors I had witnessed.'

That was another lie. The prisoner had found her way to a provincial landing pad where, bedraggled and shaken as she was, she had drawn a constable's attention while attempting to contact her orbiting vessel. Her incoherent answers to his questions had only inflamed his suspicions, and so it was he who had alerted the governing priesthood.

So, the lady had found herself shackled in the vaults beneath their tower. So the Inquisition had received an astropathic message, and so Idelax had been despatched to this backwater world. He didn't tell her that he knew all this. He had just one thing left to say to her.

'As soon as it can be arranged, you will be taken from this cell and executed by beheading.'

He had made such pronouncements to many beaten wretches like her, and their reactions varied wildly. In Lady Emelian's case, her shoulders sagged in resignation. She seemed almost relieved to know her fate. It would not last.

'I suggest you use your short remaining time to reflect upon your sins and pray for absolution.' The witch hunter turned on his heel and strode out of the cell, his acolytes straggling behind him. The servitor jailer slammed the door shut, turned its heavy locks and drew its bolts.

The prisoner had told Idelax little he had not already deduced. Oleris III had been thought well rid of its witches, but evidently some had escaped the brutal purges and had since grown in power. *To have drawn an entity from the immaterium, given it corporeal form!*

He shuddered at the thought and cursed the fools who – albeit in ignorance – had abetted this ultimate transgression. Nor had they been the first, for how else had the rumours spread that had lured these fools here? Their weakness had endangered every soul upon this planet and perhaps across the galaxy itself.

Halfway up the winding steps, from far below Idelax heard the inevitable pounding of fists upon plasteel. He heard the muffled voice of a condemned woman, protesting her innocence anew.

'I acted through faith and love alone,' she screeched in vain, 'and... and I am a noblewoman of Vostroya with friends in the highest courts. You cannot treat me like this, you have not the authority. Do you hear me? Come back! Come back at once, I command you, and unchain me.

'Do you know who I am?'

When the lady's throat was raw and her knuckles skinned and bleeding, she sank back against her cold stone wall and wept.

She wallowed in her misery until it was punctured by an unexpected sound. A whisper from inside the cell itself. She stiffened, her eyes seeking out shapes in the gloom. Was there a patch of deeper darkness over there? A patch in the shape of a proud, young Vostroyan soldier?

'Leave me be,' she croaked in fear.

'Mother,' came the whisper. Was it really there, she wondered, or a breath of stale air through her prison bars, or merely her imagination?

'I know what you are now. Leave me be. Unless you can save me from this torture.'

'Mother!'

'No, begone with you!' she shrieked.

'You should be happy, mother,' the whisper persisted. ***'Why else did you come here but to find me and be with me? Now, we both have our hearts' desires.'***

Pulling on her heavy chains, she clapped her hands over her

ears, but the voice was already in her head. She thought to drown it out with prayer, but the words turned to ash on her unworthy tongue. 'No, no, no, no,' she moaned.

'Now, we shall spend eternity together.'

II

Colonel Graven heard the screams of the dying again.

He woke with a start on the floor of his troop ship cabin. Beside him, the bunk provided for him was untouched. He had laid out his bedroll beside it because it was comfortable, familiar, moulded over the years to his shape.

He slept in his uniform, including its heavy black greatcoat and rebreather mask, because this too felt familiar. He had tried to imagine himself back in the trenches, surrounded by his comrades. It had not stopped the nightmares.

They were worse in transit, when jumping through the immaterium. The domain of the dead, it was sometimes said. Though the ship was insulated by its Geller field – a bubble of realspace around it – always he felt the horrors of this cursed realm, scratching, clawing in the corners of his mind. Awake, he could easily resist them. Not in sleep.

Graven served in the Death Korps of Krieg, reputedly the arm of the Astra Militarum with the highest mortality rate and fiercely proud of it. Always, here he felt the presence of the countless billions of Korpsmen who had served faithfully before him, their lives given for their world's atonement.

He counted too many of his own regiment among them, too many of his closest comrades. When he slept, often he relived the day of their deaths, the horrors he had seen and the far worse ones his mind's eye pictured. He heard his comrades' voices and sometimes they even spoke directly to him.

They were angry with him.

Colonel Graven checked his wrist chrono. They were not due to reach their destination for another four hours. The last thing he wanted was to sleep, but he knew it was his duty to be rested for his next trial. He would not be found wanting this time.

He lay back down and closed his eyes, and heard their screams again.

It was raining on Oleris III as the drop-ships descended. On Oleris, it was almost always raining.

There were fewer ships than Colonel Petrakov had anticipated. The 401st Krieg Regiment, it seemed, was more depleted than he had been told. That was an inconvenience. He might have to redraw his plans.

Busy with deployment lists, he had sent a captain to greet the new arrivals. Hearing her transport pulling up, he dismissed his tacticians and scribes. He fastened his red greatcoat's brass buttons and donned his brimless black fur hat, which boosted his unimpressive height by six inches. He waited for a rap on his office door.

'Come,' he instructed, and the captain ushered in two dark-clad figures.

'Colonel Graven of the Krieg, sir, and, ah, his watchmaster.'

The Vostroyan colonel introduced himself in turn. He hid

his mild distaste as he regarded his opposite number. He could smell the dirt ingrained in Graven's dark fatigues and frayed black coat. His carapace armour plates and crested helmet were dented and scuffed. Just as Petrakov had heard, he wore a gas mask, even here, from which a hose snaked over his shoulder into a battered backpack.

One thing drew Petrakov's eye: the fine-looking and obviously well-kept sword slung at Graven's hip.

His unnamed 'watchmaster' – no such rank existed in the Astra Militarum's formal command structure – was similarly clad, minus the visible breastplate, a rebreather unit worn over his chest. Or over her chest? The mask and shapeless uniform made it impossible to tell.

Petrakov dismissed his captain and invited his visitors to sit. For a moment he thought they might decline. Rain drummed on the tin roof of the prefabricated building. He took a bottle from his desk drawer.

'No, thank you,' said Graven. 'I do not dull my brain with alcohol.'

'Ohx, then?' suggested Petrakov. 'A hot drink from my own world, containing powdered grox meat, rich in nutrients and stimulants.'

'Our feeding tubes provide us all the nutrients we need.'

'You will not need those tubes here, nor the masks. The air is safe – auspexes confirm that no trace of the plague remains – and no intelligence suggests that our foes have chemical weapons.'

The Krieg colonel sat and said nothing. His lack of body language and expression irritated Petrakov. The large, dark lenses of his mask were like the eye sockets of a skull. Petrakov considered demanding its removal. He was in charge here, after all, as commander-in-chief of this world's Imperial forces. A role bestowed, he recognised, by virtue of his regiment having reached Oleris first. He couldn't judge Graven's age from his voice. It was likely – highly likely – that, of the pair, the newcomer had the greater experience.

Petrakov sat behind his desk and tried again to break the ice. 'Our peoples, I believe, have much in common.'

'Oh?' said Graven.

'We both offer more than the standard tithe of soldiers to the Emperor.'

'With good reason.'

'Indeed,' said Petrakov. 'Both our worlds seek redemption for our forefathers' blindness.'

'My world immolated itself in civil war,' said Graven pointedly, 'to rid itself of its fickle rulers and resume the path of faith.'

The Vostroyan sighed and poured himself a glass of amasec. *So much for small talk,* he thought. 'Let me brief you on Oleris III,' he said.

'Oleris was once a thriving agri world,' said Colonel Petrakov, 'until, half a millennium ago, it was ravaged by a plague of Chaos.'

He mouthed the final word rather than giving it voice. Graven had never seen the need for such genteelness. To him, it felt like cowardice.

'No crop has since grown in its soil,' the Vostroyan continued, 'and its population still numbers in the tens of thousands, concentrated in the temperate zone. Oleris' stock-in-trade now, one might say, is death.'

'A cemetery world,' said Graven. He had seen the stones outside.

'Whose bones run deeper than you might expect. Plague victims lie alongside unnamed soldiers, brought here for burial en masse since a long-dead planetary governor decreed that anyone martyred for the Emperor in this sector deserved to rest in his world's hallowed ground.'

'Hallowed?'

'You know not of Saint Josefina?'

Colonel Graven shook his head.

'A venerated priest who came here to tend to the suffering. She is said to have bathed them in a holy golden light in which their lesions melted, but she couldn't heal herself. She died here and was subsequently canonised.'

'Then it would indeed be an honour to rot alongside her.' *My honour, perhaps?* Graven couldn't help but wonder.

He knew there was a good chance he would die on Oleris III, as on any world to which he was deployed. His comrades, for expediency's sake, would leave him in a shallow grave here, even though he hadn't earned the right. *I will have to ensure that I survive,* he told himself.

'Saint Josefina's Grand Mausoleum stands not five miles away,' said Petrakov. 'Perhaps you might pray there. I found the experience uplifting.'

'Perhaps,' said Graven, 'once our work is done.'

He saw the flicker of a scowl across the Vostroyan's face. For a colonel, he was young – not by Krieg standards but by most others. His thin moustache might have been intended to indicate maturity. It might have been darkened with dye. The male Vostroyans seen by Graven thus far had all sported similar moustaches. He said, 'I was briefed to expect witches?'

'Oleris has seen more than its share of those,' said Petrakov. 'The Ordo Hereticus believes the plague awakened… powers in the few survivors.'

'And in their descendants?'

'Indeed. The centuries since have seen no fewer than three full-scale Inquisitorial purges – and of course the Ecclesiarchy now governs here – and yet somehow that malignancy continues to resurface.'

'So needs cutting out once and for all,' Graven's watchmaster muttered.

'What is the current situation?' the Krieg colonel asked.

'A witch hunter named Idelax raised the alarm this time. He came to investigate rumours of an active coven, and found the rot ran deeper than anyone suspected. He requested military intervention, but before my regiment arrived the witches made their most audacious move.'

Graven nodded. His terse briefing had covered this too. 'By storming the Ecclesiarchal Tower.'

'In truth, we believe many were inside already,' said Petrakov, 'affecting to serve the priesthood while biding their time, until compelled to act in haste.'

'The priests?' asked Graven.

'As far as we can ascertain, all dead, but we have the tower surrounded.'

'Defences?'

'Scant. Oleris III has no strategic value, no mineral wealth and little industry. The tower is only lightly fortified. I suspect the Departmento Munitorum would almost be willing to abandon this world.'

'But for fear of what forces may have been unleashed here.'

The Vostroyan nodded. 'With sufficient artillery and manpower,' he continued, 'I believe we can retake the tower in a matter of days.'

'Ah,' said Graven.

'Hence I requested a Krieg siege regiment once I knew one was available.'

'My regiment is not what it once was.'

'Yes, so I am informed. An incident with orks and a nuclear device, I hear – clumsy, ignorant brutes, I've always found – and your old colonel perished alongside his Guardsmen?' Graven nodded stiffly. 'At least, then, we can say he died with honour, facing the consequences of his failure.'

Graven bristled. 'Colonel Kleber did not fail us.' He took a breath. 'My point, Colonel Petrakov, is that our fighting strength is diminished to fewer than four hundred. We also lost much of our artillery to the firestorm.'

'Which means?'

'Certainly our tacticians can lend you their expertise. Since taking command of the Four Hundred and First, however, I have dissolved its companies. We operate as semi-autonomous ten-strong squads – kill teams when needed. I believe that is how we are best employed now – remaining apart from your main force, offering a swift response to incidents as they arise worldwide.'

'Colonel Graven, an Attilan regiment already–'

Graven carried on talking, quietly but forcefully. 'There have been incidents, I understand? You said yourself, the malignancy here runs deep, and we must excise its every tendril.'

'Before they too can grow,' his watchmaster added.

'My methods,' said Graven, 'have thus far yielded positive results.'

'I do not doubt it,' said Petrakov with tight-lipped politeness. He took a long sip from his glass. 'I hear that, among you Krieg, in a short time your regiment has earned quite the reputation – and a nickname to go with it.'

'Yes,' said the Krieg colonel. He had nothing more to add.

'Do you think he will take note, sir?' the watchmaster asked.

'I believe so,' said Colonel Graven, 'though he'll have more to say before we reach a compromise. His confidence in his own judgement is mostly affected.'

'Perhaps a commissar could speak to him?'

The colonel ignored the suggestion.

The rain had lessened but still pattered on their helmets as wet ground sucked at their boots. Vostroyans beetled about between the tin huts of the compound, the stark red of their uniforms the only splashes of colour in view. A junior officer, spying the winged skull on Graven's helmet as he passed him, snapped to attention and threw up a smart salute, which he returned.

A drop-ship rose above the southern horizon with a scream of engines, returning to its orbiting berth. Behind them, some distance to the north, the brutalist edifice of the Ecclesiarchal Tower touched the clouds. Worked into its grey stone was the symbol of the Adeptus Ministorum, a skull glaring from the pillar of a giant 'I', encircled by a spiked crown. A reminder that the Emperor's eyes were everywhere – for what that had been worth.

'What did he mean,' the watchmaster asked, 'about our worlds being alike?'

'Vostroya's shame predates even Krieg's,' said Graven, 'originating in the Age of Darkness. I don't know the details, only that to this day each Vostroyan family sends its firstborn son or daughter to fight for the Emperor.'

'Only their firstborn?'

'They also maintain a rigid class system in which ranks are assigned by birthright, not earned through experience.'

Krieg Centaurs were starting to arrive, their spinning tracks throwing up mud, carrying the regiment's command staff along with sundry aides and quartermasters. A smaller assemblage by far than it had been. Colonel Graven went to brief them and direct them to the hut allocated for their command centre.

The watchmaster was distracted by a sound, a familiar one, which caused him a melancholic twinge: a thundering of hooves as five horses swept through the gates in the vehicles' wake. Atop them were five squat figures, clad in leather. Each wore a leather greatcoat, boots and gloves, and a wide-brimmed, spiked riding helmet, with leather straps swaddling their ears and chins. All carried a hunting lance, while most had lasguns slung beside their saddles.

Attilan Rough Riders. A long way from their feudal home world. At the orders of their sergeant – distinguished by her stripes and her helmet's fine plume – they halted by a dirty metal trough, well filled by rain. They loosened their horses' barding, removing the chamfrons from their heads, and let them drink. A couple of riders dipped mugs in the water for themselves.

Approaching, the watchmaster exchanged a nod with the Attilan sergeant, acknowledging each other's equivalent ranks. 'He seems a sturdy beast,' he said.

'He is, but ill-tempered. Keep your distance.'

Undeterred, he stroked the horse's mane, kneaded its shoulder. It turned its head to size him up, harrumphed and returned to its water. He noted the variant of the winged-skull symbol branded into its hindquarters.

The Attilan looked impressed. 'I rode one a little like him,' the watchmaster explained. 'On Krieg too, our steeds are bred for strength and aggression and require a firm hand on the reins, but there is no more loyal creature in the galaxy once they have accepted a master.'

'My people say only the bravest take horses to a tank fight.'

'And must take the bravest horses.'

A grin broke across her brown, weather-beaten face. Removing her headgear, she allowed matted black hair only partly tamed by braids to unfold down her back. The white scars on her cheeks were symmetrical enough to suggest deliberate cuts. The watchmaster saw the same scars on the sergeant's comrades, the same unkempt black hair.

She extended a gloved hand towards him. 'Batu.'

He took the sergeant's hand. She didn't seem fazed by his mask as many were. She was expecting a name from him. He had once chosen one in case of need, when he had become a ridemaster. Never had it been formally recorded. He had almost forgotten it.

'You've been out fighting?' he asked.

'Searching,' Batu grunted in her guttural, thickly accented voice.

'For witches?'

'And witch hunters.' The watchmaster frowned – which of course the Attilan couldn't see, but she took his silence as a prompt. 'Idelax?'

'The Vostroyan mentioned him. I assumed he had died with the priests.'

'Maybe, but no sign of his body in the tower. Eat with us?'

'Thank you,' he said, 'I am on duty.' As a Korpsman, rarely was he off-duty. Life was duty. 'Maybe we'll chance to meet again.'

Sergeant Batu shrugged. 'Maybe.'

Her comrades had tied up their horses and had gathered, waiting for her. They were chattering raucously and laughing, a far less familiar sound to the Krieg watchmaster. Batu joined them and they disappeared into a hut.

The watchmaster nuzzled the horse that reminded him so much of his own. The one lost to a radiation sickness that had almost killed him too. The last of the 401st Krieg Regiment's mounts to die, leaving him a ridemaster no longer. Having been spared for a reason, he hoped one day to find out what it was.

With a sigh, he turned to find his new colonel again.

Colonel Petrakov outlined his battle plan in his war room.

With a polished swagger stick, he pointed out details on a tactical hololith, around which the command staffs of three regiments crowded. The Krieg colonel asked him several questions as if testing him.

The Attilan Colonel Tegana spoke less, but neither did he seem to listen much, drawing his own conclusions. Petrakov considered him, his regiment, too casual by far in their approach to their duties. Given a chance, he would have drilled some discipline into them.

His prime concern remained the siege of the occupied tower. He had stubbornly assigned most of the Krieg Korpsmen to this task, though he had left Graven a few to employ elsewhere as he chose. Most were already headed to the front lines with entrenching tools in hand. The flimsy walls around him rattled with the passing of huge artillery platforms, bearing powerful Earthshaker cannons.

According to Petrakov's scouts, the tower was still dark and silent. The last firing of its defensive guns had been three days ago. Its small stockpile of ammunition might have run dry or been close to so doing. The guns, however, were not the primary threat. Not when dealing with rogue psykers, whose strength remained unknown, whose profane powers could manifest in almost any form.

The witches, he had to assume, were waiting. Waiting in their stronghold for their enemies to walk into their clutches. Waiting to employ those profane powers at close range. A few days' bombardment of their walls would soften their resolve, and might bury some of them in rubble.

He had almost finished talking when he heard a commotion outside. The war room door burst open and in marched two imposing figures in black power armour. Their crimson robes and headdresses were festooned with holy symbols, notably the fleur-de-lys. Their appearance was greeted by awed intakes of breath, even from the hardened veterans present, as heads were reverently bowed.

The shorter, more wiry of the pair appeared to be the one in charge. She had short snow-white hair and angular features. 'Colonel Petrakov,' her clear, commanding voice rang out, 'we must speak.'

'Sister Superior, of course. My office may be more suitable?'

'There has been another incident.'

'The mausoleum?' asked Petrakov, fearing the worst. 'An attack?'

'No attack, but more than one of my Battle Sisters has noticed a... nocturnal presence of late.' Such reticence was unlike her, and Petrakov wondered what she was reluctant to reveal. On firmer ground, she said accusingly, 'You assured me that you had the wretched witches confined within the tower.'

'I am certain of it. Most of them.'

'Be that as it may, we cannot overlook the chance that others may be plotting to defile our sacred shrine. I require that you provide additional protection.'

Colonel Graven cleared his throat. 'Sister Superior, the Krieg would be honoured to oblige you however we are able. We can spare as many Korpsmen from the trenches as you deem sufficient to the task.'

The Vostroyan bit his tongue. He had no wish to disappoint this ordained holy warrior, nor incur her wrath, though technically he outranked her. Her brawnier colleague stood scowling at her shoulder, a hand resting on her holstered boltgun. So, he made the required introductions.

'Sister Superior – Colonel Graven of the Death Korps of Krieg, whose siege regiment joined us today. Colonel, may I present Sister Superior Serafina of the Adepta Sororitas, who maintain an honour guard around the sainted Josefina's place of rest.'

'My privilege,' said Graven. 'I suggest we set up watch points on every approach to the area, maintaining a respectful distance, of course.'

He earned himself an approving nod, making Colonel Petrakov's heart sink. He supposed his plans would have to be redrawn again.

That night, Graven slept more soundly.

Though he had a room to himself, it adjoined the large mess hall in which some eighty Korpsmen – those he had succeeded in keeping back from the trenches – bedded down. They needed nothing more than this, as they were moving out at dawn. He heard their soft snores through his door.

He was not spared the dreams entirely.

He was underground, captain of an engineer company again, leading his command squad through pitch-black tunnels. He was trying to reach his colonel with a warning, but the tunnels turned and twisted and kept bringing him back to where he had started. He was growing more frustrated as the labyrinth shifted around him. Stumbling into dead ends, he would turn to find the passageway behind him also closed. He had a growing sense of dread. He feared that time was running out.

Time skipped, and Captain Graven was attacking a rock wall with a pickaxe, blasting at it with a shotgun, screaming for a breaching drill, and it was all too late.

His chrono woke him with its tinny fanfare and the dream receded as he lay on his bedroll, on his back, but he knew it would not have gone far.

Graven lowered himself into the turret of an idling Chimera.

His watchmaster took the gunner's seat beside him, a driver below him in front. The remainder of his handpicked command squad, his readymade kill team – seven more veterans, rendered all but indistinguishable by their uniform masks – dropped into the passenger compartment.

More vehicles were starting up around them, wreathed in morning mist: three more Chimeras, two Centaurs and even a venerable Ragnarok, tired and battered remnants of a once-mighty fleet. His repeated requests for more resources had been refused. Krieg high command was winding his regiment down.

A familiar sound reached Graven's ears, even over the grumbling of engines – a distant booming of Earthshaker cannons. The siege of the Ecclesiarchal Tower had begun under Petrakov's direction. A part of him wished he could be there, back in the trenches, back in the world he knew, but that was not his path now.

He bellowed the order to move out, and the transports crawled through the compound gates in convoy. His was among the first to peel away. As they bumped along muddy tracks, Graven stood in the open turret, surveying his surroundings. He followed his progress on a map provided for him by Colonel Tegana, whom he had found more agreeable than the Vostroyan.

He had noted that they would pass close to the mausoleum. Soon enough, its ornate spires rose above the flat terrain. He saw no sign of the Korpsmen he had sent out here last night, though they must have been concealed nearby. The Sister Superior had approved the plans he had submitted to her.

Graven felt she approved of him too. He wondered if, when all of this was over, she might deign to take his confession. Might it even stop the nightmares?

They ploughed on through field after endless field of crumbling headstones. Occasionally they saw grimy workers tending to these, but the dead of this world vastly outnumbered its living. Graven tried to read names from the nearest stones, but erosion had faded them. 'Too many,' he muttered to himself. 'Too many names to be remembered, so none will be.'

Few Krieg lived long enough to need a name. Others, such as

Graven, chose honoured names of the past from the walls of the many mausolea that rose in grim defiance from their home world's ashes. When had a new name last been inscribed upon those walls? He didn't know.

Like many of his comrades, he carried an ossuary box. Inside, wrapped in velvet, was a bone from the finger of a Korpsman killed during Graven's first engagement. He had not known the man. That was the point. The bone represented every nameless comrade, every sacrifice. This was how he remembered them, every one of them. That was what he told himself.

His mind returned to Serafina, to her Sisters of Battle, skilled and ferocious warriors. Any witch would have quailed at the sight of them, but they stood sentry over desiccated bones instead of fighting for the living. An unworthy thought, which he quickly suppressed.

He thought about his regiment instead. When its end came, as soon it must, how would it be remembered? For a lapse of judgement leading to annihilation? Not if Colonel Graven could help it. His goal was to stave off that end for as long as he could, long enough to atone for past mistakes. The memories of his dead comrades demanded it. Their lives had to matter.

Colonel Petrakov had spoken of reputation. He had heard of the name attached by some to Graven's regiment. That ought to have pleased him, but the proffered honour had still felt unearned. *Soon,* he swore to himself.

Soon, the 401st Krieg Regiment would be known not for its failures, but because its survivors had walked through nuclear fire and only been tempered by it. They had refused to lie down when their time had come.

Soon, they would deserve their soubriquet of the Relentless Dead.

* * *

Oleris' grave workers subsisted in tiny, squalid hamlets, clusters of ramshackle huts squeezed into the few spaces reserved for the living. Perhaps it was this, each hamlet's isolation, that had made close oversight impossible, allowing heresies to take root in the cracks.

The Chimera passed several such settlements, headed for one in particular. Graven had held one detail back from Petrakov, from everyone. Before arriving on Oleris III, before even receiving his assignment, he had been contacted by a grey-faced Imperial emissary with impeccable credentials but no name to share. The agency she represented was eager to locate the missing Idelax, keener still that, were he to have been 'compromised', as few eyes as possible should see him. The inquisitor's last report to his superiors had included a list of coordinates, locations that he planned to visit.

The first of those now loomed ahead of Graven. After driving for three hours, he looked forward to stretching his limbs. He tapped his driver's shoulder with his foot, a prearranged signal for him to pull up.

According to his dataslate, forty-seven workers and sundry dependants occupied this hamlet. Despite this, no one walked its tracks and the surrounding fields were empty. No one came from the huts to greet them, no faces appeared at their dark windows. All was still and, once the echoes of the Chimera's engine had died down and the rain had let up for a moment, deathly silent.

'Emperor grant we have not reached this world too late,' Graven muttered as he clambered out onto the sponson, then dropped down into the mud.

He didn't catch his watchmaster's soft reply.

He turned to ask him to repeat it, but his comrade was not standing by his ear as he had thought. Confused, he raised his eyes to the turret, in which the watchmaster was still seated, looking down at him.

'Is there a problem, sir?'

Colonel Graven shook himself. 'I thought I heard... But it was nothing. A trick of the wind, no more.'

III

The afternoon was growing late as they approached the second hamlet on Inquisitor Idelax's list. At first sight, this one too appeared deserted.

Colonel Graven fretted. The last thing he wanted was to have to report to Petrakov that his kill team had only wasted time.

Then, beside him, his watchmaster stiffened – 'Sir!' – and Graven too glimpsed shapes flitting between the huddled buildings, heard the slamming of a door, saw a shutter being hastily closed.

He tapped his driver's shoulder and the Chimera grumbled to a halt. The watchmaster was ready on the trigger of its multi-laser. Graven stood up in the turret. He bellowed, 'Show yourselves, in the name of the Emperor!'

A muzzle flashed in an upstairs window. He ducked as a burst of autogun fire pinged off the armour plating by his head.

'Return fire, sir?' the watchmaster asked.

'Not yet.' Graven waited for more shots, but silence had settled once again, reminding him of the stillness of the other hamlet.

Cautiously, he raised his head. 'I am Colonel Graven of the Astra Militarum. I repeat, show yourselves. No faithful citizen need fear us.'

A minute passed, then more, with no response of any kind.

Then Graven heard a door unlatching, boots squelching in the mud.

Three ragged, dirty workers approached the Chimera, trembling with nerves. Graven clambered down to meet them. Their empty hands were raised before them, so he kept his weapons sheathed. Ten feet from the delegation, he signalled it to halt.

The foremost worker was an elderly man with leathern skin and a straggly grey beard. 'Please, sir,' he croaked, 'is it true? Has He sent you in answer to our prayers?'

'That depends,' said Graven. 'Who fired on us?'

'Forgive her,' the old man entreated. 'She is young and was afraid, and with all we have seen and heard lately, and when she saw your fearsome mask...'

'This is Settlement One-Three-Dash-Seven-Beta?'

'As the priests label it, yessir. To us, it is just home.'

'A grave worker voxed the Ecclesiarchal Tower,' said Graven. 'He claimed to have witnessed witchcraft, but was cut off before he could elaborate.'

The old man frowned. 'Yes, sir, but that was many moons ago.'

'What is your situation? What has made you so afraid?'

'The witch hunter didn't tell you?'

Graven seized on the reference. 'Idelax made it here?'

'Is that not why you...? It's the spectres, sir. The witch hunter saw them for himself. The spectres haunt us in the night. The spirits of the immaterium, the dead returned with vengeance in their darkened souls. They blame us, blame the living, for their tragic plight, and they plan to torment us unto death.'

* * *

'When did the witch hunter come here?' asked Graven.

'It must've been a moon ago now, sir.'

'Tell me all you remember.'

He was sitting on a cushioned chair in the main room of a single-storey shack. Pails were arranged about the floor to catch rain from the leaky roof. His watchmaster sat on a similar chair beside him, while workers craned about them. A young boy hid behind his mother's legs, clutching at her skirts.

Their elderly spokesman – he had given his name as Rayoul – perched on a three-legged stool across from his distinguished visitors. 'The spectres had bedevilled us for many moons by then,' he said. 'We'd sent word to the tower, but given up hope that the priests…' He checked himself.

'Describe them to me, these "spectres".'

'I haven't the words.'

'As best you can.'

'To begin with, we felt them merely as a presence. We heard their moans on the wind, glimpsed them out of the corners of our eyes. We weren't sure they were even real. At morning prayer, we pleaded for the strength to resist their whispered lies, see only what was true.'

'Such creatures prey on the weak-minded,' the colonel agreed.

'They only grew stronger. Night after night, the screams of the tortured woke us, till one night…' The old man shuddered. 'The screams came from Torven's hut, my nephew. His face was pale, his eyes staring.'

Graven almost wished he had brought a commissar with him. One might have had something to say. Impatiently, he awaited more information.

'His goodwife had seen the spectre, right there in their room. She saw right through it, to the wall behind it, as it hovered over him, as if it were suckling on his very soul.'

'He was dead?'

Rayoul's choked sob confirmed it.

'And the spectre?'

'Fled through the wall as soon as light was shed upon it.'

'May I speak with your nephew's wife?' asked Graven.

Rayoul shook his head. 'She fled too, with the sunrise, as did others, and more have left us since. You've seen how few of us remain – fewer than half of us. We felt that, if we ran, they'd only follow. So, we kept up our duties and prayed and slept in shifts, till the day the witch hunter arrived.'

'Inquisitor Idelax?'

'Yessir, I think that was the name.'

'You said he saw the spectres too?'

Graven never got his answer. From outside the hut, he heard a scuffle, angry shouts and the distinctive crack of a Lucius-pattern Type XIV heavy lasgun. He snatched his pistol from its holster as he leapt to his feet. He suspected treachery, but the workers in the room seemed only startled and afraid.

He pushed past them to the door, his watchmaster on his heels, as a second shot and then a third rang out.

Outside, Graven sized up the situation in an instant.

A worker lay dead at the feet of two Korpsmen, whose weapons were drawn. Crowding around them were eight or nine workers with mutinous expressions, and one on her knees, bleeding from her temple, an autogun beside her in the mud. There was one more gun among them and a shovel raised in threat.

The Korpsmen were yelling orders as their comrades converged upon the scene, the colonel and watchmaster among them. The workers lost their nerve but not their anger. Weapons dropped, but voices were still raised. Graven's voice rang clear above them.

'I will shoot the next person to speak out of turn!' That quietened the workers, so he turned to his Korpsmen. 'What happened?'

'Colonel, he cursed the Emperor's name.'

'You lie!' a worker cried. 'Malek was devout – he would never...' His voice trailed off as Graven trained his laspistol upon him.

He held the weapon levelled for a second. Then, his point made, he lowered it and asked, 'You were present? You heard?'

'I heard nothing. Nothing was said,' the worker spat.

'The curse was muttered,' said the Korpsman, 'not intended to be heard, but I was by the heretic and heard it clear as day.'

'So you shot him?'

The new voice was Rayoul's. He and others from the shack had joined the scene, as had workers from elsewhere across the hamlet, more farm tools and one more autogun among them. A small assemblage threatened to grow into a mob.

'I challenged him,' the Korpsman said, answering the old man's question. 'He spat at me. He drew back his fist to punch me.'

His claim sparked howls of protest. 'They barged into Malek's hut and trashed it for no reason!' someone shouted.

'He stood up to them, so they killed him!'

'Hit his sister with a rifle butt when she tried to help him!'

'They tell us they're soldiers of the Emperor, but how can we trust them when they hide their faces?'

The crowd was regaining its confidence with numbers. Korpsmen were reaching for their weapons. Graven had to defuse the situation. Looking for a way, he saw what looked like ink through a las beam hole in the dead worker's smock. He stepped up to the body and crouched by it.

Someone shrieked, 'What's he doing? Stop him!'

Graven tore the smock open, exposing an ugly tattoo across a burn-marked chest. He had guessed correctly. The eight-pointed star of Chaos. It was lopsided, likely self-inflicted. No further words were necessary. Around him he heard stifled gasps and sobs. The crowd's defiance had instantly deflated. Already, some on its outskirts were slinking away.

One who stayed was the worker who had called a Korpsman a liar. His callused hands trembled as they clutched a cloth cap to his chest. 'Colonel, sir, I swear I didn't know. None of us knew. He fooled us all.'

The woman with the cut head scrambled to her feet, agreeing: 'The traitor did his work and said his prayers. How could we know?'

'How indeed?' the Krieg watchmaster rumbled.

A curt nod from Graven dismissed the workers, and they scurried away in relief. He didn't yet know if he believed them. Their regret had seemed genuine enough, but the Krieg distrusted displays of emotion. Emotions were irrational by nature and often used to manipulate. He based his decisions on hard facts, of which he still had few.

He sent his Korpsmen to continue their search of the hamlet. He doubted they would meet more resistance. Rayoul said his people would see to the body's disposal, this being their calling after all. They wouldn't bury it, though. With a disdainful curl of his lip, he said the body would be burnt to keep its taint from spreading.

Graven approved.

Rayoul said, 'Sir, forgive us, please. We truly did not know.'

'Tell me Malek was the first,' said Graven shrewdly. They were back in the leaky shack, but this time he chose to stand. He glowered down at Rayoul, balanced on his uncomfortable stool.

The old man dropped his gaze in shame. 'There have been others.'

'You said nothing of witches here.'

'I thought... We believed they had been purged.'

'By Inquisitor Idelax?'

'Sir, we know we have been blind, but these were our neighbours, co-workers, friends and family, and once they were faithful, I'd swear to it – they all were. It must've been the spectres, sir. You don't know how their voices worm their way into your head. They make you think dreadful thoughts.'

'How many of you?' Graven demanded.

'Four, before Malek. One, young Lydda, when she was exposed, she threw green fire from her hands and tried to run, but she was gunned down in her tracks. The others...' Rayoul swallowed.

'Go on.'

'The witch hunter marched them out at dawn, weighted down by chains. Sir, we know there was no other way. Each spat and cursed His holy name before the axe fell on them. He is merciful and just, praise be to Him.'

Dutifully, Rayoul's fellows murmured, 'Praise be to Him.'

One spoke up: 'Tell him. Tell him about the other one.'

The old man, nodding, looked up at Graven again. 'The fifth witch, sir.'

'You told me there were four.'

'Four among us, I said. One was shot, three chained in the old barn overnight. The fifth was set to guard them, but during the night he... he turned on his partner. He stabbed him in the back.'

'Be sure you speak the truth,' Graven warned him.

'I do, sir.' Rayoul met the colonel's shuttered glare with confidence. 'The fifth witch discovered by the witch hunter was one of his own attendants.'

'Impossible!' the Krieg watchmaster barked, and Graven was inclined to agree with him. The workers around them, however, insisted otherwise.

'His victim died, but not before he could raise the alarm. The traitor went to free his fellow witches. I never saw myself, but them that did say the witch hunter marched into the old barn after him. They say he wielded a burning whip, and that green fire and red flashed through the timbers.'

'It's true, but the flames never caught,' an older woman said. 'When the witch hunter came out again, he was holding the traitor's severed head, which he cast into the mud. I'd show you the body, sir.'

'But you burnt it,' the colonel guessed.

'So you see, sir,' said Rayoul, 'we have cause to beware of strangers. It could as well have been your soldier as our neighbour who'd been touched by–'

'It could not,' the watchmaster snapped.

'Be assured,' said Graven stiffly, 'that no Death Korpsman would ever succumb to such corruption.'

'As you say, Colonel Graven, sir,' the old man deferred, but he sounded less than convinced.

'The inquisitor left here, I assume?'

'Three mornings after he came, in his brass-plated tank, prayers blaring through its speakers. He said his work was done. His attendants had been through our homes. He'd checked every one of us for marks and found us clean.'

'Including Malek, I presume,' Graven said.

'He said the traitors brought the spectres to us, so they'd not be back again, even though... Pardon the impertinence, sir, but it seemed to us the spectres made the traitors, not the other way around.'

'Did he tell you where he was headed?'

'No, sir, not in my hearing, but he travelled eastward, if it helps you.'

Still following his list, thought Graven.

'He said there'd been other calls from other hamlets, tormented like ours. More traitors, more witches to be rooted out and dealt with.'

The watchmaster asked, 'And your spectres?'

'For a few days, the next few blessed nights, it seemed the witch hunter had been right.' Rayoul released a heavy sigh. 'Until today. Until Malek. Maybe he was the only one we missed. Maybe now it can finally be over.'

The Krieg laid down their bedrolls in the hamlet's largest building, the old barn mentioned by Rayoul. It was hardly secure, its timbers rotting, but as a Korpsman remarked wryly, what mattered that against a reputedly intangible foe?

The barn was in use as a storehouse, grain sacks stacked against one wall. More empty sacks than full. Graven recalled what Petrakov had told him, that no crop had grown on this world since its plague. Therefore, food had to be imported and distributed by archdeacons in the tower. The captive tower.

The workers here knew little of that yet, only that supplies were overdue. The colonel had deflected all questions on the subject, but certainly Rayoul had been relieved when informed that his visitors could sustain themselves. There was plenty of water – troughs and barrels brimmed over – to replenish their reserves.

He asked his watchmaster, 'Do you believe their story?'

'That a nest of traitors could have hidden in plain sight in a settlement this size? Possible, but doubtful.'

'Highly doubtful,' agreed Graven.

'That a witch hunter's acolyte could have been persuaded to their side?'

'Yes, even more so.'

The watchmaster ventured, 'Unless this world's dark forces have already grown so powerful…' He hesitated to expand upon that thought.

Graven thought about what they had seen that morning. A hamlet like this one, abandoned. A thorough search had turned up nothing. No sign of any struggle. No evidence of misdeeds of any kind. No bodies, though perhaps they had been buried. No clue as to what had happened there, but the odour of death had played about his nostrils, a faint but only too familiar stink.

'At least we can be sure the witch hunter came this far,' his comrade said.

'Less certain that he made it further,' Graven growled.

'The acolyte, perhaps, was just a novice.'

'Perhaps, and either way not Krieg-born. Our people know the cost of treachery too well. We know the very worst of what can happen when a single soul strays from the Emperor's light.'

The two men stood in pensive silence. Graven thought about the radiation-scarred surface of his home world, the barren, hellish landscape in which he had been raised and trained. The tragic result of one man's unthinking treachery. Before he knew it, however, his mind had drifted and he found himself picturing another world entirely, reliving a fresher trauma.

He asked his watchmaster, 'Do you ever wonder why we were chosen to survive when–' He checked himself. He was a colonel now, a commanding officer. To talk to a subordinate this way was inappropriate. 'Belay that,' he said gruffly.

His squad's final four members had entered the barn, reporting to him. One pair had searched their quadrant, finding nothing to concern them. The other had voxed the command compound from the Chimera, relaying their coordinates. In the worst case, they would not now simply disappear as had Idelax's retinue.

Another two Korpsmen were stoking a peat-burning stove, provided by Rayoul. Though Oleris' days were mostly warm, if wet, its temperatures dropped cruelly overnight. Not that the Krieg were unaccustomed to sleeping in the cold, but since the offer had been made, they had gladly accepted it.

Graven's gaze lingered on another soldier, sitting in a corner with an engineer's shotgun between his knees, threading a cleaning rod into its barrel. Only the weapon and his shorter tunic jacket distinguished him from his comrades, though Graven felt he would have known him anyway.

Korpsman 319-938-25549-04 had served longer under him than any other. A member of his first command squad. He had been at Graven's side that day. One of the few people left alive who knew exactly what had happened. Of course, he never talked about it. He kept his thoughts to himself, as was only right, as was required – which didn't stop the colonel from wondering.

He instructed his watchmaster, 'Draw up a rota. Two guards outside the barn throughout the night, two on patrol. I'll take the first shift. Whatever the truth about this place, it's time we saw it for ourselves.'

Colonel Graven's feet were wet, though he had recently reglued his boots. He needed a new pair, but the regimental stores had none left in his size.

His lumen cube's anaemic light washed over the hamlet's wooden huts. Shadows fled from it, but no further than they had to, lurking at the edges of its reach resentfully. Clouds obscured Oleris' red moon and its stars. Graven saw contorted shapes in every shadow, acutely aware that they stretched for miles around, reaching outwards through the fields of headstones.

His watch was almost over. Thus far, it had been uneventful. Occasionally he saw faces at windows, insomniac workers hearing his footsteps and looking out in fear. Candlelight glimmered in the rooms behind them, keeping the darkness at bay.

He heard a sound behind him. A sudden scrape of movement.

Graven whipped around, as did the Korpsman at his side, so at least he knew this sound had been real. His pistol was already in his hand. He was about to voice a challenge when his lumen light fell upon the culprit. A fat, hairy rodent – far from the first he had seen – took fright, disappearing through a hole in the planking at one hut's base.

'All clear, sir?' the Korpsman whispered.

He nodded. 'All clear.' Perhaps, he thought, Rayoul's prayers had been answered. Perhaps no spectres would appear tonight, nor any other night. Perhaps the death of one more traitor had been all it took.

They had almost completed their final circuit. As Graven turned back towards the old barn, something caught his eye. The dark, brooding shape of the Krieg Chimera sat nearby. His light had glinted off something underneath its chassis.

He signalled to his Korpsman and they approached with caution. Graven squatted, shedding light on a battered length of metal. He reached between the vehicle's tracks, drawing it towards him. It ran deeper than he thought, and he wrestled with the sucking mud for it.

He found himself holding a mottled tube, around two feet in length, with an obtuse bend. 'What does this look like to you?' he asked.

'An exhaust pipe, sir,' said his Korpsman, with which Graven concurred.

'How many vehicles have you seen here?'

'A single truck, but plenty must pass through.'

Including, he thought, *farming vehicles long ago.* The pipe could have lain underground for years or decades, until tank tracks had churned it to the surface. It was rusted, but hardly more so than some of the Chimera's working parts. He told himself, *It probably means nothing.*

Standing up, he dropped the pipe. Still, he took a detour on his way back to the barn. He peeled back a sheet of tarpaulin from the workers' own old crop sprayer. He found its exhaust pipe intact and rusted into place.

He bedded down behind a ladder leading to an empty hayloft.

As he drifted off to sleep, a voice whispered in his ear, and wearily he resigned himself to the nightmares once again.

A parade of figures marched behind his eyes, each identical to all the others in their gas masks. *'Why?'* they demanded of him, echoing his own earlier question. *'Why did we have to die before our time, before we could fulfil our purpose? How can that have been the Emperor's plan for us?'*

'I cannot believe it was,' said Colonel Graven. 'Believe me, I fought for you with all the strength I had. I prayed for you.'

'Why not you? Have you not had your time, many times over?'

'I know. I know that is true, and I swear I will make recompense.'

'How can you? How can one life atone for so many hundreds wasted?'

'I'm sorry!' he cried, and realised that he had woken, a Korpsman leaning over him, and that he might have yelled the words aloud.

Embarrassed, he struggled to come up with something to say. Until he realised two more things. The first was that, despite his thick blanket and the stove's gentle heat in the air, his heart and lungs felt frozen.

The second was that the figure above him, the one into whose blank face he stared in dawning horror, was no Korpsman.

It was barely even humanoid and very far from human. What he had mistaken for eyes, or rather a gas mask's lenses, were no more than shadows. The whole thing was just a shadow, like the ones that had stalked him on patrol, imaginary monsters on the edges of his vision. He almost felt that, if he blinked, then it would fade, except that he could feel its presence, not least by the numbing cold emanating from it.

This monster was indubitably real.

He managed to croak a warning – 'Intruders! We're under attack!' – as his fingers quested for his pistol, never more than an arm's length from him.

He found the weapon, raised it, squeezed the trigger, barely taking time to aim. A beam of focused light sliced through the shadow, which shrieked as it recoiled, a high-pitched nails-on-chalkboard sound.

As Graven scrambled to his feet, reassuring cracks of las fire filled his ears. His shout had woken his five Korpsmen in the barn, bringing two sentries running from outside. Their weapons lit the dark space in staccato bursts, revealing not one but two spectres floating in the air between them, shadows wreathing them like tattered cloaks.

He added to the furious barrage. It was hard to discern the spectres' ever-shifting outlines, but he knew some las beams had struck true – and had passed through them, having no discernible effect other than to scorch the rafters.

A spectre swooped towards a Korpsman, who stumbled as he tried to back away. 'Target that one,' Graven yelled. 'They must become solid to attack!'

He was pleased to see he had deduced correctly. The Krieg redirected their fire as instructed, despite the risk of striking their own comrade, and now they made their target scream again and writhe.

Graven's sword lay by his bedroll in its scabbard. Holstering his pistol, he stooped to pull it free. He turned back to the spectre. Though it had aborted its attack run, still it was assailed by las beams, thrashing in midair. He thumbed his power weapon's activation stud, wreathing its blade in bright blue flames. Its hilt thrummed in his hands. *Six steps and strike upwards,* he reckoned. *I don't expect it has a heart, but all the same...* He started towards his target.

'Have you not had your time, many times over?'

The voice, the deathly whisper in his ear – no, not in his ear, but in his head – froze Graven's heart again. The other spectre – still hovering beneath the old barn's roof, the one that had attacked him, he just knew it – had turned its gaze upon him. For an instant, he made out vengeful eyes and a forked tongue uncoiling over razor teeth. But then the shadows shifted, resolving themselves into gas mask lenses and a flexible rebreather hose.

Then came the voice again, the impossible, accusing voice of a faceless, nameless comrade long deceased. The voice of all of his dead comrades. *'Your life is undeserved. Give up your life. Your life for ours.'*

A scream bubbled up from Graven's lungs. He just about caught it in his throat, clenching teeth and fists to keep the scream contained. He was dimly aware that he had dropped his sword. It burnt blue at his feet, but his vision had tunnelled and he saw only grim-faced masks around him, half-melted, splitting at the seams to reveal horrific, suppurating burns beneath.

An instinct he had never felt before, certainly not so strongly, warred with a lifetime of conditioning. The urge to run and hide. 'I will not shame myself!' he howled. 'I will not let you down again!'

And then the urge was gone, and Colonel Graven found himself on his knees, the inside of his mask damp with sweat, his heart beating like a Hades breaching drill as the barn snapped back into focus around him. He looked up at the spectre, still glaring blankly at him, and breathlessly, defiantly, told it, 'You do not know the Krieg if you thought to make us fear you.'

It looked at him a moment longer, and then, without turning, drifted upwards through the roof and disappeared.

Graven's hand closed around his sword hilt. Something solid, reassuring, to hold on to. Something real. He heard his watchmaster barking orders: 'Get out there. Find them. Protect the hamlet.'

As the barn emptied out, the watchmaster stayed behind. 'Sir?'

Graven stood, to prove to his comrade, to himself, that he was capable. His legs still felt a little shaky, but already the effects of his brief ordeal were fading. Like a dream. His heart was slowing to its normal pace. 'The other one?' he asked. 'I didn't see what happened to it.'

'Escaped too,' the watchmaster said with chagrin, 'through the wall, before we could finish it off. It seems the workers spoke true after all.'

'About some things, at least,' the colonel growled.

IV

The remaining hours of the night passed in the usual cocktail of anxiety and tedium. The spectres remained unseen. In the dark they could have hidden anywhere around the hamlet, but as a misty sunrise banished shadows, Graven grew in confidence that they too had fled back to their own hellish realm.

Until night falls again, he thought.

Bleary-eyed workers emerged from their homes. They trudged towards a long, single-storey building at the settlement's centre. This, Graven knew, was their meeting house, where among other things they joined in daily prayer, the nearest chapel being some miles away.

The ten Death Korpsmen joined them, finding plenty of spaces to sit on wooden benches. Rayoul led the service, which was barely an hour long. A lectern, serving as a makeshift altar, stood on a rumpled rug into which a holy symbol, the Imperial aquila, was sewn.

Rayoul thanked the Emperor for sending His soldiers to watch over them as they slept. Graven doubted many workers had slept peacefully last night, although only the barn had been attacked. He was tired too, having not slept again since being woken. Joining in the prayers, he drew strength from them.

He gathered his Korpsmen as they filed out of the hut. 'Search the hamlet again,' he ordered them, 'from top to bottom. Nothing must be overlooked.'

'Sir, is that necessary?' asked Rayoul, overhearing. Graven turned his back, the question unworthy of the breath to answer. His watchmaster split the squad into pairs again, assigning a quadrant to each.

The colonel marched back to the Krieg Chimera, sliding into its driver's seat. He operated the vehicle's vox-caster and searched for a signal. Command headquarters was a hundred and thirty miles away, too far to vox directly. During this time, however – this prearranged time, the second hour after dawn – his intervening units would be at their casters too.

He was able to speak to some officers in person, receiving relayed messages from others. Squad Lambda-Two had found its assigned hamlet deserted, but its meeting house defaced by spray-painted heretical symbols. They had burnt the building. Squad Gamma-Four had fought a mob of traitors, who had posed them little threat. The commissar attached to Squad Omicron-Two was satisfied that the workers in his hamlet, though afraid, were loyal. Graven had him question them again.

No problems were reported around the mausoleum, for which he was grateful.

He also made contact with a couple of Attilan squads, one of whose captains told him, *'A few of my riders say they've been hearing voices. Could be nothing, could be something. Just thought it should be noted.'*

He warned each squad in turn about the spectres and had an account of the night's events sent to headquarters, describing the creatures' tactics and known vulnerabilities. He was still awaiting a reply, an acknowledgement at least, when shouting rose from the hamlet's centre. A Korpsman had found something.

There was a hole in the meeting house floor. The watchmaster stood at its edge, looking down into darkness.

A Korpsman had felt that the floor was uneven, something missed yesterday. She had shifted the lectern and rolled back the rug to find the reason.

The hole was jagged, hammered through old floorboards, gouged from the mud beneath. A flakboard square had lain over it, keeping careless feet from plunging through. It was long and wide enough to fit a person, but of unknown depth.

The watchmaster had sent Korpsmen to bring a worker to him. They returned with Rayoul himself. 'We found him lurking right outside,' one said.

'Hardly lurking,' the old man protested as the watchmaster fixed him with a suspicious glare. 'You know, this is my home you're turning upside down!'

Still, the watchmaster didn't speak. Rayoul sweated. His eyes flickering to the uncovered hole, he asked defiantly, 'What of it?'

'Where does it lead?'

'The catacombs. Where else? You don't know of them? This world is riddled with them – some natural, but others dug centuries ago when burial space was running out and the plague's return was feared. We move the older bones down there to make room for the new. It's a large part of our job.'

'An ossuary,' the watchmaster said in realisation.

'As the priests call it.'

'Then why was it hidden?'

Rayoul shrugged. 'There are plenty of other ways in. It's hardly a secret.' The watchmaster didn't know whether to believe him.

A Korpsman had brought up a lumen cube, casting light into the hole. The watchmaster could see its bottom now, some twenty feet below. 'How do I get down there?' he asked.

'Why would you want to?' Rayoul countered.

'How do I get down?' he asked again.

Within minutes, the watchmaster was descending a rope ladder, which Rayoul had called for and lashed to an anchoring bench. He had left four Korpsmen in the meeting house, lest someone think to trap him underground.

His flimsy lifeline swayed with each rung found by his questing feet. His shoulders scraped against soil. Then the hole's sides dropped away and there was only space around him. Judging himself close enough, the watchmaster jumped the last few feet to the floor. He pulled the lumen cube from his pocket, held it up.

He was in a broad tunnel that curved and branched away in each direction. Shovels and pickaxes lay scattered about him. The cold air made him glad of his greatcoat. As the walls glimmered white in his light, the only light, the watchmaster blinked in surprise.

Embedded in the walls were disassembled human skeletons, bones stacked one upon another. They stretched further than he could see, neat row after neat row. Perfectly preserved white skulls leered out into the tunnels. The Krieg lived cheek by jowl with death and so the sight did not disturb him, but it made him curious. He wondered at the point of this display, which must have consumed years of labour.

The voice of his commander intruded from above. 'What do you see?'

'Tunnels, sir,' he summarised, 'and… bones.' He took a few steps to peer along another branch. More bleached skulls stared from its walls. The tunnel ran a few yards before branching again.

He heard Graven asking, 'How far do they extend?'

Then Rayoul's muffled voice: 'I told your sergeant, all the way across Oleris.'

Returning to his starting point, the watchmaster called up, 'Anyone or anything could be concealed down here and never found.'

Rayoul's face appeared at the hole. 'I wouldn't stray too far. Workers who know those tunnels a deal better than you have been lost in them for days.'

'Can anybody hear me?' the watchmaster shouted, cupping his mouth. 'If anyone is down here, identify yourself!' Only the echoes of his own voice came back to his ears.

He took a last look about himself, then stepped onto the ladder. He scaled it, back to the meeting house. Though no judge of expressions, he thought he saw relief on Rayoul's face. Testing him, he said, 'I could take a few Korpsmen down there. We could search and map the tunnels to a radius of, say, a mile to begin with.'

Colonel Graven contemplated the suggestion.

As all present awaited his decision, the watchmaster heard muffled sounds outside the hut. Low voices. He marched to the door and yanked it open. A group of four workers quickly looked away from him and dispersed, finding other things to do. He looked back at Graven, who had also seen it.

'I think we might look closer first,' the colonel said.

It was raining again as the ten Death Korpsmen reassembled by the Chimera.

Though they hadn't used their entrenching shovels in months, still they carried them in their backpacks. Colonel Graven sectioned up the ground around the vehicle and set them to digging.

He did his share, of course, but also kept a shrewd eye on the workers in the hamlet and the fields. Whether it was a washerwoman sitting with her tub, three men tying ropes around a subsided headstone or the small group building a pyre for Malek's corpse, every one of them looked nervous. Over and over, heads turned in his direction, even while their eyes avoided his.

When a shovel blade struck metal, Graven was not remotely surprised.

The Krieg converged upon the spot, making short work of layers of clinging mud. Barely a foot beneath the surface, ten shovels scraped a large, unyielding mass. More scraping uncovered a shape familiar to them. A circular gun mount attached to the roof of a tank, although the gun itself had been removed.

A brass-plated gun mount attached to a brass-plated tank.

While Graven had been busy, the fields had slowly emptied, workers slinking out of sight between their huts. 'They know,' the watchmaster said.

'A Land Raider stripped and buried in plain sight of their homes. They could hardly not know,' agreed Graven, 'and now they know that we know too.'

'Your orders, sir?'

'Round up the workers, every one of them. Secure them in the barn. Kill any who resist, but keep some alive to question.'

His Korpsmen snapped to attention, drew their weapons and moved out across the hamlet.

'This... this is inexcusable!'

Colonel Petrakov glared at the dataslate as if by force of mind he could rewrite the words upon it. He shifted his attention to the young captain in front of his desk, standing to attention. 'How could you let this happen?'

'Sir, the Guardsman in question arrived with the recent intake. I didn't know him well, but his record until now has been spotless.'

'From a good family, I see.'

'Yes, sir. His uncle is a lieutenant in Fourteenth Company. His sergeant tells me he was nervous, which is common, but keen to make his parents proud. There were no indications that he might...'

'Might take his Imperial-issue lasgun and kill two members of his squad as they slept in their trench!'

The captain looked shamefaced. 'Yes, sir.'

Exasperated, Petrakov muttered, 'Had it been an Attilan who succumbed, I might almost have understood it. A Vostroyan, though!'

The captain frowned. 'Colonel?'

'Have any other Guardsmen had nightmares? Heard voices in their heads?' A report from the Krieg Colonel Graven, which had reached him just minutes before, had made disturbing reading.

'I doubt they would report it if they had, lest they appear weak.'

'Find out,' snapped Petrakov.

'Sir.' The captain hesitated. 'Sir, have you read to the end of my report?'

He had not yet. He looked back at the slate in his hands. 'I read that the traitor was killed as he tried to escape.'

'But the truly disturbing part,' said the captain, 'is what happened after.'

'Emperor-loving lickspittles, why can't you leave us be?!'

Another spray of bullets was unleashed from a window of the shack. Colonel Graven kept his head down behind a rain barrel, bracing it against repeated impacts. It was holed, spewing out into the mud.

He returned fire and the shooter's head dropped out of sight. He signalled to the three Korpsmen with him, sending two around the structure to its rear.

Sporadic bursts of gunfire reached his ears from all directions. Few workers were giving up without a fight, but those fights were inevitably one-sided. Rayoul and his fellows in the shack were the best-embedded of them.

Graven had been counting shapes at windows. 'Five or more hostiles in there,' he called out, 'three autoguns between them.' His regiment had battered down the ferrocrete walls of thousand-year-old strongholds. Even without cannons, mere planks of wood would not deter them.

He gave his Korpsmen time to get into position. He nodded to the one still with him, his old engineer, who rolled a smoke grenade towards the shack. They charged into the black cloud pumped out by it, breathing clean air through their filters. Two guns fired blindly at them, missing wildly.

Graven's comrade smashed a window with his shotgun and fired through it as the colonel shoulder-charged the door. Its old latch broke, as did a hinge, and he ploughed through into a startled worker.

A rear door splintered open, allowing in more smoke and Korpsmen. Workers tried to run but were suddenly hemmed in. They panicked, shrieking with fear and anger. Only one got off a shot, which ricocheted off body armour. Reluctant to likewise fire into the crush, Graven wrestled his opponent's weapon from him and drove its butt into his skull. Another, unarmed, leapt at him, impaling herself through the stomach on the autogun's readied bayonet.

* * *

In less than a minute, it was over.

Two workers were dead, three more restrained. Graven located Rayoul in the thickening miasma. He was on his knees, bleeding from a head wound, the fight knocked out of him. Graven seized him by the armpits, hauled him out into the light and sent him sprawling in the mud.

He levelled his laspistol at the old man's head. 'The truth this time!'

'You know the truth,' Rayoul mumbled. 'I told you the truth.' He looked up at the colonel and a shadow crept across his face, hardening his features. 'Most of it.'

'What happened to Inquisitor Idelax? What did you do to him?'

'You won't find him.'

'Then he is still alive?'

Rayoul held Graven's gaze. His entire demeanour had changed, no longer subservient but self-assured. 'You'll join us someday soon.'

'The warp I will!'

'Another fallen soldier, his life traded for a false promise. If not on this battlefield, then on another like it. Death is life's only certainty.'

'And not to be feared,' said Graven.

'You would not say that if you knew.'

The words chilled him to his core. *Lies,* he told himself, *intended to weaken my resolve.* 'If you value life so much, then answer my questions!'

'I am you, Colonel Graven, you and all the others like you. The nameless in their billions, marching blindly to their fates. How many will it take, do you imagine? How many more deaths before your Carrion Lord feels sated?'

'Shut up!' he hissed.

'I am all of your comrades-in-arms, the Korpsmen who burnt for your mistake and cry out from beyond the veil for justice.'

Graven cocked his pistol. 'I warned you.'

'It's all so clear to us now. No sacrifice can ever be enough. For Krieg, there can never be atonement. Your God-Emperor will never set you free.'

A las beam through Rayoul's head stilled his vicious tongue forever.

The gunshot turned more heads towards the colonel: Korpsmen and their prisoners en route to the old barn. 'At ease,' he called to them. He worried, *How much did they overhear?* He had spared them the ravings of a heretic, he assured himself. Spared himself too. The old man lay in the dirt, face down. There was no doubt that he was dead – until his body moaned and spasmed.

Rayoul's very shadow was alive. Graven leapt back as it seeped out from underneath him, writhed about him. Like oily black smoke, it billowed up into the air, where it collected into a humanoid shape. Hovering above Graven, the spectre leered at him with its semblance of a face as if in mockery. Then, before he could recover himself to shoot at it, it dispersed on the breeze.

His watchmaster and two Korpsmen hurried to him, weapons drawn. Graven poked Rayoul's body with his toe, but it had fallen still now.

'Are all of them... influenced?' asked the first Korpsman to find her voice. 'Do all have spectres clinging to them?'

'They can't, not if the body's death reveals them,' the watchmaster said, 'for we've seen others die.'

'Just him, then? Just their leader?'

To Graven, both sounded oddly distant. The hamlet's wooden buildings seemed to shrink away around him. He was back in the previous night, back on his bedroll with the spectre looming over him. He felt its cold in his heart and lungs again. He had been briefed about a lord and lady coming to Oleris in search of the dead and finding them. Rayoul, if he could still be called that, had described an attack upon a nephew: '*...as if it were suckling on his very soul.*'

'No,' he said aloud, and snapped back to the moment. 'The spectre, the spectres, last night,' he said dully, 'weren't seeking to feed off us as we thought. Rather, it seems they wish to recruit us.'

Sixteen prisoners lay in the old barn, secured by ropes.

Some glared at Graven as he marched in, cursing him. Others were wrapped up in self-pity, sobbing to themselves. 'Murderer!' hissed the boy he had noticed before, no longer retiring but seething with malevolence.

He confirmed Rayoul's execution and threatened that it wouldn't be the last. He told them their only hope lay in confession. He picked the worker with the most mutinous look and asked him the whereabouts of Inquisitor Idelax. Barely had the worker drawn breath to spit defiance when Graven shot him dead.

This had an effect upon the others. This time, Graven chose the one who looked most fearful. Staring down his pistol, she couldn't find her voice, so he had her dragged whimpering outside to where her fellows wouldn't hear her.

Rainwater trickled down her upturned face in grimy rivulets. 'Please, sir, I had no part in this, I swear. The spectres whispered to me like they did the others, but I... I never listened. I did no harm to no one.'

'Nor did you try to stop it.'

'What could I do? Rayoul... One night, he changed. We'd always followed him, he was the wisest of us, but now he was so cold and cruel. He said we weren't to work no longer, and when he led morning prayer, it was not to the Emperor but...' Shuddering, the woman made the sign of the aquila.

'You could have spoken out.'

'Some tried, but, sir, we didn't know... we didn't realise how many had been listening till they turned on the dissenters. We had to do as Rayoul told us, or else... They took my neighbour in the night. Her screaming woke me. Others tried to run, but he had them hunted down, and... and...'

'And what?'

'And taken underground, to be fed to... to the creature.'

Graven exchanged a look with his watchmaster. 'The creature?'

'I heard it once, just once, while I was down there. Its terrible roar, echoing along the tunnels. It must be the size of... I... All I could do was pray, sir. I prayed for someone to come and save us, and it worked. It worked because He sent you here, so I did right, sir, didn't I?'

'And yet still you said nothing.'

'I wanted to – I tried – but there was always someone watching.'

'The witch hunter,' said Graven. 'Was he taken underground?'

'Yes. Yessir, he was, but not to the creature like the others. What they did to him...' The woman made the aquila again.

'Then you can take us to him.'

Her cheeks paled even further. 'No, sir, I can't. I can't go back down there. Please, please, don't make me go, I beg you, sir.'

Graven nodded to his watchmaster, who hauled the wretch to her feet. Brusquely, he said, 'If you still have faith as you claim, then you will be protected. No creature is a match for ten Death Korpsmen.'

'No, no, not just the creature!' the worker cried. Graven turned his masked face towards her and she swallowed. 'That... that's where they always come from. From the catacombs. The... witches.' She whispered the word.

The colonel waited.

'Rayoul sent a message when we saw your tank coming. He sent us back to work as if everything was normal. Like the last time, sir.

Like when the witch hunter... He fought them, sir, so hard, but the witches had the green fire in them and they burnt him with it.'

'You set an ambush for us,' Graven said in realisation, 'and all of your lies and your pretence were meant to keep us here until it could be sprung.'

The watchmaster asked, 'How long before they come?'

'Last time it was less than a day,' the woman said. 'They'll be here any minute, sir, and we... we must be gone before they are, or else they'll kill us too. Or something worse.'

Colonel Petrakov took a short tour of the trenches. He thought an appearance by him might reassure his Guardsmen. His commissars had warned him that word of last night's events, one of their own turned traitor, had spread quickly.

He was surprised to see for himself how much the trench network had expanded. This was due to the Krieg, of course, several squads of whom he saw labouring with shovels. Others manned their giant Earthshakers, loading, firing, reloading with clockwork regularity. Petrakov wore ear defenders, but the booming of the guns still almost deafened him.

Each officer with whom he spoke, his throat raw from having to raise his voice, told him the same. They had pounded the walls of the Ecclesiarchal Tower, destroying gun emplacements, but their scouts had seen no sign of life within.

Loath as he was to admit it, Graven may have been right all along. Petrakov had the creeping feeling that the tower was only a distraction, the true threat lying elsewhere. Sister Superior Serafina had contacted him again. She had been monitoring vox-traffic and was also concerned, piling further pressure on him.

He found the highest-ranking Krieg officer he could in Graven's absence: a commissar, who led him to a claustrophobic dugout some way behind the guns, where mud walls deadened their sounds to a tolerable level. Krieg bedrolls lay on shelves scraped out of the walls. As there was nowhere else to sit, Petrakov remained standing, the low roof pressing down on his fur hat.

The commissar, of course, was not Krieg-born, and though she wore a gas mask, she removed it to speak with him, a gesture very much appreciated. Her face was set like rockcrete, her voice rough like gravel. She heard his proposal and remarked, 'This could still be an ambush.'

'It could,' the Vostroyan acknowledged.

'In which case, the cost of hasty action could be my regiment's ruin.'

'Are you saying the Krieg would fear to take that risk?'

'If you knew them as I do,' she said sharply, 'you wouldn't ask that question.'

'Then?'

'A large part of my role with the Krieg,' said the commissar levelly, 'has been to rein in their penchant for self-sacrifice – and the tendency of others, not many but some commanding officers, to take advantage of it.'

Prickling at the implication, Petrakov said, 'Then what would you suggest?'

'In two more days, we can tunnel half the distance between the front trench and the tower.'

He shook his head firmly. 'No. We can't afford to wait that long.'

'If that is your assessment, Colonel Petrakov.'

'It is,' he said, finally decisive.

'Then I suggest we step up the bombardment overnight and send the first infantry wave over the top at dawn.'

'I will issue the orders,' he said.

'And of course,' said the commissar, in a studiedly neutral tone of voice, 'the Krieg will lead the charge.'

* * *

Graven rested his laspistol's stock on the window sill, into which he had carved shallow grooves to keep it steady.

Through half-drawn shutters, he had a perfect view of the door of the meeting house below him. From his vantage point he could also see two Korpsmen, crouching behind rain barrels. The rest were hidden from him. They had been in position for two long hours and more, but the Krieg were nothing if not patient. Graven stretched his muscles to stave off cramp, but kept his eyes firmly on the door.

A Korpsman tensed and signalled up to him. He had detected something. A moment later, Graven too glimpsed movement through the meeting house window.

At last the door was opened from within, revealing a man behind it. He was tall and emaciated, wrapped in a tattered brown cloak. He was hairless and his forehead was horrifically swollen, pockmarked with suppurating sores. Though Graven would have assumed it anyway, he was certainly a mutant.

He swallowed his disgust to fix his target in his sights. Said target, however, remained on the stoop of the hut, the door-frame obstructing his shot. The witch looked around with sharp eyes narrowed in suspicion. He must have wondered why no one had come to greet him.

The colonel held his breath, finger tensed on his trigger. The witch murmured something and, behind him, Graven saw a second figure, as he had been led to expect.

More seconds crawled tortuously by.

Then the first witch stepped out of the meeting house, into the rain.

And, at this pre-agreed cue, the Krieg kill team opened fire.

The witch reeled, gloriously, caught in a las-beam crossfire. His leg buckled, dropping him to his left knee. He gesticulated wildly, and in his hand Graven saw a bleached-white human femur. The witch drove one end of the bone into the mud while from the other, green sparks flew. The air around him shimmered, and suddenly the Krieg found their shots deflected by an almost invisible shield.

Graven cursed to himself.

The second witch stepped out into view, but the shield also protected him as he helped his ally to his feet. Graven took the chance to yell to his squad, 'Las fire won't penetrate that thing from this distance. Get in closer!'

The second witch turned to glare up at him.

This one was shorter, wizened, his bones twisted, leaning on an old, gnarled cane. Sewn into his brown cloak, three circles formed a triangle, arrows pointing out between them. The hateful symbol of the Plague God. Green fire ignited in his eyes, casting his face into malevolent shadow.

Graven tensed himself to leap for cover, but then the witch stepped forward through the barrier, which didn't impede him in the slightest, and he couldn't help but seize his chance to get off one more shot – but it only grazed his target's shoulder.

Faster than he had thought possible, green flames erupted from the witch's eyes and from his nose and open mouth, and streamed towards the colonel like a flamer's cleansing discharge, only with a sicklier quality.

The blast struck the window squarely, blowing its shutters inwards. Graven flung himself aside but was engulfed by overwhelming heat and light and searing pain. Determinedly, he held tight to his senses, but felt them slipping from him. Headfirst, he fell into a yawning pit of darkness, at the foot of which dead comrades reached for him with eager hands and vengeful cries.

Graven fell into their unforgiving grasps.

V

The sound of gunfire drew the Krieg watchmaster.

He had been stationed behind the meeting house lest someone try to slip out through a window. Now he crept along a narrow passageway between that building and the next. His back against the meeting house's wall, he peered around its corner. He saw the witches at its open door, mere feet away.

Having heard his commander's shout, he was just in time to witness the furious response. The watchmaster recoiled from an outpouring of unholy fire.

When he dared look again, the hut across the way was burning. Smoke belched from the window at which he had last seen Graven. He couldn't have reached him, even had the imminent threat not taken precedence.

The fire-wielding witch had stepped back to the other's side and now they advanced together, the shimmering dome around them moving with them. Two Krieg were flushed out from behind barrels as the psychic shield rolled over their position. They had nowhere to fall back to. They charged with bayonets fixed. The fire witch twisted out of one's way, his cane parrying the other.

His gaunt partner pointed at a Korpsman, clenched his fist, and his target convulsed and dropped his weapon, clawing at his throat. The fire witch pointed at the other, eyes flashing, and flames burst from the Korpsman's greatcoat. He dropped and rolled to quench the blaze. The first Korpsman too fell to his knees, struggling vainly against an invisible chokehold.

More Krieg were appearing in surrounding doorways, however, closing on their foes as instructed. The watchmaster yelled, 'Their shield is down!'

The shimmer around the two witches had indeed vanished, presumably dropped in favour of offensive action. The Krieg brought their guns back to bear, distracting the witches' attention from their victims, who lay gasping in the mud. The watchmaster left his own bolt pistol in its holster. The telekine was again waving his arms. A las beam to his back appeared to pierce whatever armour he was wearing, wrenching a howl from him, but he quickly recovered himself and restarted his ritual.

The watchmaster was still closest to him. From his belt he unclipped a frag grenade. He stepped from behind the meeting house and bowled it underarm. It landed with a plop between the witches' feet, even as their dome of force sprang up again – around them and the bomb.

He relished their looks of horror as they saw it, recognised it, did the only thing they could. They leapt for cover, through the shimmer, ahead of the inevitable explosion. Fire blossomed inside the dome, marking its borders plainly, and sent a tidal wave of boiling mud out through it over both the witches.

The fire witch was first to stand, but only to find Death Korpsmen streaming at him from every direction, their war cries merging into a discordant scream for vengeance. The witch recovered his dropped cane and tried to cast another hex, but screamed himself as bayonets tore into his flesh.

The watchmaster started towards the melee, but saw the telekine, lying on his back, stirring. He drew his pistol now, bellowing a warning.

The witch brought his hands together with a clap like thunder, and the Korpsmen around him were sent flying through the air as if by a sudden tornado. Rain barrels were uprooted with them, bursting open. A Korpsman slammed into the burning hut, which creaked and groaned, straining to break free of its too-shallow foundations. Others landed, winded, in the dirt up to a hundred feet away. Even the watchmaster, far from the epicentre, felt the blast, which sent him reeling back towards the meeting house.

Only the fire witch emerged unscathed, and he helped the other to his feet as their enemies lay groaning all about them. The watchmaster took a shot at him, but the witch gestured, the shimmer reappeared between them, and his las beam was easily deflected.

He had a sick feeling in his stomach, one he recognised having felt it just one time before. The feeling that the tide had turned decisively and that the Krieg, so close to triumph mere seconds ago, were now fighting a losing battle.

But then a new sound reached his ears. An old, familiar sound to give him hope. The sound of the watchmaster's prayers answered.

A thundering of hooves.

Graven came to with a hoarse scream of defiance.

He thrashed against imaginary foes, which dissipated into smoke. He was sweating. He was alone. He was in a burning building. Flames licked across the ceiling, and suddenly a blazing timber came plummeting towards him. He rolled out of its way as it crashed down by his head.

His scattered thoughts were reordering themselves. He remembered the witch's attack. He remembered where he was. He could make out a glow from the window at which he had been stationed. He had made it across the room from it. Just as well, as the inferno was spreading from there.

Graven couldn't see the door, but he remembered its position in relation to the window. He crawled on hands and knees towards it. Smoke was thickening around him – without his respirator, it would likely have choked him in his sleep. How long had he been out, and why hadn't his comrades come for him?

Was the battle still ongoing? Over the roaring flames, he couldn't hear.

The door was burning too. Its latch burnt his fingers through his gloves. He pushed the door open, tumbled through. The flames pursued him down wooden steps and out through the front of the hut.

Out here, the air was clearer, cooler, and he almost ran into an armoured horse. Graven drew his power sword and lit it up. He needed a moment to process all that he could see.

He saw Death Korpsmen and mounted Attilan Rough Riders. He saw the two witches, separated, both surrounded, desperate, wounded. Horses wheeled about them, riders slashing at their targets with curved sabres. The Krieg provided covering las fire and, where they saw an opening, bayonet charges.

The fire witch gesticulated, and green fire filled his eyes and mouth. He was preparing to unleash another blast. Before he could, a shotgun shell burst against his kneecap, causing him to shriek and buckle. His fire fizzled.

The telekine pointed at a charging horse; the animal stumbled, unseating its rider, who rolled expertly, tucking his chin and knees into his chest. The witch took his chance to flee towards the meeting house, but another Attilan rode him down: their sergeant, whom Graven remembered from the compound. Her horse reared up behind the witch and cracked his skull with its hooves. He fell in a welter of blood, and the gleeful sergeant's mount trampled his body into the mud.

Graven had seen enough.

The fire witch was kneeling, attempting to cast again, his hands trembling such that he could barely hold his cane. He saw the Krieg colonel bearing down on him and began to speak – whether to curse him or plead with him, no one would ever know. Briefly, Graven wondered if the witch knew him from his crested helmet, if he recognised a foe he had thought slain, and if that stoked his fear in his final moments. *They call us the Relentless Dead!*

His sword cleaved through the witch's neck.

The battle was over, but much remained to be done.

They searched the meeting house in case more witches lurked within. They dragged the altar back over the hole in the floor, along with a bench for good measure, to impede any new arrivals.

The witches' corpses they cast into the burning hut. They let the fire burn itself out, but contained it when it threatened to spread to other buildings. They didn't lack for rainwater for this task.

They tended to their wounded. Thank the Emperor, there had been no fatalities, only bruises, minor burns and, for the Korpsman thrown into the hut, cracked ribs. The watchmaster thanked Sergeant Batu for her squad's assistance. She grinned at him. 'Sorry we couldn't get here any faster. We rode as hard as we could after picking up your colonel's call.'

'Your timing could hardly have been better,' he said.

They checked on their prisoners in the barn. They had heard barely a peep from them, but that changed when they saw Death Korpsmen in the doorway. They must have heard the fighting and, now they knew its outcome, realised that they were doomed. Their anguished howls rang out across the hamlet, and the watchmaster wondered how many regretted their transgressions.

'It wasn't our fault,' one wailed, 'we only did as we were told.'

The watchmaster thought about the spectre that had attacked Graven in the night. What if his leader too had been overtaken? What if he had spoken with the spectre's voice today? *I would have known,* he told himself. *I would have seen it right away.* Still, it was an uncomfortable thought.

The Krieg were conditioned, above all, to follow orders, not to question. How much damage could an enemy have done that gave those orders? *It could not happen,* he decided. *The colonel resisted his spectre as any Imperial officer would. It does not control him and never could.*

They had kept their informant apart from the others, in Rayoul's old hut, tied up the same. Graven had her brought to him and told her that the witches were dead.

'Only two of them,' she moaned. 'There are others, many others, more each day.' She still feared to enter the catacombs, but he made it very clear to her that she had no choice in the matter.

The Attilans agreed to watch the hamlet while the Krieg searched underground. Sergeant Batu grinned and said, 'No room to ride down there.'

They uncovered the hole in the meeting house floor. Graven descended the rope ladder first. By lumen light, he surveyed his new surroundings. He felt his stomach tightening. His watchmaster's description of the ossuary tunnels had hardly done them justice.

I don't think I have ever seen anything quite so... He didn't have the words, but something was stirring in his chest. He clenched his teeth and quashed the feeling. *They are only remains,* he told himself, *only what we leave behind.* If it looked like the bleached skulls suspended in the walls were glaring at him, resenting his presence, it was only a trick of the dim light, a shifting of shadows.

The rest of his squad joined him, regardless of their injuries. The pain of a few cracked bones was easily negated by dialling up the stimm content of their water supplies. The informant froze on the ladder, insisting she could go no further, so Graven shook its ropes until she lost her grip and, shrieking, fell into his arms. 'Take us to the witch hunter,' he demanded, and with a pistol to her head, she did her best to pull herself together and obey.

For close to an hour, they trudged through the frigid darkness in their cocoon of lumen light. The informant led the way, hands bound behind her back, frequently stumbling. They followed tunnels that twisted this way, that way and back upon themselves. They came upon dead ends, including freshly dug tunnels not yet implanted with bones, and had to retrace their steps. They were watched all the way by the blank eyes of the dead.

Rayoul had been right about one thing. They could easily have lost themselves down here, but for the Krieg's experience in similar environments. Two Korpsmen mapped their travels with handheld wayfinders, and one of them spoke up: 'Sir, we have come round in a circle.'

The other concurred: 'The ladder can only be a hundred yards away in that direction.' She indicated a side tunnel.

Graven rounded on their informant, who shrank away from him. 'I… I'm trying, I swear – I'm doing my best.'

'To mislead us?'

'No. I've only been down here a time or two and always with someone to lead the way, and I… I just don't know…'

Graven turned to his watchmaster. 'Return her to the barn. Find someone who can be of more assistance.'

'Please, sir, you can't… can't take me back to them. They'll know. They'll know I turned against them, talked to you, and…

Give me another chance. I know where I went wrong now, and I swear I can do better.'

'She's no use to us,' said the colonel. The watchmaster signalled to a Korpsman, who seized the woman's arm.

'East!' she blurted out in desperation. 'They took him east!'

Graven turned back to her, slowly.

'I remember now. I was there when Rayoul told you. He never lied to you, only kept parts of the truth back. He laughed about that behind your backs, said you were easy to deceive, and he... I heard him say...'

'He said that when Idelax left, he "travelled eastward",' said the watchmaster. Graven recalled that too.

They returned to the ladder and, from there, followed their wayfinders. Graven pushed the informant ahead of him again and, before long, saw her confidence growing.

'Yes, this is the way, I'm sure,' she told them. 'You see how these crossed bones form a line of Xs? The entrance is just at the end of that line, but hidden.'

She ran her hands over the tunnel wall, plucking and prodding at its embedded bones. Graven stood back and watched her for a minute, but became increasingly convinced that she was stalling him again. He was about to say so when he heard a soft click, and the informant whooped with delight.

A section of the wall, bones and all, swung smoothly open, and Graven sent the informant through first.

The rest followed, filing into a broad, round, smooth-edged cavern.

Its centrepiece was a squat black altar, and Graven sucked air between his teeth as he saw the profane symbols carved into its stone sides, inlaid with silver thread. Atop it sat a dagger with a twisted blade, black candles in a holder, and a tarnished silver goblet containing dregs of what might have been blood.

There were bones in the walls, albeit fewer than in the tunnels.

Some had been gouged out and smashed, their remnants heaped about the cavern's edges. *Only what we leave behind,* the colonel reminded himself, but still he felt a flush of indignation at such flagrant disrespect.

Driven into the walls were the poles of tattered green-and-yellow banners, flying the Plague God's triangular symbol. Wooden benches, the same as in the meeting house but older, were scattered about. Clearly, this blasphemous church had been here many years.

Graven smelt the prisoner before he saw him. He lay behind the altar, chained to it by his wrists, curled into a foetal ball. His satin-lined cloak was torn and soiled, as was his synth-leather armour. He looked like he might be dead, until he flinched as light washed over him.

The watchmaster reached him first and crouched beside him.

'Is it him?' asked Graven.

'Hard to say. He answers the description, but any symbols he may have carried have been stripped from him.'

The watchmaster shook the supine body, which roused and swore at him. 'You'll gain nothing from me, I have told you. The Emperor protects those whose faith in Him is staunch.'

'Inquisitor! Inquisitor Idelax, I am His servant too.'

The prisoner opened his eyes for the first time, regarding the watchmaster with a watery gaze. 'Praise be to Him,' he whispered, then passed out again.

Inquisitor Idelax woke.

He felt like he had slept for a very long time. He lay in a soft bed, with sunlight streaming through windows and vague memories of being hoisted from the earth's bowels in an improvised sling. He had been undressed, cleaned, shaved and his wounds tended. Fresh clothing was piled on a wooden chair beside him. Worker's clothing.

His entire body ached. Manacles had left their imprints in his wrists. He didn't trust his newfound comfort, fearing it some kind of dream or trick – but no, his mind was too strong for the former and he would soon see through the latter.

Instinctively, he felt about himself for his Inquisitorial rosette, though it had been wrested from him weeks ago. He felt the deep pang of its loss afresh.

He heard movement below him, on the ground floor of what he surmised was a grave worker's hut. His throat was raw, so he banged his headboard against the wall until he heard footsteps on the stairs. On second thoughts, the bed was far from soft, only compared to the cavern floor.

Two masked soldiers – Krieg Death Korpsmen, Idelax had dealt with such before – entered the room. One brought a jug of water, from which he filled a chipped mug. 'It's laced with stimms, sir, if that is acceptable to you,' he said.

Snatching the mug, the inquisitor drained it in one gulp.

He turned to his other attendant, whose shoulder bore the chevrons of a sergeant – no, a watchmaster. 'Are you the one I saw down there?' he croaked.

'Yes, inquisitor. You are Inquisitor Idelax?'

The witch hunter nodded. 'You command this unit?'

'No, sir, I serve under Colonel Graven. I'll have him informed that you have woken.' The watchmaster motioned to his Korpsman, who set down the jug and left the room. He asked the inquisitor if he had any other needs.

'Only information,' said Idelax, 'of which I have plenty to exchange.'

'As soon as you feel stronger, doubtless the colonel will oblige you.'

'Only my flesh has been abused.' Against his muscles' protestations, he hauled himself into a sitting position. 'My mind and soul are fortified, as strong as they have ever been. No, stronger. I am ready.'

Idelax gestured to the chair. The watchmaster, standing to attention, seemed undecided for a moment, then set the pile of clothes aside and took a seat.

'Thank the Emperor for heightening your senses,' the witch hunter muttered, 'allowing you to pierce this coven's cowardly deceptions.'

'Inquisitor, I'm sure that given time you would have done the same.'

He glared at the watchmaster sharply. 'Not for a second was I duped!' Then his chiselled features softened, and he sighed. 'What I was unprepared for was that they should turn an acolyte against me.'

'We had heard such a tale.' The watchmaster spoke with caution.

'The spectres didn't show themselves to us as they did you. They targeted Djallon in secret, I believe, because he too was warp-touched. I fought him in the old barn, where the spectre that possessed him made use of his psychic talents, before it fled his shadow once I took his head.'

'Yes, we observed the same.'

'The distraction, I regret to say, proved more than sufficient to its purpose.'

'We know the workers summoned reinforcements.'

'By the time I emerged from the barn, the battle was already lost.'

'The same witches we encountered?'

'One, perhaps. A fire-wielding man and a woman with power over lightning. There were six more in my retinue all told. Two had already fallen, in addition to the psyker and the one slain by him, while I myself was weakened – and the workers too assailed us, held us back, while...'

Idelax trailed off. The watchmaster could see in his eyes that he was no longer in the room but reliving his ignominious defeat. It felt strange to see a witch hunter like this. Lacking his vestments, he could have been any civilian, weak and vulnerable. He was young by the standards of his ordo, old by those of the Krieg, blue-eyed and blond. The watchmaster didn't know what to say to him, so was glad when they were interrupted.

Colonel Graven remained in the doorway. He introduced himself and asked if Idelax was fit to travel. 'Colonel Petrakov is keen to speak with you, inquisitor, and I believe our work here done.'

'No witch has aught to gain by returning to this hamlet,' Idelax agreed.

'Nor were there any spectres in the night. With your assent, I plan to move out at ten-thirty local time, which is eighty-six minutes from now.'

'What of the prisoners?'

'I leave them in your hands, inquisitor. Should you wish any kept for interrogation, the Attilans will take them to the tower.'

'No. I want them dead,' snarled Idelax. His handsome face had hardened, his blue eyes no longer haunted but piercing and cruel, and now at last the watchmaster saw in him the Emperor's wrath personified and was heartened to be one of the devout.

'Sir,' he said, 'one of them led us to you.'

'None are to be spared,' the witch hunter reiterated.

Graven nodded, turned and left the room.

To the watchmaster, Idelax said, 'All have been touched by Chaos. They pray to the green fire now, that one day they might wield its power. From the cult to which they have pledged their allegiance, there is no return – and we have nothing more to learn from them.' He took another drink.

When he had finished, the watchmaster prompted him, 'They spoke of a creature in the catacombs?'

'I never set eyes upon it, only heard its bestial roars. I couldn't tell you what it was, only that my captors spoke of it with fearful reverence. They made sacrifices to it, among them my retinue's survivors. I believe it may have taken cultists too, on occasions when they failed to sate its hunger.'

'They never took you to it?'

'No. The witches had other plans for me. A darker purpose. They chained me to their altar and they...' The witch hunter took a breath. 'You know about the incident that brought me to Oleris III? The lord and lady?'

'The witches tried to place a spectre in your body?'

'I thank the Emperor that my heart and mind were pure, my will sufficient to resist their incantations.' Idelax's eyes faded for a moment, but he hardened them again. 'No, watchmaster, not a spectre, but something far more vile.'

They set light to the old barn with the remaining cultists in it.

Graven had had each cultist shot first, an act of mercy. He hadn't wished to hear their screams as they burnt. His Korpsmen had used the workers' own autoguns, conserving Imperial resources.

Some had died with curses on their lips, some pleading, others accepting their fates with quiet dignity. His informant had been among this final group, to his surprise. He had no sympathy for her, nor for any of them. They had made their choices in full knowledge of the price. Even the youngest of them. Everybody had to die, but they had squandered the lives they had been given.

Graven no longer doubted that there were others like them, many others. Other cultists, other witches. He had been right to insist on coming here. He took no pleasure in that fact; it only made his mission harder, thus more probably his last. His regiment's last chance to earn its name.

The Chimera's tracks had sunk into the mud. Korpsmen dug busily around them, sliding duckboards under them for traction.

Inquisitor Idelax stepped out of his hut, wearing plain grave worker's clothes but standing tall in them. He basked in the heat from the burning barn. Then he turned to survey his surroundings, located Graven and approached him. 'I hear my Land Raider is out of commission.'

Both glanced towards the nearby half-dug pit. 'When we've time, I shall send a squad back here, equipped to salvage all we can,' said Graven.

Idelax waved away the offer, turning back to the Chimera. 'I'll ride in the turret with you. It will give us time to talk.'

'Are you sure that's best, inquisitor? You have been through a punishing ordeal. We can make you more comfortable in the troop compartment.'

Deep blue eyes rested on the colonel. 'I believe a spectre tried to take you over.'

'Yes, inquisitor, two nights ago.'

'Why do you imagine it chose you?'

Graven had asked himself the same question and so had an answer ready. 'They targeted our leader, as they did the workers' leader.'

'Hmm. They did not target me,' said Idelax.

'Perhaps because your psyker posed a greater threat to them. My watchmaster tells me that was your assumption too.'

The witch hunter pursed his lips in doubt, but said no more.

The watchmaster saw off Sergeant Batu and her mounted squad.

Wistfully, he watched them cantering along the muddy tracks

until they were only specks to him. He had hoped to ride with them – ostensibly to make space for Idelax in the Chimera – but they weren't returning to the compound. They had business in another hamlet, from which Graven's call had diverted them.

The watchmaster turned to find the witch hunter standing behind him. He blinked. 'May I help you, inquisitor?'

Idelax said bluntly, 'Tell me about your commander.'

That was unexpected. 'The colonel?'

'You work most closely with him.'

'For almost five months, sir, since he took command of the Four Hundred and First Regiment and assigned me to his command squad as his deputy.'

'For many Krieg, that would be a lifetime of service.'

'Indeed.' The watchmaster realised that Idelax was waiting to hear more. 'The colonel is… efficient. Pragmatic. Dedicated. He is…' He struggled for the words. 'He is a Death Korps officer.'

'You trust him?'

'With my life. I know he will make it count. Colonel Graven has sworn to make each life in his regiment count, to compensate for prior losses. Sir, if I may ask, has my loyalty been called into question?'

'You need have no worry on that score,' said the witch hunter. 'I have encountered Krieg before, and you, watchmaster, typify them. You do not flinch from my examination. You answer my questions directly, without obfuscation.'

'Only the guilty fear to speak the truth.'

'Yes, that is so. All the same, it is natural for even the most faithful, in the presence of one such as me, to find doubts in their hearts, to fear that I might see them too. Your people I have found to be exceptions, possessed of a rare self-confidence. I believe that you, that most of you, are free of doubt.'

'Your pardon, inquisitor, but I fail to see your point.'

'Colonel Graven is a Death Korps officer.'

'Yes, sir.'

'Efficient. Pragmatic. Dedicated. Strong enough in heart and mind to fight off a spectre's attack.' The witch hunter took a step closer. Something dangerous flashed in the blue depths of his glare. 'Then why can't he look me in the eye?'

VI

The Ecclesiarchal Tower had been retaken.

Colonel Petrakov rode to it in his Salamander command vehicle. It was a slow, uncomfortable journey, juddering over trenches and along narrow pathways cleared through rubble by heavier artillery. It ought to have been a triumphant one, but nothing had been won today.

At dawn, at the sound of a whistle, hundreds of Krieg Death Korpsmen had clambered from their trenches to swarm across no-man's-land. Reports had quickly reached command headquarters, in equal parts expected and concerning. No fire had been drawn from the tower.

Vostroyan Guardsmen had queued at scaling ladders, awaiting the second whistle, which had never come. The Krieg had reached the tower unmolested and were searching floor by floor, but so far had found nothing but the mutilated bodies of the priests who had once ruled here.

The Salamander pulled up in a cobbled courtyard. Its walls

had crumbled under shelling, the unmanned cannons behind them broken. The tower's main body, though holed in many places, stood defiant. The Ecclesiarchal skull glowered down from its grey setting, as if resentful of its mistreatment.

Petrakov was met by a masked Krieg commissar and captain. They escorted him into the tower, told him where to safely step, showed him the vandalism wrought even before the bombardment. Not one symbol of the priesthood had been left intact. Heretical slogans were spray-painted on the walls.

The upper floors were in a similar state, he was assured. Rather than climbing, however, the colonel was led down winding, worn stone steps. Cold shadows wrapped themselves about him.

He descended for what felt like an age, until he reached the tower's dungeons. Sconce-mounted torches provided a flickering light. He peered through the bars of a cell door and was not surprised to see bodies stacked up within. 'The priests, I assume. Is this what you brought me here to see?'

'No, colonel,' said the Krieg commissar, and he recognised her husky voice, having met her in the trenches but not asked her name. 'Not this.'

A crude hole had been battered through a rockcrete wall. Sprayed above it, in misspelled Low Gothic, was the taunt, *Comme fynde us if you darre*. Tentatively, Petrakov approached it. He could hear movement through it.

The captain reassured him: 'Our people, sir. I sent two squads through to secure the immediate vicinity.' Torchlight, spilling through the hole, glimmered off a white wall comprised of… What was that, some sort of ivory tiling?

'We believe the witches fled this way, no less than four days ago,' said the commissar. 'As you can see, they broke into the catacombs, which run–' She cut off as new sounds came to their ears through the hole. A bestial roar. A warning shout. Lasgun reports.

'Stay here, sir – we can deal with this.' The captain raced towards the sounds, the commissar not far behind him.

With an indignant huff, Colonel Petrakov drew his ornate, hand-tooled Vostroyan lasgun. With just a tad more caution than the Krieg had shown, he followed them into the breach.

The journey back to command headquarters felt twice as long as the outward leg had.

The difference was Inquisitor Idelax's presence, beside Graven in the turret. The colonel felt under constant scrutiny, even when the witch hunter's eyes were closed. Little as he had to say, he felt as if his silence were being judged.

Idelax asked questions about recent days' events – all perfectly reasonable questions – before appearing to succumb to weariness. Graven couldn't tell if he slept or not. However, as they neared their destination and the spires of the Grand Mausoleum appeared on the horizon, Idelax turned to him and asked, 'What did they say to you? The spectres?'

Graven studied the road ahead of them. 'They claimed to be the spirits of old comrades.'

'Any comrades in particular?'

'None I could identify. My regiment has many nameless dead.'

'Such as the ones who perished on Maximus Arkanos?'

The witch hunter's knowledge should not have surprised him. 'They lamented their lives wasted. They sought to take my life in recompense. They claimed I should have died that day instead of them.'

'Do you agree?'

The question, bluntly delivered, shocked Graven into turning. Idelax was still slumped in the gunner's seat, eyes hooded but intense.

'No,' the colonel said, but he knew it was a lie. 'Perhaps for a moment, in dreams. Upon awakening, I fought.'

'Djallon, my acolyte, dreamt too,' the inquisitor said. He waited for that to sink in before continuing. 'That night, his final night, he woke up screaming. I might have probed him further, but his kind are habitually tortured. I imagine it must be the shame, the knowledge that through weakness they allowed the warp into their minds. No matter how determinedly they turn their powers to the good, they know they teeter on the edge of sanity.'

'One stray thought from the abyss,' the colonel muttered.

'Djallon's spectre did not cause his shame.'

'Perhaps you're right. Perhaps they did see something in me. In unguarded moments, I might have asked myself why I was spared above so many others.'

'Survivor's guilt is not uncommon,' said Idelax, with surprising equanimity.

'But futile,' Graven insisted, 'as we Krieg know more than most, especially those of us long-lived enough to rise in rank. The divide between life and death can be as slender as a footstep in a minefield, the order in which we form up in the trenches.'

'Hence you do not take names for yourselves.'

'Only for the convenience of others.'

'To keep you from mourning individuals?'

'Because it matters not which of us die, so long as some survive to see that their deaths counted.'

'Yet still you mourn.'

Graven inclined his head in assent. 'For all that Krieg has lost and will yet lose before its debt is paid.'

'Death can often seem capricious,' the inquisitor agreed, 'but I believe the Emperor sets a path for each of us to follow.'

'I believe that, in some way I cannot know, my regiment strayed from that path,' said Colonel Graven, 'and was harshly punished for it. Since then, I confess, finding my new path has been a struggle, but I see it now.'

He sensed that his answers were meeting with approval, but still the probing continued: 'Then you harbour no guilt over your regiment's failure?'

'No,' said Graven, and repeated it to reassure himself. 'No, I do not. The tribunal ascertained the truth. Krieg high command appointed me to lead this regiment, and I would not presume to doubt their judgement.'

He regretted his candour as, in a quiet growl, the witch hunter asked, 'There was a tribunal?'

The Krieg were battling some kind of mutant creature.

Petrakov only glimpsed it through the Korpsmen pressed about it, in the narrow confines of a bone-filled tunnel, by the sputtering light of a lumen cube dropped and kicked between pairs of muddy boots. He glimpsed its furry chest, its backward-jointed legs, its horns. *A beastman!*

It lacked the room to wield its massive sword, whereas the Krieg made full use of their shorter blade bayonets, stabbing and rending at it. Petrakov levelled his lasgun, but doubted he would see a clear shot, nor need one. The beastman howled in pain and fury as a bayonet was thrust through its wrist, its sword relinquished.

Now he saw another like it, lying twitching, being trampled on the ground. The situation, he judged, had been well controlled.

Until he heard a snort behind him.

He whirled to see another creature, head down, charging at him on two legs, hooves pounding, the points of a pair of curved horns jutting out, threatening to gore him. He couldn't get out of its way. Though there was a tunnel opening between them, he couldn't have reached it in time.

That knowledge brought calm upon him. His fate in the Emperor's hands now, Petrakov dropped to one knee, switched his gun to its full-auto setting and squeezed the trigger, filling the tunnel with a blinding light barrage that the beastman in turn could not avoid.

It had almost reached him when, blessedly, it stumbled, failing its endurance test. It planted its repulsive goat's face in the dirt before his feet, and already the Krieg were streaming past him and falling upon it.

Standing, the Vostroyan colonel stiffened his legs. He didn't want anyone to see how they were trembling with a delayed adrenaline release.

The battle was soon done, three beastmen dead. At their captain's instructions, the Korpsmen fanned out through the tunnels to guard against any more approaching, but called back that none were to be seen.

'What happened here?' the captain asked the squad's watchmaster. 'An ambush?'

'I believe not, sir. I believe the creatures heard or smelled us coming and attempted to withdraw, knowing we outnumbered them, but by a fluke of the tunnels' layout we already had them cornered.'

Petrakov stepped forward. 'This concerns me. How were we not aware that Oleris III had bred these abominations?'

No one had an answer for him. Never had he seen a beastman for himself before, and the sight revolted him. They dated back millennia, to the Age of Strife, their origins unknown.

'Invariably,' the commissar said, 'such creatures are drawn to worlds upon which the Ruinous Powers have gained footholds.'

Petrakov feared that she was right. Along with the priests, scores of servants had lived on the tower's lower floors, and just a handful of corpses had been found. The rest must have left with the witches – whether willingly or otherwise.

He decreed, 'I want that tunnel entrance sealing up. I intend to relocate command headquarters to the tower, to send a message to the people of this world that the Emperor still has oversight here.'

He also intended to leave these gloomy catacombs as quickly as he could, only, when he turned to do so, he saw tunnels branching off and didn't know which one to take. Not wishing to admit this, he reluctantly waited to be led again.

He felt as if the walls of bones were closing in around him. He found this place unnerving, a monument to death. He thought that only mutants like the beastmen, like the witches, could bear to be down here.

'What needs to be done now seems obvious,' said Colonel Graven.

Petrakov had assembled his army's command staff in the war room: the old one, in the compound, as the new one was still being cleaned up and equipped.

Sister Superior Serafina had turned up for the meeting, along with the same Battle Sister as before. 'This taint must be scoured from the face of this world,' she agreed, 'and from beneath it.'

'So our saint may once more rest in peace,' her larger comrade said.

'Indeed.' Petrakov gestured with his swagger stick, and technicians rushed to light up a freshly prepared hololith. Graven recognised the shape of Oleris III's largest and only habitable continent. 'Unfortunately, no reliable schematics exist of the catacombs beneath us.'

'The ossuary,' Serafina corrected the Vostroyan.

'Quite. The ossuary, which has expanded over generations on an ad hoc basis.' He gestured again, and hundreds of glowing red dots overlaid the map. 'We do, however, know where they... it can be accessed. Could be accessed, I should say, as even this information is decades old.'

'I hear these tunnels run hundreds of miles,' said the Attilan Colonel Tegana.

'Then we have much work ahead of us,' Graven said flatly.

Inquisitor Idelax spoke up. He looked healthier than he had that morning, his blond hair cut and washed, the colour returning to his cheeks. His synth-leather armour had been cleaned and stitched, and he wore a new black, fur-trimmed cloak over it. Sewn into this with silver thread – perhaps in the past few hours – was the Ordo Hereticus' symbol, the ubiquitous Imperial 'I' with three crossbars. Beneath the cloak, Graven had already glimpsed a finely crafted Vostroyan plasma pistol.

'I have sent a report to my ordo, recommending that Oleris III be purged.' Through gritted teeth, the witch hunter added, 'For a fourth and final time.'

'Is the Inquisition claiming jurisdiction here?' asked Petrakov.

Idelax shook his head. 'It may be many months before action can be taken. I believe the situation too urgent to wait.'

Graven said, 'These witches and their followers have hidden underground for decades, centuries, growing in both numbers and power.'

'What is it the rumours say?' mused Petrakov. 'That the veil between life and death is thin here?'

'If left unchecked, who knows what other horrors could be summoned,' commented one of the two Krieg captains whom Graven had brought with him. He noticed Idelax suppressing a shudder at that thought.

'Action must be taken now,' said Serafina, stridently.

'Every sinner on this planet must be rooted out and slain!' proclaimed her Battle Sister.

'Their leaders, at least,' said the Sister Superior, 'must be found and executed, before they can bring whatever schemes they are hatching to fruition.'

'We must be methodical,' said Graven. 'My regiment has the most experience in subterranean manoeuvres and so should take the lead. Each of our squads should attack the ossuary from a different entrance and chart a course towards the others, leaving our foes nowhere to run.'

If Petrakov was irked by his presumption, he managed not to show it, having more pressing concerns. He agreed that most of his Firstborn regiment would enter the tunnels, but that the Attilan Rough Riders would stay above ground, where they were most effective. They would keep searching the hamlets, catching anyone who might try fleeing to the surface.

A Vostroyan captain asked, 'Sir, what of the spectres?'

'What of them?' Graven snapped.

Petrakov said, 'My regiment has four sanctioned psykers attached. Against immaterial beings, they may be our best defence.' He looked to Idelax for support, which came in the form of a silent nod.

'Then I suggest,' said the captain, 'we set them to guard the mausoleum.'

'No!' barked Serafina. She steadied herself with a breath. 'As I understand it, our defence against these wraiths is strength of faith, the last thing my Sisters lack. Your sanctioned witches would be best employed elsewhere.'

'Sometimes, Sister Superior,' said Idelax quietly, 'it takes a warp-touched mind to fight a warp-spawned horror.'

'No witches in my regiment,' Tegana grunted.

Petrakov asked, 'Colonel Graven?'

'Never have I heard of a Krieg-born psyker,' Graven said with a measure of pride, once again drawing Serafina's approval. 'We are prepared for spectres now. We know their tactics. They are vulnerable when they attack, so will soon learn not to attack us. I am more concerned with this other, more bestial creature.'

Idelax filled in the details for those who didn't know.

'Presumably,' said Graven, 'its lair is close to where the inquisitor was held, as he heard it often. Finding and dealing with it will be my kill team's primary mission. We have already mapped part of the area.'

'Could it simply be another beastman?' asked the Vostroyan captain.

'From the way my captors spoke of it,' said Idelax, 'unlikely.'

Tegana had stepped away from the table to speak with an Attilan messenger. Returning now, he said, 'I have new information. A squad of mine unearthed another cell of cultists, persuaded one to talk. About the creature. He took sacrifices to it, glimpsing it once in shadow. Twice a man's size, he says it was. More beast than man and ravenous for human flesh, flying into a fury when denied it.'

'Very much as I suspected,' said Idelax.

'Our informant named the creature,' Tegana said, 'Devourer.'

Idelax retired early for the night.

His well-appointed quarters in the tower were unfit to occupy at present, he had been informed. Petrakov had given him the best he could, a private bunkroom adjoining his own. The drumming of rain on a tin roof, surprisingly, soothed him, lulling him into a deep, unguarded sleep.

In dreams, he was back in the hamlet, fighting witches with his loyal retinue. Djallon, his psychic acolyte, fought harder than the others, having more to prove. A halo of pure white light surrounded him, from which the anaemic green flames of his foes retreated. Idelax's neural whip cracked, the witches shrieking as it lacerated their backs. He blinked and they lay dead in the mud, alongside their misbegotten followers. He looked down at them, satisfied.

He looked up to meet Djallon's green-flashing eyes. *'Is this what you wanted to see, inquisitor? Is this your only dream now, of what might have been?'*

'Who are you?' Idelax demanded, and lashed out with the whip, which passed through Djallon's insubstantial body.

The psyker laughed at him. *'Who am I? I am your failure manifest, the weakness blinding you to what was underneath your nose. You know who I am.'*

'No. No!'

'Not only him but everyone who ever trusted in you, dead because of you.'

'You are a spectre, playing on my guilt, and I deny you!'

Idelax blinked and was back in the underground temple, chained to the black altar, with witches gathered about him, faces hooded. Sweet, cloying smoke from black candles teased his nostrils. The iron tang of blood, poured from a silver goblet, lingered on his lips and tongue and clogged his throat. A twisted blade was poised above his heart, and he could feel... something – a cold, oily, evil presence, probing, worming its way into every pore of his exposed skin.

'Wouldn't it be so much easier to give in?'

He screwed his eyes shut, clenched his teeth, focused his will to resist. He heard the witches' rhythmic chants disturbed by doubt, felt oily tendrils flinching from him as if burnt. Opening his eyes again, he was dazzled by his own bright light, but it was green rather than white. With a final supreme effort, he directed the light outwards, screaming not at the witches but at the spectre in his dreams: 'Begone!'

And found himself back in his bed, sitting up with arms outstretched, as a pair of Vostroyan Guardsmen burst through his door.

'Did you see it?' he demanded of them.

'Sir, we only heard you shouting.'

'There was a spectre here, but it is gone now. My faith repelled it.'

'Nothing passed us outside, inquisitor.'

Tetchily, he said, 'Then it must have entered through the wall and fled the same way. Search this block. Search the compound. Look in on Colonel Petrakov. Something may still be hiding in the shadows.'

'Yes, sir,' one of the Guardsman said, before saluting unnecessarily, but Idelax was accustomed to that. As both hurried out, he sank back into his soft pillows, which were damp. He wiped cold sweat from his brow with the back of his hand.

The watchmaster also dreamt.

He was back in the saddle, wind whipping through his greatcoat, heart pounding to the beat of hooves against the rocky scrubland. He leaned forward, closer to his mount, shifting their combined centre of gravity, increasing their velocity.

His comrades were behind him. In his sights was an ork battlewagon, an ugly-looking scrap metal hulk. Its cannon belched out fire, but its gunner had misjudged the speed with which its foes were bearing down upon it, or lost its nerve at the fearsome sight, and so the shell shrieked overhead.

The watchmaster – ridemaster as he was again – thrust his lance into the wagon's armour plating, wheeling his mount away from the shaped explosion. Six more lances in turn scraped plasteel, and the grotesque xenos that had clung to the battlewagon's hull leapt from it as flames burst from its engine.

Slaughtering the burnt and scattered orks, then, was only a formality. The Death Riders encircled them, any attempting to escape the cordon mauled by hooves and teeth. The orks waved crude stone spears and axes, but never knew from which direction the next charge, the next thrust of a Krieg sword, would come and so could not defend against it.

Within minutes, they lay in a broken heap and the ridemaster's facemask was spattered with dark ork blood.

He gave his squad a break to adjust their mounts' drug intakes and dress the few cuts they had suffered without feeling them. His own mount was untouched, so sliding from it he simply thanked it for its service with a pat. It snorted with something like scorn as the ridemaster turned his attention to his objective.

The ancient city's skeletal remains squatted on the near horizon, a silhouette against the darkening sky. Almost within his reach. He monitored reports through his vox-earpiece, learning that half of his regiment, approaching from other compass points, were already at its outskirts.

Then, without warning, the ground shook.

'God-Emperor, no!' Barely had the ridemaster breathed the words before the shockwave struck him: a noisy blast of hot, dry, debris-peppered air, which almost bowled him over and sent even the Death Riders' stoic mounts skittering back on their splayed feet with startled whickers. *The forbidden weapons!* Never had he believed that the xenos, even they, would be so stupid, reckless, clumsy. *So bold?* For hadn't the Krieg once burnt their own world too, when they had seen no other path?

The city's skeleton was collapsing, melting, and then it was visible no longer, engulfed by thick black smoke, which continued to build upon itself and spread into a top-heavy mushroom shape, suspended like a death shroud above a killing field miles wide.

The ridemaster had a sick feeling in his stomach. He should have been giving orders, but he had none. His earpiece was silent too. In that dreadful, timeless moment of slow-dawning comprehension, all voices had been silenced. He thought about his comrades at the blast's centre, who would not have stood a chance. *How many comrades?*

He looked around his squad, still stunned and gaping at the mushroom cloud, and in the present, in his dream, the watchmaster knew what, in that moment, he had feared but hoped and prayed might not be true.

He knew that their layers of protection, their rebreathers, would not save them. Not as close as this. Not even their mounts would survive. Not even his own venerable steed. Death would come upon them slowly but inexorably. All of them. All but him. From that moment, they were truly dead men walking.

Graven didn't sleep.

He lay on his bedroll, listening to his Korpsmen's breathing in the next room. He was not afraid of spectres, so he told himself. He had posted sentries inside the mess hall, in addition to the ones Petrakov had patrolling without, so any spectre thinking to harm him would find itself shredded by las fire.

He couldn't sleep because his mind was whirring. Endlessly, it replayed his conversations with Inquisitor Idelax.

The latest of these had occurred outside the war room. Graven had felt a firm hand on his shoulder, turned to meet intense blue eyes. *'I will accompany your squad tomorrow.'* Why had the witch hunter said that?

The Devourer, he told himself. Idelax had an interest in that mysterious monster. He had been threatened with it, lost comrades to it, so naturally wished to see it slain. But what if there was another reason? What if the inquisitor suspected that Graven had lied to him?

No. I never lied. He had held back part of the truth, however, which was a fine distinction. *The tribunal ascertained the truth.* And Captain Graven, standing in the dock, had held back nothing from them. He had welcomed the judgement of his own people upon him, only to be confounded by it.

Things were different now. Then, he had seen nothing to live for. Now, he had found his path. Or so he had believed. Now judgement was something to be feared. The judgement that, deep down, he still felt he deserved.

I withheld the truth from an inquisitor.

He had been given every chance to speak. For one of his station, Idelax had even sounded reasonable. Subdued, as his ordo had feared, by his weeks held captive? Or baiting a trap? Graven's silence on its own was reason to condemn him, and so, although he saw no shadows shifting in the corners of his room and heard no whispers in his mind, still he was haunted through the night.

They set out in the morning mist again.

Most vehicles leaving the compound today were Vostroyan, spick and span beside those of the Krieg. They were to collect soldiers from the trenches, convey them to their new assignments. Some would travel overnight to the continent's far shores. Among them stalked Scout Sentinels, eighteen feet tall, with Guardsmen hunched in their cockpits, controlling their piston-driven legs and weapon arms, poised to lead the way across uncharted territories.

Graven paced beside his Chimera, ploughing a furrow in the mud. Last night, he had made a decision and was glad of it, but its weight lay upon him until he could put it into action.

Inquisitor Idelax failed to appear on schedule. Instead, a Vostroyan lieutenant approached Graven. The pair exchanged salutes. 'The inquisitor sends his regards, sir, but advises that he won't be travelling with you today after all, having business to attend to.'

'I see,' said Graven, numbly.

'Colonel Petrakov will procure a flyer for him, so he may join you later.'

He thanked the lieutenant and dismissed her. Surrounded by purposeful activity, the colonel stood entombed by his own thoughts. Having anticipated another uncomfortable journey, now he didn't know quite what to think.

Last night he had convinced himself that, one way or another, what he needed was something he had once possessed but lost. He needed certainty. He would add to his previous day's statement, confess and face the consequences. Now he had been robbed of that chance and knew he might not get another.

Perhaps it is best, he told himself. *If the inquisitor has asked his questions and is satisfied… Could the Emperor be sending me a sign?* But his secret, promised its release and now denied, churned resentfully inside him.

Few people living knew the truth about him, about that fateful day, not even his senior officers. He had been advised that no one else needed to know. The day of the nuclear bomb. The dark day upon which so many Krieg had died: his fault, because it had been his duty to stop it.

On that day, Graven had disobeyed his colonel's orders and, by so doing, had brought about his regiment's destruction.

VII

The hamlet appeared undisturbed since Graven's last visit. Smoke from the burnt-out barn still flavoured the air. The hole inside the meeting house was covered.

His kill team spent the day here, with little to do but maintain their equipment. Other squads needed more time to reach their starting points so that they could all attack the tunnels simultaneously. Long months in trenches had taught Graven patience, but the memory of the ghosts he had faced here three nights ago kept him on edge.

They slept in the downstairs rooms of Rayoul's shack. The alarm was raised only one time in the night, as a sentry saw a shadow at the window. If there had been a spectre, however, it evaded their questing lights and slipped away.

Next morning, they moved aside the meeting house's altar, unfurling the rope ladder. Graven sent his engineer into the pit. He had almost reached the bottom when, in a loud whisper, he called up, 'Someone has been back here. The ground beneath me is freshly dug.'

The engineer clung to the lower rungs a while, examining the tunnel floor by lumen light. Then, shifting his weight, he set the ladder to swinging back and forth and, as it reached its apex, jumped from it.

Landing clear of the area beneath the ladder, he returned to crouch by it. Shrugging off his backpack, he rummaged through it for a trowel. Above ground, Graven moved everyone back outside the meeting house. They waited.

Twenty minutes passed before the engineer reappeared in the doorway. Gingerly, he held a metal disc about ten inches in diameter. His comrades gave him a wide berth as he carried it clear of the huts. He laid the mine down in the mud, packed grain sacks around it. He fired his shotgun from a distance and his second shell hit, causing a muffled detonation.

'Was that the only one?' asked Graven.

The engineer confirmed that it had been, and so the Krieg descended, one by one, into the catacombs.

They followed the maps sketched on their prior visit to the profane temple. Graven wanted it checked before they turned their backs to it.

The engineer examined the bone-filled wall with its secret catch and declared this also booby-trapped. His comrades withdrew again until he made it safe. This time, it required only one snip of a wire, which would otherwise have pulled taut as the hidden door was opened.

The temple was empty, but not as they had left it. The altar had been dragged across the floor as if in hope of relocating it until its weight had proved too great. The items that had lain upon it had been taken. The cut wire led to a frag grenade, wedged between a skull's teeth in the wall.

They were about to move on when Graven heard a faint noise

in the distance. It could have been an animal growl. He raised a hand for silence and all ten Krieg listened intensely, but the sound was not repeated. Even had it been, it would have been drowned out by the next one: the shriek of jet engines, descending above them.

The cavern shook, dislodging small stones from its ceiling.

Graven had no wish to split his forces, so returned them to the ladder. He sent the watchmaster up to greet Inquisitor Idelax and invite him to join them.

Graven led the way through the catacombs, alongside his engineer, who scanned ahead of them with a handheld auspex. Though he found no more traps, still the threat of them impeded progress – which, the colonel ruefully acknowledged, may well have been the point.

His Korpsmen followed in two files, the watchmaster bringing up the rear. Graven was hyperconscious of Idelax's eyes on the back of his head. The inquisitor walked in the formation's centre, at Graven's suggestion, despite having stated tartly that he needed no protection. Each time Graven gave an order, involuntarily his gaze flickered to the witch hunter, thinking he might countermand it.

They followed the left-hand wall, a precaution against losing themselves in the labyrinth. In the underground silence, every sound they made returned to them, amplified. Their own footsteps clattered in their ears, often forcing them to pause to be sure they weren't being pursued. Their own breaths merged into a constant susurration, not dissimilar to the spectres' whispers.

Rounding a bend, Graven found his path blocked by a wall. A particularly large white skull in its centre glared at him, hissed at him: *'You lead them to their doom as you did us.'*

He halted his squad. 'Spectres! Can anybody see them?'

His Korpsmen, gripping their lasguns, checked the walls, the ground, the roof before reporting in the negative.

'More voices, colonel?' asked Idelax, sounding like he was accusing.

Denial would have served no purpose. 'I will not listen to them,' Graven swore.

'Remember, the mind is poisoned only by the words we hear.'

They doubled back, took the next left turning, and he tuned out the susurrations, telling himself that if syllables seemed to form within them, they were only a trick of the mind and they meant nothing.

It was probably due to this effort that he didn't hear what most of his squad did, what made them halt again.

'No doubt about it this time, sir, something is stalking us,' reported his watchmaster. 'Some kind of… snuffling creature.'

'The Devourer?'

'From what we've heard of that, I'd say much smaller.'

They listened, breaths bated, for a minute, but heard nothing. Eventually they moved on, but very soon a whispered message from the watchmaster made its way up the ranks to Graven. The creature had been heard again.

There was only one thing to be done.

Briefing his nearby comrades with hand gestures, Graven slipped away from them through an opening in the right-hand tunnel wall. The Korpsman immediately behind him followed him. The rest continued on their way, behind the engineer.

Graven waited in the tunnel mouth.

He drew his sword but didn't activate it. As his team moved away from him, following their tunnel's curve, they took their lumens with them, so that absolute darkness stole over him and now only his ears could guide him.

He heard the footsteps of his squad receding, but beyond this only his own breathing and that of the Korpsman beside him. *'We remember what you did and we are down here, waiting for you.'*

Graven heard no creature. He wondered if his watchmaster might have been mistaken, though he never had been before.

He would never know what it was that saved his life. A noise, after all, but not coming from the expected direction and almost subliminal? A subtle shifting of the tunnel's air currents? Had it simply been instinct that alerted him, in that instant, to the threat?

He whirled around, yelling to his Korpsman, lighting up his sword and, in its pale blue glow, seeing claws, fangs and blood-crazed eyes.

The beastman flew at Graven, a spitting, snarling ball of matted hair. He had underestimated its intelligence, let it split his forces after all. It wouldn't profit from it. It would find even two Death Korpsmen more than a match for it.

His comrade, lacking time to fire his lasgun, stepped to meet the charging creature, slid a bayonet between its ribs. Hardly wincing, it raked him with its claws. The Korpsman grunted, falling back, as Graven swung his sword. Aiming for the neck, he sliced instead into a human shoulder.

Close up, he saw scarred, blistered red skin through the beast-man's fur. It had a wolf's pointed ears and elongated snout, and the latter thrust towards him, open wide, spittle spraying from its jagged teeth. He could smell the rot on its hot, wet breath. He thought that, were it not for his rebreather, it would likely have infected him already.

He threw up his free arm, lodging it underneath the creature's jaw, keeping it at bay. But it was strong, far stronger than he was, scrabbling at him with clawed hands and feet.

Just as well, then, that he was not alone, that no Krieg ever truly was. Rallying, his comrade stabbed the beastman in its wounded side, working the blade inside its body. Evidently he pierced something vital, and it reeled, allowing Graven to draw back his sword and thrust it into the beastman's stomach, sending it howling to the ground.

They continued to hack at its thrashing body until it was definitely dead.

Footsteps clattered up behind them: his squad, returning having heard the sounds of battle. Graven checked himself for injuries. There were tears in his greatcoat, but not in the breastplate beneath it. His Korpsman's flak armour had been shredded, but his skin had not been broken.

'One down,' the colonel growled, 'but many more to go.' He watched as the beastman's entrails burnt to ash in the blue fire of his blade.

Rain dripped through the tunnel roof and pooled along its floor. The Krieg sloshed through cold, muddy water, which seeped into Graven's split boots. More and more, they heard activity around them, grunts and scampers, as if there were many creatures circling them, afraid to come too close.

'It could be that we are being tracked,' said Idelax, 'by witches with some kind of second sight.' Graven found this a discomfiting idea.

His engineer halted, holding up a warning hand. Hunched over his auspex, he whispered, 'Sir, I have a reading. Life signs.'

'How many? Where?'

The engineer made some mental calculations. 'Ahead of us and left, around a hundred feet away, two, perhaps three of them, clustered, stationary.'

'Directly in our path, then. An ambush?'

Graven filled in the rest of his squad, and they advanced with caution. The tunnel branched, and once more they followed the left wall as it curved back on itself. Lumen light fell upon an opening in the same wall. Graven looked at his engineer, who nodded. They withdrew a step.

The Krieg took up firing positions, two Korpsmen on their stomachs in the water, two crouching over them, two standing behind. Six guns brought to bear, with four more standing by. Idelax stepped back and watched as, at a signal from his colonel, the engineer pitched a lumen cube along the tunnel. It landed with a plop, a few feet short of the opening – from which Graven heard a rasping breath caught in anticipation.

Long seconds passed.

Then, just as he had hoped, impatience overcame their waiting foes. First one and then a second sprang from hiding with triumphant roars, which froze in their animal throats as they saw that their targets were not where they were expected to be. The ambushers had become the ambushed.

These beastmen were goat-faced, like the ones described by Colonel Petrakov. Scraps of leather armour were lashed to their muscular frames and one carried a holstered autogun, for which it reached too late. In a furious few seconds, they were ruthlessly gunned down. Clinging to its final thread of life, a beastman tried to crawl back into cover, but shuddered with the impacts of more las beams and fell still, its face submerged in filthy water.

The auspex found nothing else lurking. Graven heard more scampers and suspected that more creatures had closed in as the battle had begun, thinking again upon its abrupt cessation. 'If we are indeed observed,' he said, 'then our path is easily foreseen. We must be less predictable.'

He consulted with his two navigators. Comparing the crudely sketched maps on their dataslates, they found them broadly in agreement. From now on, their role would be more crucial than ever.

They passed the tunnel opening from which the beastmen

had come and took the next right turn. They marked their route with a boot-polish arrow, daubed onto a prominent skull beside the junction. At each turning thereafter, Graven chose a way at random, while his Korpsmen pored over their maps, sometimes stopping while the engineer checked bearings and distances.

Having travelled a short way in this fashion, they were halted by a new and chilling sound. It was a loud, deep-throated roar, which came from some indeterminable distance away, reverberating through the tunnels. A roar of wounded anger, but one also tinged with arrogance. It sounded like a challenge.

The Devourer was calling its foes to itself.

'Do we take the bait?' asked the watchmaster.

'If we do, we make our path predictable again,' said Graven. Catching Idelax's narrowed gaze, he added, 'The Emperor wishes that monster slain. What other option do we have?'

They came upon an upward-leading tunnel, where the ground was dry again. The higher they climbed, the further it narrowed about them. The bones embedded in the walls soon petered out.

They had not passed a turning in some minutes. For the third time, they heard their quarry's roar and there was no doubt about it this time – it emanated from behind them. 'The monster only finds its voice when we have strayed off course,' the watchmaster observed.

Graven pressed on regardless and, soon enough, saw his hoped-for reward – a grey patch of daylight ahead. The passage took a sharper upward turn before ending at a rusted metal grille, through which he could see the sky.

It didn't take long for two Korpsmen to work the grille free. The Krieg climbed out of a small round hill into a field, where rows of headstones and a desultory drizzle greeted them. It was mid-afternoon.

Graven allowed his squad a short break. He saw wooden huts in the distance and considered making for them to find a vox-caster and report to headquarters, but he judged them too far away, and anyway, who knew what might be waiting there?

It concerned him that Idelax, slumped on the hillside, looked weary, his blue eyes red-rimmed. 'Inquisitor,' he warned, 'we cannot rest here long. We may still be watched.'

'Yes, yes,' agreed Idelax, tetchily.

'This seems a good spot for us to sleep tonight,' said Graven. 'If you wish, you could stay here, with guards of course, until the rest of us return.'

'Only my flesh is weak,' the witch hunter muttered, and from a pouch inside his black cloak, he produced a small bottle of tablets and thrust one into his mouth. He swallowed, closed his eyes and breathed deeply for a minute.

He opened his eyes to find Graven still looking down at him. 'Was there something else, colonel?' he asked sharply.

There was, but now was not the time, not least with nine comrades within earshot. 'No, inquisitor,' said Graven, 'that is all.'

They filed back down the access tunnel, back into the catacombs.

'If our foes know our location,' the watchmaster had pointed out, *'they know we must come back this way and have had time to prepare.'*

Already well aware of this, Graven kept a hand on his laspistol. The auspex, however, picked up nothing of concern, and soon they were back in the ossuary, once more surrounded by its bones.

'Perhaps we have shaken off the witches' sight,' the colonel said, but even as he spoke, their lights found something on the tunnel floor.

It looked like a shapeless mass of rags as they approached it, but Graven had seen enough corpses, too many, to know better.

Kneeling, he peeled back a torn cloak, stiff with encrusted

blood. A cracked and dented skull gaped up at him. Grey scraps of meat clung to the skeleton's ribs, marking it as more recent than it looked, its flesh having not had time to decompose entirely but rather been stripped from it.

Only what we leave behind.

Idelax loomed over Graven's shoulder. His jaw was taut with anger. From the remnants of its clothing, he identified the corpse as one of his former acolytes. 'The cultists kept her alive for days. They threatened her to force compliance from me, which only underlined their lack of understanding. Finally, they took her to the monster. They took pleasure in preparing me to hear her dying screams, but she was silent almost to the end.'

He knelt beside the body too and prayed over it.

'Inquisitor,' said Graven at length, 'we could bury her.'

'No,' said Idelax, standing. 'No, clearly she was placed here to test our will and slow us down. Instead, our foes reveal to us that they are close at hand and give us yet another reason to–'

He was cut off by the Devourer's roar.

It seemed like they were closer to it now, which made it easier to pinpoint its direction. 'No time to lose,' said Idelax, and they set off towards it, but even as they did so, from behind them came another sound.

Las fire. A sustained volley of it. Someone, somewhere in the labyrinth, was fighting for their life. It could only have been another squad, Krieg or Vostroyan. Perhaps they had heard the roar and been drawn towards it too. Graven's instinct was to go to these comrades, but he didn't know the way.

They walked for half an hour longer, glimpsing no more beastmen, hearing no more gunfire, but the roar of their quarry twice more. Graven heard no further whispers. He began to wonder – hope or fear? – that he had imagined those before.

Then torchlight spilled into the tunnel they were following, and soon it opened out into a small, almost circular cave, three torches fixed at equidistant points about its edge. 'For our benefit?' the watchmaster wondered aloud.

'Or the monster's,' said Idelax.

A Korpsman pointed out moss clinging to the roof, some fifteen feet above them, evidence that there had long been light here, as nothing could have grown without it. The cave seemed empty, but five more tunnels led from it. Six ways from which an attack might come, including from behind them.

One opening was taller than the others and framed by a polished black stone archway. Embedded in its lintel, a row of six bleached skulls clutched gems in their eye sockets, glittering red, blue and green. Graven realised that every other skull in the walls of the cave had been angled towards them.

He motioned to his squad. In pairs, they crossed the cave to shine their lights along each exit tunnel. In the mouth of one, they found a beastman, which routed with a squeal. They fired after it, but Graven held them back from pursuing it. He had only glimpsed the creature's hairy form as it dropped onto all fours to run, but it had been faster than human, and even had they caught it, they could have lost themselves or found another ambush.

The Devourer was more important. A threat to every soldier in these tunnels and, he thought, some kind of figurehead to their foes, if not an object of their worship. Though it hadn't been heard in a while, the path to it could hardly have been clearer. The archway was like an invitation. *Or a goad,* he thought. As if it made any difference.

Graven re-formed his squad. He glanced at the witch hunter, who gave him a nod of approval. The colonel checked for tripwires in the archway and, finding none, stepped through it.

* * *

The tunnel behind the archway bent sharply to the right.

Another torch was mounted in a sconce on its right-hand wall, whipped by a cold, damp breeze. A Korpsman, checking her rebreather unit, confirmed that the temperature had dropped two degrees. Opposite the torch, a shaggy, horned, two-legged figure was sketched crudely on the wall, human skeletons scattered at its feet.

'The sacrifices must be brought along here,' said Idelax, 'with the torches placed to ensure they miss no detail of their grisly fates.'

Graven started down the tunnel. After just a hundred yards or so, it split into three narrower, rough-hewn branches, each with torches too, their light showing him that each soon branched again. There were no bones in these tunnels.

'These look like natural faults,' he said. 'There appears to have been a small amount of excavation, but not lately.'

'The Devourer has claimed this as its territory,' said Idelax, 'possibly even during the Chaos plague, and its servants have kept the ossuary from encroaching upon it.'

Before Graven could reply, he heard a sound behind him – a grinding of ancient gears, followed by a resounding clang of metal upon stone. Whipping around, the Krieg snapped up their weapons, finding no targets for them.

The watchmaster took a few steps back along the tunnel. 'A gate, sir,' he reported. 'A gate has come down across the opening.' He leapt back as an autogun barked and a bullet ricocheted off the wall close by him.

Now, Graven could hear rasping breaths and what sounded like satisfied snickers. 'A mechanism, hidden in the archway,' he said ruefully, 'with beastmen sneaking up to trigger it as soon as we walked through and seal us in here.'

'With the monster,' a Korpsman said.

'Exactly where we wished to be,' Graven reminded him, though inwardly he remonstrated with himself: *I should have been more cautious, should have searched for more than merely wires.*

Idelax hefted his new plasma pistol. 'I could turn those bars to slag, if I could reach them without coming under fire.'

The engineer said, 'A demolition charge tossed down there would blow out the gate, but it would likely bring the roof down too.'

Graven nodded. 'Leaving us as trapped as ever. We go on.'

He picked a random tunnel branch and marched along it, then another, his squad falling into step behind him, now forced into single file. 'Keep an eye on that auspex,' he instructed the engineer.

'I will, sir, but the way these tunnels wind, we could be inches from a foe before I get a reading from it.'

Graven was well aware of that. In these confines, they were at a distinct disadvantage. A foe could be in melee with them before they could employ their guns, and if that foe had claws and teeth and animal strength…

He activated his power sword. *A waste of its charge with no foe in sight,* he chided himself, but its light would give them heart. 'We must keep moving, keep a step ahead of it, seek out an arena more suited to our strengths.' He was a Krieg Death Korpsman, after all, a former engineer himself. Tunnels like this were his element. Tunnels every bit as claustrophobic and oppressive as these felt.

The tunnel he was following, however, narrowed further and became impassable. Quickly, Graven turned the squad around, knowing that if anything was coming up behind them they were well and truly cornered.

At the junction, he made another choice, which after its initial promise brought them to another blind alley. Here, the

Krieg discovered scraps of bones and blood-soaked grave worker's clothing. An extinguished torch lay on the ground beside them, as if it had been snatched to use as a weapon, in vain.

A navigator spoke up: 'Sir, I need a moment with the wayfinder.'

'Keep moving,' said the colonel, gruffly.

In the next narrow tunnel, the roar of the monster reached them, and the torches seemed to gutter with its force. It sounded dead ahead of them, almost on top of them.

'Not guiding our course this time,' a Korpsman breathed.

'No,' Graven concurred, 'but playing with us.'

He chose a path away from their tormentor, but feared that he was being herded. When next he had a choice to make, rather than maintaining his heading, he picked a tunnel that switched back, encouraged by the breeze emanating from it.

They continued in this fashion for what felt like many hours, although Graven's wrist chrono gainsaid this.

A couple of times, the auspex picked up life signs, faint enough to be mistaken, but they steered clear of them all the same. Wherever Graven felt a breeze, he took that tunnel, even when it seemed to lead them back towards the Devourer. Especially then. He was tiring of this game of cat and mouse, and almost wished for the monster to tire of it too and make its move.

Despite this, in a twisting tunnel, where the torches seemed more widely spaced than usual, the definite sound of hooves on rock caused the colonel to signal a retreat. *There must be a better place to make our stand!*

The Krieg's mapmakers had conceded defeat. They traversed tunnels that Graven thought he recognised. Sometimes they found boot-polish arrows left by their former selves and ventured into new directions from them.

As the breezes from the tunnels strengthened, Graven grew

more confident in his decisions. He realised that he had stopped looking elsewhere for approval.

He turned into a tunnel definitely new to him. It was longer, straighter than most, and at its end, bright light blazed through a large round opening. He signalled to his squad behind him to proceed with stealth. The floor of the tunnel was well trodden and, increasingly as they travelled down it, strewn with broken bones and bloody scraps of clothing. A faecal stench assailed his nostrils, growing ever stronger.

The monster's lair, it has to be! Halfway along the tunnel, he halted, sent a single spotter ahead. *We weren't supposed to find this, weren't supposed to get this far, but I outsmarted it. Now we can turn the tables on the monster, set our own trap for when it returns.*

And then he heard its roar again, blasting out through the opening.

The Devourer was in there.

It was no longer stalking them around the labyrinth, if indeed it ever had, but rather it was waiting in its lair. Waiting for them.

Now Graven was no longer so sure of himself. His spotter had frozen, turned to him for orders. The rest of his kill team looked to him too, Inquisitor Idelax's face as inscrutable as any Krieg gas mask. Was he the one outsmarted after all? Did the Devourer know its prey were here? He felt it must. It must have heard them, smelled them or been tipped off by its psychic allies. Did they go on and face it, knowing this was what it wanted, or turn back?

Then came the roar of anger, of challenge, again, the same as every other time but this time from behind them, from no further than the end of the tunnel they were in. Which was impossible. Unless...

'God-Emperor!' the witch hunter breathed, and Graven felt his throat constricting. 'Two of them.'

And they had the Krieg surrounded.

VIII

In the end, it wasn't such a tough decision. Graven gestured to his squad and, as quietly as they could in the circumstances, they raced up the tunnel.

At least this way they had a chance. A slim chance that the trap around them hadn't yet been closed. A chance of getting through that opening and into the Devourer's lair before they were expected. A chance to put up a good fight and not simply be slaughtered.

Their lone spotter raced ahead of them, into whatever might lie in wait, expecting the nature of his death to be a warning to his comrades, thus worthwhile. For a second, he paused in the opening, eclipsing its blazing light. Then, firing his lasgun repeatedly, he plunged through it.

Graven followed his lead without a qualm. A cavern opened up around him. A brazier burnt at its centre, assaulting his eyes with its brightness, its smoke being drawn up through a flue pipe in the roof. The walls were draped with dusty tapestries.

He saw heaped furs and piles of broken skeletons. This was a charnel house, and in its centre, by the brazier, his spotter was duelling with three creatures.

Goat-faced beastmen. Two attacked with knives, which the Korpsman's bayonet parried. The third, with an autogun, looked for a shot between its allies. Graven charged that one with his power sword. Startled, it sprayed bullets in his direction. Most pinged off the wall around the entranceway, forcing a Korpsman on his heels to duck back through it.

Eyes still adjusting, Graven swung at the beastman's still-blurry mass. It howled as he severed its arm below the elbow, sending its gun skittering away. Weaponless, it lunged at him, trying to bite his throat, impaling itself on his readied blade. Its sudden weight on him sent him reeling all the same. His boot went through the ribcage of a brittle skeleton, ankle twisting under him. He hit the ground, the creature's wet corpse slamming down on top of him.

He wriggled out from under it, took stock of his surroundings. His kill team had poured into the cavern, so the two remaining beastmen were outnumbered, fighting no less fiercely for it. Hanging back beside the wall, Inquisitor Idelax levelled his gun coolly and, seeing his chance, squeezed his trigger. With a flash of superheated plasma, a beastman fell, clawing at its melted flesh.

Where was the Devourer?

Graven's eyes searched the stacked furs, presumably its bed, which could have concealed a giant. An angry roar from right beside him made him start. It emanated from a vox-speaker lashed to a trolley. The audacity of it took his breath away, that these animals had employed a mere recording to mislead him.

The last one fell, blood gushing from its many cuts. Graven stood, breathing a sigh of relief not for his life but for his regiment's sake. His first instinct had been right, however – they hadn't been meant to reach this place – and now they had pierced its last deception too. He hoped.

Two Korpsmen hurried back to the entranceway, taking up positions to each side. Peering through it, one reported, 'Nothing coming up behind us, sir.'

'Perhaps there never was a monster after all,' the other said. 'Though if there is, it can't have failed to hear the battle.'

But the skeletons were evidence enough. One, lying sprawled across the bed, was not yet picked wholly clean, still bloody. 'I only see one entrance to this cavern,' said Graven. 'Should anything appear, we would be cornered here, but at least there is some cover and room to manoeuvre.'

'Or we could mine this lair,' the engineer suggested, 'and hide out in the tunnels till the thing returns.'

He never heard his colonel's reply, as a hanging tapestry by his shoulder trembled.

'Behind you!' a Korpsman yelled, and barged the engineer aside. Simultaneously, Graven heard a thundering of hooves. He snapped up his laspistol as a massive, black, horned beast ploughed into the cave, through the tapestry, shredding it in the process.

The Devourer, like the beastmen, was a cross between animal and human, though Graven saw little of the latter in its shrivelled yet blazing red eyes. It had a bull's broad head, thick neck and horns, but was mutated far beyond that even. Its hirsute torso swelled with undulating muscles, and slimy tentacles extruded, writhing, from between its ribs.

It snorted, pawed the ground and tossed its head, shaking fabric from its horns. The Krieg were already fanning out, seeking cover, taking their first shots at it. The Devourer was naked but for a soiled loincloth and a clattering collection of bead necklaces – tributes of some kind? – but las fire hardly made it flinch. Its hide was tough like armour plating.

With startling speed, the monster whipped around and pounced upon a pair of Korpsmen. Its right arm was a giant, snapping claw, like that of some hideous crustacean. The claw crashed down between its targets as they separated, and bit into the cavern's rock floor.

The monster's roar, at such close quarters, made Graven's ears ring and stirred the daemons in his mind. He pumped his pistol's trigger, loosing off shot after shot. His target, at least, was too large to miss, and it had to have a weak spot. He aimed for those tiny, puckered eyes, but the monster swung away from him. Another claw swipe demolished a pile of bones behind which a Korpsman had been crouching. Two others rushed up behind the monster, gambling that blades might harm it more than beams, but again it was too fast. It rounded on them, forcing them to backpedal desperately, an inch ahead of evisceration.

They had had the right idea, thought Graven, just the wrong equipment. Holstering his pistol, he gripped his power sword two-handed.

He heard a plasma pistol's distinctive *woomph*, and flames engulfed the Devourer's claw arm. It had had another Korpsman in its sights, but now it recoiled with a howl, its fur alight, giving her a chance to scramble from its shadow.

Its huge head snapped around. The monster stared up at the roof as it sniffed out the source of its pain, and Graven suspected it was blind. Still, it found Idelax across the cavern from it, his back to the wall. Four Krieg stood between him and the Devourer, to whom it paid no heed whatsoever.

With a snort that blew steam from its nostrils, it lowered its horns and charged the witch hunter, and the Korpsmen in its path had to move fast or be gored or trampled, though some thrust their bayonets into the monster's black mass as it thundered past them. One found his lasgun snatched from his hands as its attached blade lodged in its side, while flailing tentacles lashed others.

Idelax stood his ground, levelling his plasma weapon – until he seemed to realise that it needed more time to recharge, whereupon he could only tense himself to try to dodge the monster, as futile as this surely was.

Graven, racing up behind it, was too late to help. The inquisitor looked doomed, but a Korpsman threw himself onto the Devourer's curved horns, baffling whatever senses it possessed and throwing it off course so that Idelax, by a hair's breadth, was able to dive out of its way.

The monster rammed the wall with an impact that made the cavern shake – and, in the process, crushed its masked attacker.

Graven screamed with rage and stabbed it in the back, cutting into muscle, drawing blood. Throwing back its great bull's head, the monster carried its victim with it, impaled upon one horn, and had there been hope left for him at all, it was quashed as his body was shaken like a rag doll and flung across the cavern, landing with a force that broke it further.

With the Devourer thus occupied, if only briefly, half a dozen Korpsmen rushed it, swarmed it, leapt upon it. Over and over, they thrust bayonets into its freakish form, and Graven was among them, his energy-wreathed blade slicing all the deeper. Its tentacles impeded him, discharging thick, green-glowing pus as they were severed to flop and wriggle snakelike on the ground.

With a mere shrug of its malformed muscles, the Devourer flung four attackers from it. Whirling, it lunged at the one hurting it the most, and Graven had to duck beneath the arc of its smouldering claw, before recoiling from its grasping tentacles and almost being felled again.

Preparing for the next attack, he was glad to see his watchmaster still on the monster's back. One hand clung to a bead necklace as the other drove a sword bayonet into a brawny neck. That certainly got his unwilling mount's attention. The Devourer bucked and thrashed, then, when it failed to dislodge its tenacious rider this way, threw itself into a wall to scrape him off.

The watchmaster hit the ground and, winded, barely evaded a stamping hoof that would have cracked his skull. The foot was raised to stamp again, but the monster, leaking blood like a strainer, teetered, and Idelax, circling the brazier, keeping it between him and his foe, now took his second shot.

His plasma stream burst against the back of the Devourer's head, raising a ferocious burnt-meat stink – and making it, finally, buckle, although clearly it had no intention yet of giving in. Snorting with the effort, it employed its remaining tentacles to lever itself back to its feet, as the Krieg regrouped around the cavern's edge and blasted it again with las beams, bolts and shotgun shells, widening its wounds, causing them to gush more copiously.

'Keep it up, it can't stand this punishment much longer!' Graven crowed, slapping a fresh power pack into his pistol.

The Devourer turned his way again, and with a roar louder and more furious than ever, it propelled itself towards him. Graven dived to avoid it, landing in its earthy-smelling furs, in which he floundered. He rolled onto his back, to get off one more shot before the monster trampled over him. Instead, it stumbled under his comrades' sustained assault and never reached him.

Lying on its stomach, it jerked and thrashed and snorted under las fire for a minute more, until the colonel ordered his squad to cease firing. The Devourer raised its burnt head at his approach, snorting at him, too weak to do anything more. Even its horns had half-melted into impotent nubs.

Graven hacked through its neck with his power sword until it died.

* * *

'Hmm. Smaller than I expected it to be,' said a Korpsman with disdain, standing over the huge black carcass.

'More ancient, though, and powerful,' said Idelax, 'gorged on centuries of sacrificial offerings. Your handling of it was impressive.'

'Thank you,' said Colonel Graven on his squad's behalf.

The Devourer's viscous blood was everywhere they stepped, and it was bleeding still. It seemed like it would never stop. Two Korpsmen dropped a heavy fur over it to slow the spread.

'One guard on the entranceway,' the watchmaster ordered. His gaze fell upon the torn tapestry and the wide crack in the wall behind it, through which the Devourer had come. He corrected himself: 'On each entranceway, and someone to check for others behind the wall hangings.'

Idelax noted that he didn't assign these tasks to particular Korpsmen. They looked to each other and, silently, those most able volunteered. Others had been injured in the fight, at least two bleeding badly. One appeared concussed and sagged against the cavern wall, his head against his drawn-up knees. Or was that the female Korpsman whose voice the inquisitor had heard? He couldn't tell.

One was dead, of course.

Idelax joined Graven and the watchmaster, praying over the body. When the monster had targeted him, when his plasma pistol had failed him, he had thought his life at an end. *Not yet,* he had prayed, *before my comrades are avenged!* and the Emperor had answered through a loyal servant's actions. A life given in exchange for his, by a soldier who had thought his life worth less.

Not that the witch hunter disagreed, but others might have been more reticent.

'Did he have a name?' he asked.

The two men of Krieg exchanged an uncertain glance.

'His life counted,' he assured them, knowing this would please them.

Around them, Korpsmen had broken out their medi-kits, applying sterilising fluid and gauze to cuts and bruises, sealing deeper gashes with sprays of synthskin, rubbing blessed lotions into strained muscles.

Graven took a look around his squad. 'The day is growing late, and absent the discovery of more hidden ways into this cavern…?'

'Nothing so far, sir,' his searching Korpsman called over on cue.

'Then, being in a fairly defensible position, we might consider sleeping here.'

Idelax wrinkled his nose. 'Does not the smell concern you?' It emanated from a dark alcove at the cavern's rear, its floor lined with straw.

Graven said, 'You're welcome to our spare rebreather, to filter out any toxic particles.' It took the inquisitor a moment to realise that he meant the dead Korpsman's rebreather, another to be certain that this wasn't some morbid example of Krieg humour.

In the absence of a quartermaster, the watchmaster was scavenging equipment from the body. He called to a comrade, 'Is your lasgun still shorting out?' Hearing that it was, he tossed the fallen Korpsman's weapon to him.

Graven turned to ask him, 'What size are his feet?'

Idelax's gaze lingered on the colonel as he swapped boots with the corpse. He had meant what he said – he had found no fault with Graven's squad, and thus his leadership, today. It was clear that the Korpsmen under his command had faith in him, but faith, as he well knew, could be misplaced.

'Colonel,' said the watchmaster, 'might the jewelled archway be the only way back into the ossuary?'

Graven was ahead of him. 'If so, then once our enemies know we have slain their Devourer, they might well seal the opening and entomb us with it.'

'I should take the fittest Korpsmen and find a way back there.'

'Agreed.'

'I am unhurt. I will come with you,' Idelax offered.

'Inquisitor, that is not necessary,' said Graven.

'Even so.'

'Your stimms are close to wearing off. Unless you take another dose – which I would recommend against, for your own health – your weakened state would only be a hindrance.'

Idelax glared at Graven, unused to being spoken to so plainly, but knowing he was right. He gave in with a silent nod and stepped away. He watched as the watchmaster gathered three Korpsmen to himself and led them out into the tunnels. He watched as Colonel Graven helped another dress a wound on his – or her? – back, regardless of the difference in their ranks.

The words whispered to him two nights before still echoed in his mind, the accusation that complacency had blinded him.

He would not be blind again.

The watchmaster led his four-strong team around the labyrinth.

No longer being stalked, they could afford to be methodical. They followed the left-hand wall again, knowing that in time it had to lead them to the exit. The engineer had brought along his auspex, while another Korpsman had taken a wayfinder from an injured comrade.

Turning down another narrow tunnel, the engineer noted a boot-polish arrow at its mouth. 'It's been crossed through to mark this as a dead end.'

The watchmaster asked, 'Then why do I see light down there?'

As they proceeded cautiously, he heard low voices too and

felt a warm, stale breeze. At the end of the tunnel, light seeped through a crack in the wall, and the watchmaster knew now what to expect.

'I remember that rock there,' said a Korpsman, 'but it's been moved aside by something with inhuman strength.'

The watchmaster stepped through the crack, through the tatters of a hanging tapestry. He found himself back in the Devourer's lair, blinking in its brazier light, with several lasguns pointed at him until their wielders recognised him.

Acknowledging his colonel and the inquisitor, he turned back around.

The torches on the walls were burning down and out, plunging some tunnels into darkness. In one such tunnel, by the glow of his lumen cube, the watchmaster saw a shadow shifting and halted his squad. 'Life signs?'

The engineer studied the auspex. 'No, no life signs. Almost the opposite. A cold spot, directly ahead of us.'

'Speak up if you hear voices,' the watchmaster ordered.

'Watchmaster, I… I think I do,' said the engineer.

'Then you know what to do.'

The engineer nodded and, gripping his gun tightly, stepped forwards. The shadows seemed to coalesce before him as if to block his path, and now the watchmaster could make out a definite shape in them and trained his bolt pistol upon it.

'I know what you are,' said the engineer loudly and firmly, 'so you have no power over me. I trust my commander and will not hear your lies. So, if you wish to stop us, you will have to become solid, in which case we are more than ready for you.' He worked his shotgun's action.

The spectre continued to hover, regarding him impassively.

'Yes,' said the engineer more quietly, 'that is what I thought.' Then, taking a fortifying breath, he marched along the tunnel, through the shadows, which smoothly dissipated as if they had never truly been there. *A trick of the mind.*

'Well done,' the watchmaster said as he and the others followed. He wanted to ask what the spectre had whispered to the Korpsman. He did not.

Not long later, they encountered their first beastman after hearing its scampering footsteps. The auspex showed it approaching, so, extinguishing their lumens – a dwindling torch was nearby, in any case – they waited in readied silence in the tunnel mouths around a four-way junction.

The beastman's misshapen shadow fell between them, but its movements ceased. The watchmaster, hearing it sniffing, knew it had caught their scent.

In the instant that it scampered away, he charged from cover, firing, a cue for his comrades to do the same. The creature – small, dark-furred and lupine – was fleeing on all fours. It might have been the one that had escaped before. A bolt from his pistol nicked its ear. It hared around a corner, with the watchmaster hard on its heels. The labyrinth's twists and turns slowed it, kept it in his sights, and he shot it twice more until, whimpering, the creature missed a turn and ran full tilt into a wall, which snapped its neck.

The watchmaster's comrades caught him up as he ensured that it was dead. 'A scout, I should think, come to check on the Devourer,' he said. 'It won't be reporting back to whoever sent it, but any within earshot will have learned enough.'

They continued on their way until, some minutes later, their navigator spoke up.

'Watchmaster, the layout of these tunnels matches those mapped on our way in.' He showed his dataslate as proof. 'The wall markings confirm it. I believe we are close to the archway, and I can guide us to it.'

The watchmaster bade him do so, and soon they turned into a well-remembered tunnel, with a warning scratched into its wall. At its end, they saw two figures crouched by the familiar archway. Two men, draped in black hoods and robes over grave worker's smocks. Cultists, no longer caring to try to hide it. The watchmaster saw right away what they were doing. Just as he had feared, they were setting explosive devices.

They hadn't seen him yet, but they would at any moment. He ran at them, and as the cultists' heads rose in alarm, he strafed them with a three-round burst. One took the brunt: the closer and younger of the pair. The elder ducked behind him and, whether through panic or self-serving guile, gave him a hefty push along the tunnel.

The watchmaster and the young cultist collided. The latter's eyes rolled back into his head and he expired. Frustrated, the watchmaster bundled his dead weight aside, but the older cultist had made use of the distraction, escaping through the archway, and already gears were grinding as a thick barred gate descended.

Not this time! the watchmaster swore, and he propelled himself towards the gate, dived, and rolled underneath it before it could slam down.

Out in the cave beyond it, a skull had been wrenched from the wall to reveal a wheel behind it at which the cultist stood, startled by his foe's appearance. His eyes flickered towards a tunnel entrance, but as the watchmaster picked himself up, instead he reached into his robes for a curved, long-bladed black knife.

The watchmaster in turn drew his bayonet. Three Korpsmen, trapped behind the gated archway, could only watch as he and the cultist closed in battle – which proved to be savage, short and predictably one-sided.

The vanquished fell at the victor's feet. The watchmaster yanked his blade out of the cultist's guts. Mindful of the cave's six entrances, he wasted no time in reflection. Hurrying to the control wheel in the wall, he turned it back and raised the gate, allowing his comrades to join him.

Two shone cubes into each of the cave's other openings, disturbing nothing but hearing ominous snorts and scrapings in the distance. Returning to the archway, the engineer ran his hands over its inside surface. He rooted a couple of spikes from his backpack, drove them into the intrados with his shotgun butt. 'That should keep the gate from being brought down on us again.'

In the meantime, the watchmaster found blood on his glove. It came from his forearm, where the cultist's knife had found a torn part of his greatcoat, nicking him through it. Stepping through the archway, past the engineer, he had him keep watch while he dealt with it. 'It's nothing,' he insisted when asked, 'as long as I can stop the bleeding. Can you find your way back to the lair?'

The question was addressed to the navigator, who claimed that he could.

'Good. Two of you go, I'll stay here with the other. Some beastmen may have slipped past us, so be careful, and watch out especially for spectres.'

'Yes, watchmaster,' said the Korpsman without trepidation.

'Tell the colonel we have found the archway and will hold it as long as we are able. Until morning, if we must, if that is the colonel's decision. But tell him his watchmaster recommends that he come quickly.'

Graven led his squad back through the narrow tunnels.

They were weary but keeping themselves alert, some increasing their stimulant intake. He had judged that, on balance, it was worth the exertion – and risk – of further travel to leave this labyrinth behind them, now that they had a way out. Idelax had seemed pleased with this decision, despite looking more drained than ever, grey-faced and sunken-eyed.

Before moving out, they had had one last thing to attend to.

The explosion, when it came, made the walls shake and Idelax stumble, but the Krieg neither winced nor looked back. They walked for another minute before the aftershocks and echoes died away, and Graven knew the job was done.

He had personally placed the mining charges, lit the fuses. The Devourer's lair was destroyed, the monster itself buried with its hybrid lackeys and its victims, and one unfortunate member of Graven's own squad.

His mind kept picking at that scar, which was unusual. He found it both frustrating and concerning. *He was only one man,* he thought, *one of so very many, and he died well to boot.*

His squad's first loss. Their fourth assignment. Graven had been proud of their resilience. Too proud? Never before had he served alongside anyone so long, not to his knowledge. His old engineering squads had each been disbanded, their survivors sent to bolster others. *Even before the orks.* That was just the way it was. The way it was meant to be. He wasn't meant to grow accustomed to his comrades, wasn't meant to get to know them.

This comrade had never had a name. Few people, even after talking to him, could have told him apart from any other Krieg, but Graven could. Though rarely had he seen his face, he knew the Korpsman who, high up on the gantries of an occupied forge, having broken his blade and drained his power packs, had jumped a crazed ogryn from behind, choking it with a chain. He remembered a sniper in the window of a ruined chapel, whom he had spied too late, his life saved by that same Korpsman's lasgun and reflexes.

He had shared sentry duty with him only the previous night, sitting side by side with him in the rain.

Graven wasn't meant to mourn him.

Are the spectres doing this to me? he wondered, but he knew that wasn't it.

Gunfire ahead of the Krieg speeded their footsteps. It was over by the time they reached its source. The watchmaster and engineer flanked the gem-studded archway.

'There are beastmen out there, sir, but we've been keeping them at bay,' the former reported, sounding uncharacteristically subdued.

'Tunnel mouth at four o'clock, watchmaster!' the engineer cried, firing his shotgun through the archway. 'Some kind of bird thing, but I clipped its feathers for it.' That explained the squawk of pain.

'The tunnel we first came along?' asked Graven.

'Clear as far as I can see,' said the watchmaster.

'Who still has a smoke grenade?'

There was no time to mourn dead comrades, not while the living needed him. Graven couldn't be distracted by thoughts of mortality.

A grenade was duly produced and rolled out through the archway. It burst in the centre of the cave beyond it, sending frightened beastmen scuttling away, though undoubtedly not for very long.

'Go, go, go!' Graven yelled, and his squad raced through the smoke, across the cave.

In broader, bone-filled tunnels once again, they took a moment to consult their hand-drawn maps before proceeding. Their goal was to reach the exit to the surface that they had earlier discovered, and their colonel led them there.

His fallen Korpsman, he assured himself, had accomplished

more than most. He had outlived most of his regiment, compensated in part for lives wasted, died with honour. He had helped to kill a monster, leaving his comrades alive and free to hunt down the ossuary's other horrors. He could rest in this world's hallowed soil, content that he had nothing to regret.

We should all be so fortunate, thought Graven.

IX

The Krieg erected three small tents leeward of the hill. They changed their air filters and nutrient packs. They refilled water bottles from the rain.

Inquisitor Idelax had his own superior field rations, rehydrated rice and protein, which in the absence of an acolyte he heated himself over a campfire.

The watchmaster set three sentries, one on the hill, two underneath it. He slept dreamlessly until woken for his own watch six hours later. He tested his arm, felt the stiff patch of synthskin pulling on it, but he retained full motion.

A persistent drizzle had put out the fire. The sky was a ponderous black. The watchmaster saw someone sitting on the hillside and was surprised to make out Idelax, his blue eyes clear and piercing. He acknowledged his presence with a nod, but neither of them spoke.

The watchmaster headed underground, alongside the engineer. The downward-sloping access tunnel to the ossuary ended at a T-junction. Only as they reached it did the two sentries stationed there appear.

'Anything to report?' the watchmaster asked.

'Another burst of las fire,' one said, 'thirty-four minutes ago. Roughly north-west of here, some distance away, soon over.'

'Same as yesterday. The same squad, perhaps?' At least that would mean they were still fighting – or had been up until this latest incident.

'Otherwise, watchmaster, all quiet.'

'We'll take over now. You are relieved,' he told them. The Korpsmen snapped to attention, then relaxed. They reslung their weapons and made their way back to the surface.

Each way from the junction, there was a sharp tunnel bend. The watchmaster separated from the engineer. He took the left-hand tunnel and soon reached a vantage point where it branched into three.

As the echoes of his footsteps died down, a deathly silence settled. The world seemed to end at the edges of his lumen light. His world for the next three hours. He knew his comrade was a shout away, but he felt no less alone. Alone but for the skulls leering at him from the walls.

The watchmaster chose not to sit, because standing would keep him more alert. Still as a statue, bolt pistol drawn, he waited.

Korpsman 319-938-25549-04 was doing push-ups.

Half an hour into his watch, he wanted to keep his muscles limber, blood circulating. He had just checked in with his watchmaster along the tunnel. All was well. He was troubled, then, to hear footsteps behind him.

An ally, he assumed, as the pace was unhurried and a foe would have had to pass another sentry. The watchmaster again?

Still, he sprang to his feet and pressed himself against the wall, his shotgun readied.

A figure appeared around the bend. 'Inquisitor?'

'As you were, Korpsman.' Idelax's blue eyes glowed in the lumen light, but he looked tired.

'Can I do something for you?'

'I am told you heard a spectre.'

'Yes, sir, yes I did.' He should not have been surprised. It was a witch hunter's job to know such things.

Idelax lowered himself stiffly to the ground. Sitting with his back to a bone-embedded wall, he motioned to the engineer to do the same. Clearly, he anticipated a long conversation. The engineer sat, ensuring that he still had sight along each tunnel.

'What did it whisper to you?'

'I wouldn't know,' he said. 'I did not listen.'

'Tell me what you heard!' the inquisitor demanded.

He was taken aback. He had thought his answer the correct one, the expected one, but evidently not. 'Lies, inquisitor. The spectre told me lies.'

'What have you done to feel guilt over?'

'I swear, there is nothing.' It was a statement rather than a protest. It was the witch hunter's job to ask.

'And yet you were targeted by a thing that senses guilt and wields it as a weapon. It would go better for you, Korpsman, to confess to me. Unburden yourself of your sins, pray for His absolution and such creatures lose their power over you.'

The engineer hesitated. Only for a moment, but Idelax had surely seen it. 'I don't wish to be disloyal,' he attempted to explain. 'The spectre spoke to me not of my own actions, but rather of another's, and as I said, it lied.'

'Whose actions?'

'Colonel Graven's, sir.'

The witch hunter leaned forward. 'Tell me everything,' he said.

The engineer remembered:

The siege was almost over. The orks had been routed from their defensive walls. Imperial forces – Krieg forces – were closing in around the ruined city. Above ground, the roar of both sides' guns was deafening.

Below, the shriek of a Termite assault drill chewing through the earth deafened only the five engineers inside the burrowing vehicle.

The Termite surged as, demolishing a brick wall with ease, it broke into a long-disused sewer tunnel. Its occupants braced themselves against the inner hull as it dropped four feet to flop onto its stomach, straddling a drizzle of sludge.

Before the Termite had stopped juddering, its hatches were flung open. Captain Graven leapt out, followed by his squad. 'Fan out,' he instructed, 'make sure nothing has seen us.'

Barely had the words left his lips when a shotgun blast rang out and a pair of snotlings – filthy, ratlike scavengers with green skin and orkoid features – took fright. They didn't get far along the tunnel before more shells cut them down.

'I don't see any more, sir,' said a Krieg soldier – Korpsman 319-938-25549-04, indistinguishable from the other three in his tunic jacket.

Graven nodded, seeming satisfied. Surprise was of the essence in this mission. As much of a racket as the Termite had made breaking in here, it was hoped the orks would be too far away – and too distracted – to notice one more reason why the earth beneath their feet was shaking.

A Korpsman consulted his dataslate. No map existed of the sewer system, only of the city above as it had been centuries before, their goal marked by a black skull icon. 'This way, captain, bearing right as soon as we are able.'

'Double time. We have a lot of ground to cover.' Graven led the way along the musty tunnel, his Korpsmen falling into step behind him, focused on the task ahead of them, none of them thinking overmuch about the chance of failure.

Unaware as they approached their tragic destiny.

'Maximus Arkanos!' Idelax realised.

'Yes, sir,' said the engineer, 'that was the planet's name.'

'You were there, with Colonel... Captain Graven.'

'I had recently been transferred to his command squad.'

'Explain your mission to me.'

The engineer obliged. 'The orks had stumbled upon an ancient weapon, thought buried in the Age of Strife. A forbidden weapon.'

Idelax nodded. 'A rad weapon.'

'They were holed up in the city, its remains, but they had few defences there and were easily surrounded. Any flyers they sent up, we could shoot down. We had the orks contained, but they were belligerent and stubborn.'

'Indeed.'

'They would certainly fight us to the death. The concern was that, once they knew they were beaten, the xenos might activate the weapon, immolate themselves and take us with them. Captain Graven considered this improbable.'

'Oh? Why so?'

'As I understand it, sir, a tech-priest advised that the weapon was unlikely still to function, even less for such slow-minded brutes.'

'But you chose not to take that chance.'

'Captain Graven led his squad – my squad – to tunnel underneath the city. Orbital scans had told us roughly where the weapon was, as it was leaking radiation.'

'And you were to capture the weapon? Just five of you?'

'No, inquisitor, not capture it.'

'Then what?'

'Collapse the sewers underneath it. Seal the weapon in the earth again, along with any xenos set to guard it.'

Idelax sucked air between his teeth. 'Would that not activate it?'

'Not according to the tech-priest, sir, unless...' The engineer took a breath himself. 'Colonel Kleber judged the risk worthwhile. The orks were thought to have called for reinforcements, so we were compelled to act quickly. They had to be kept from escaping with the weapon, for on another world, an occupied world, it would have wreaked devastation.'

'Indeed,' said Idelax again.

'At least if the bomb exploded on Maximus Arkanos, casualties would be limited.'

To the members of the Four Hundred and First Krieg Regiment, the inquisitor thought but did not say aloud. As always with the Krieg, his subject's gas mask made him hard to read. He imagined, however, that the face beneath was equally impassive.

In a frank, unwavering tone, the engineer resumed his story.

They had reached their destination without hindrance.

Twice, they had thought they saw more snotlings. They had turned out, on inspection of their corpses, to be volelike local vermin.

'This is the place,' announced their navigator. 'Directly underneath the orks' stronghold in the city.'

'And the weapon,' Graven added in a growl. This was corroborated by rebreather units, which warned of hazardous radiation levels. Even protected as the Krieg were, they couldn't safely stay here long.

They set about placing their mining charges. One Korpsman climbed onto a comrade's shoulders to adhere a couple to the roof.

They heard the roar of engines long before they saw its cause. Something was speeding along the tunnel towards them. Something loud. More than one something, closing with alarming speed. They had no time to complete their task, nor reach the cover of another tunnel. 'Kill the lights!' the captain ordered.

In the dark, they raised their shotguns.

A blinding light came thundering towards them, and now they heard guttural, ecstatic whoops behind it. 'Fire!' yelled Graven as soon as the light was in range, and a quartet of shotguns barked, alongside the captain's own laspistol, aimed in the voices' direction.

The light spilled over Korpsman 319-938-25549-04, standing forward of his comrades as he was. At the same time, the light split into a pair of sources: two ungainly, oil-stinking vehicles. Motorised bikes, jolting along on shredded tyres, each with a single glaring headlight. Each with a goggle-wearing xenos rider and a side-mounted gun that, in all fairness, should have tipped it over.

Each undeniably, almost breathtakingly fast.

The engineer dived out of their path, but the tunnel gave him scant room to manoeuvre. He flattened himself against its side as the first bike veered towards him, then away as its slug-ridden rider slumped dead across lopsided handlebars. The bike slammed into the opposite wall and fell apart.

The second bike ploughed on through the debris and over the corpse. The ground struck sparks off its gun as, from within its tarnished depths, there burst a whirling spray of bullets, pinging off the tunnel's sides but also clipping at least two Korpsmen that the engineer could see.

Delightedly, the rider bellowed, 'Dakka, dakka, dakka!' as if the gun were make-believe and needed sound effects providing.

The Krieg scattered as the bike careened between them, with just a couple managing clumsy bayonet stabs at the rider. The engineer wondered how it could possibly turn in these confines, but somehow it did. Attacking a wall with an oversized front wheel, it flipped itself around, landing with a bone-jarring thud – then it came roaring, spitting bullets at them again.

No doubt it had expected them to be intimidated, possibly to run. Instead the Krieg stood steadfast, once more bringing their shotguns to bear. A deadly hail punched into the ork, knocking it backwards from its saddle. It landed on its square green head, and they all heard the snap of bone.

The bike, now riderless, shot past them, somehow remaining upright, at least for a few hundred yards, covered in seconds, until, reaching a T-junction, it too struck the wall and a spark must have caught its leaking fuel tank. It exploded, bringing down the roof on top of it.

A wave of heat and dust buffeted the Krieg, their rebreathers sparing them from choking on it. The stretch of roof above them groaned but held – it would have been ironic had the orks done their job for them. *With hindsight, it would have changed much.*

A barking, rasping sound assailed their nerves. It took them a moment to pinpoint its unlikely source. An ork was laughing.

Clinging stubbornly to life, the second rider lay, its thick neck twisted, bone shards poking through its skin. 'Boom,' it grunted, then laughing again, it repeated, 'Boom, boom, boom!'

Four shotgun barrels swung towards its head. 'Put it out of our misery, captain?' asked a Korpsman.

The xenos' flat, brutish face crumpled in disappointment. 'Small boom. No big boom, but soon,' it grumbled in barely intelligible Low Gothic.

'Wait!' said Captain Graven. He glared down at the paralysed creature. 'What "big boom"? What do you mean?'

Its red eyes were unfocused and it gave him no response.

Graven crouched by it, thrusting his laspistol under its snout. 'Do the orks intend to use the ancient weapon?' he demanded.

The engineer saw the ork's hands twitching as if for Graven's neck, but it couldn't raise its arms. He thought it would continue to ignore him – what more could he threaten it with, after all? – but, clearing, its eyes swivelled to fixate upon him. The ork sneered, saliva dribbling along its tusks.

'Big mek wired it up,' it grunted, 'so any jolt and boom! Bullets start flying? Boom! Shell blasts through the wall? Boom, boom! See skull-faced 'oomies coming? Then big mek stamps on casing and boom, boom, boom!'

The five Krieg looked at each other.

'It's lying,' said one. 'It has to be.'

'But what if it isn't?' asked another.

'I've been up close with orks before,' said Korpsman 319-938-25549-04. 'Dull-witted as they are, they have a knack for bodging tech.'

'Look at the bikes,' said the fourth. 'Spare parts from a junk heap lashed together. No way they could function, but they did.'

'Still, to rig up a vibration sensor trigger for a weapon they can't understand… The tech-priest said it couldn't work.'

'But what if they have?'

'Boom,' said the stricken ork dreamily, its voice fading. 'I want to see it. Let me live long enough to see it.'

'No,' Graven said, and shot it through the eye.

He straightened up but didn't speak, staring down at the xenos' carcass. His Korpsmen waited expectantly until one, having taken a bullet to his arm, was forced to step aside and staunch the bleeding.

'Sir,' someone said at last. When he seemed to go unheard, he prompted more urgently, 'Captain Graven. Sir. What do we do?'

'Is your commander often indecisive?'

Another disconcerting question. The engineer duly considered it. 'I hadn't seen it up until that point.'

'However?'

'Perhaps, yes, on a few occasions since. But on Maximus Arkanos,' he hastened to add, 'the captain faced an impossible choice.'

'Had he not orders to follow?'

'But also reason to believe that if he did... Inquisitor, there was an investigation into these events.'

'A tribunal, yes, so I am led to believe. And you were called to testify?'

'No, only the captain was, but I could have said no more than he did.'

'Assuming, of course, that he held no details back.'

'Why would he?'

The witch hunter rested his head against the wall, his eyes hooded. For a minute, neither of them spoke again. Then, quietly, he asked, 'What would you have done, Korpsman? In that situation, had you been in command, what would have been your choice?'

Even as the engineer drew breath to answer, a sudden sound, a clinking of rock, jolted both men to their feet. 'Behind me, inquisitor,' the engineer whispered, and Idelax obliged but stayed close, drawing his gun.

A dim light had appeared along one of the tunnels. The engineer clicked off his own lumen cube and crouched in darkness, in the tunnel mouth, his shotgun levelled. Tentative footsteps approached, sounding like booted feet, not hooves. Four, maybe five people. He let them get a little closer, into range, before issuing a challenge: 'Who goes there?'

The footsteps scraped to a halt and there was a short pause before a man's voice answered, 'Vostroyan Firstborn. Friend or foe?'

'Friend, if you are who you say you are. Come forward one by one with weapons sheathed and let me see you.'

That prompted a brief exchange of whispers, before one set of footsteps resumed its approach, along with the light. The engineer relaxed, but not too much, as he made out a distinctive red Vostroyan greatcoat. Its wearer also seemed relieved as his lumen cube found the waiting Korpsman, although his splendid moustache twitched at the sight of the inquisitor behind him.

'How many of you are there?' the engineer asked.

'Four. Just four left from two squads of five. We were attacked in the night.'

'By beastmen?'

'Witches. We found another of their secret temples. Empty, but clearly still in use. We set an ambush for them. Suddenly, through some… profane power, without us seeing their approach, there were three of them among us.'

'You ran from them.'

The Guardsman bristled at such bluntness. 'The witches wielded fire and lightning, and in the confines of that cave… Our captain was slain before we knew it. Our sergeant ordered a withdrawal, but he too was cut down from behind.'

The engineer said sagely, 'Faced with overwhelming odds, there is no shame in living to fight again.'

The Vostroyan gave a curt nod. He called his comrades forwards, and the Krieg watchmaster had also heard the disturbance and quietly joined them. 'Might you have been followed here?' he asked.

'No, we made certain of it.'

'But the witches fooled your senses once before,' said Idelax, to which the newcomers had no answer.

He offered to escort them to the surface so both Krieg could stay at their posts. He would wake Colonel Graven to hear the Vostroyans' story.

Soon enough, the engineer was left alone again. He stood stiffly at the tunnel junction, determined to be more alert than ever. *I resisted the spectre,* he told himself, *because my faith is strong. I will resist these witches too.*

'Sir,' said Guardsman Bukharin, 'if I may make a suggestion?'

Colonel Graven nodded.

'I would wake your people and return to that profane temple right away. We wounded two witches and drained much of their power. Never will they be weaker than they are now, and... colonel, I fear they took some of us alive.'

Graven pursed his lips beneath his mask. 'How long since you escaped them?'

'Two and a half hours by now,' another Firstborn said.

'Then they can wait two more until dawn,' he decreed.

'Colonel, if it's true what we are told, that the witches offer up the bodies of their prisoners to be–'

'Dawn!' restated Graven, and though his thick moustache twitched, Bukharin did not press his objection. 'These witches too may have summoned reinforcements, and soldiers fight more efficiently when rested. An hour's sleep would also benefit the four of you.'

'We have stimms, sir,' said Bukharin, but a couple of his comrades were eyeing up the soft grass on the hillside.

'In the absence of your captain and your sergeant,' Graven asked, 'which of you has served longest?'

The Vostroyans exchanged awkward glances. A sharp-featured woman spoke up: 'Sir, that would be me.'

Bukharin said, 'But I am higher born and so have seniority.'

Yes, thought Graven. *Yes, of course.* 'Then you are acting sergeant of your squad, which I am taking under my command. Be ready to move out – and lead us to these witches, so that we may destroy them – at dawn.'

The engineer was not surprised when Inquisitor Idelax returned.

This time, they didn't sit. He kept his eyes fixed on the tunnels and was glad of the excuse. Idelax stood at his shoulder, an ominous shadow in the corner of his eye. 'Tell me,' he said, 'what did Captain Graven do?'

'On Maximus Arkanos, sir? I thought you knew.' He had thought everybody knew.

'Did he or did he not set the explosive charges?'

'He... We did not. We returned to the Termite instead. It was forty-five minutes away, and the captain had to send an urgent message to Colonel Kleber. With hindsight, we ought to have taken a vox-caster with us, but we had to move quickly and quietly.'

'This message?'

'A warning that the weapon was still active, and the orks prepared to use it.'

'Or so a single ork claimed. A dying ork.'

'The captain believed it a credible threat,' said the engineer. 'He recommended pulling back our infantry companies until the situation could be reassessed. At least, that would have been his recommendation.'

He remembered:

Huddled in the metal tube of the passenger compartment. Knee to knee with his nervous comrades, the odour of their sweat in his nostrils. The captain, losing his usual composure as he tried to make a vox-connection. His gloved fist hammering the console in frustration.

He remembered the explosion.

It had felt incongruously minor, rattling the Termite's hull, but it had rumbled on and on, and even after it was over, the five Krieg had sat in stunned silence, the only sound a harsh static crackle from the console. Each of them knowing just what the explosion portended. Contemplating their own failure.

'Inquisitor,' said the engineer, 'you asked a question earlier. You asked me what I would have done that day, in Captain Graven's place.'

'You have an answer for me?'

'Yes. I've always known. That same question played on my mind as we raced through the sewers, to the Termite, before... before we learned...' He took a breath. This time, he felt the answer he was giving was the wrong one. He also felt it needed saying. 'I believe I would have done the same as he.'

'And regretted it as sorely?'

'Respectfully, inquisitor, we don't know – we can never know – the outcome had the captain chosen differently.'

'Had he carried out the orders he was given and collapsed that roof?'

'Most likely, the weapon would have gone off all the same.'

'But earlier,' said Idelax, 'before your ground forces were so close to it.'

The engineer couldn't deny that. Another bitter irony, he thought, was that his squad had been among the few survivors, protected by the Termite's armour plating and their depth beneath the surface.

'Inquisitor, I must reiterate that high command cleared the captain of any wrongdoing.'

'Yes, and promoted him even, as the longest-serving member of your much-depleted regiment.'

'So, even were I to question his actions, it would be immaterial.'

'Your loyalty,' Idelax rumbled, 'is commendable. Which brings us back to the other question you have yet to answer. The first one I asked you.'

'The spectre.' The engineer swallowed.

'What did it whisper to you?'

'It tried to convince me that the colonel was not to be trusted.' He remembered its sibilant voice, its icy presence in his mind, and it made him want to shiver. 'It called him weak and full of doubt. It claimed that his guilt brought him to Oleris III, to where...' He paused, feeling almost overwhelmed by the thoughts he had been keeping distant, now crashing over him like waves. 'Inquisitor, the spectre told me that their bodies... that my comrades lie in the soil around us, but surely it can't be? Are we not far from Maximus Arkanos?'

'In fact, that world and this one share a sector.'

'I did not know that.'

'Though it is hardly relevant,' said Idelax. 'Who would gather fallen soldiers from a dead and poisoned world and ship them here? Who would fund such a meaningless endeavour?'

'The spectre told me lies,' the engineer restated, to convince himself. 'It blamed the colonel for its pointless death and promised he would lead me to the same. Finding no doubt in my heart, the spectre tried to place it there.'

'By exploiting the secret you were keeping.'

'No, sir, there was no secret. To speak of this was simply not my place.'

The witch hunter let out a sigh, his shoulders sagging. Then, in a weary voice, he said, 'You have naught to feel guilty about.'

And with those reassuring words, he turned and walked away.

The Krieg were back on the move, joined by the orphaned Vostroyan squad.

Colonel Graven had briefed them in the pre-dawn drizzle. He had warned them of witches with powers to baffle the senses – who might well know they were coming before they knew themselves.

The Vostroyans' acting sergeant led the way. The watchmaster brought up the procession's rear again. They were almost an hour into the catacombs when they heard an explosion and a crash of falling rock from somewhere to their left.

'Sounds like somebody triggered a trap,' the watchmaster speculated. 'One of theirs or one of ours?'

Graven said, 'Not far away. Comrades may be in need of our assistance.'

'Colonel,' Acting Sergeant Bukharin protested, 'we mustn't be distracted. That is what our enemies want. I hear no guns, do you? No sounds of battle.'

'So, it seems any comrades are either victorious or dead,' agreed the watchmaster.

The colonel weighed up his options.

'Sir,' Bukharin piped up again, 'my own comrades–'

Graven spoke over him: 'First, we deal with this witches' temple and any captives they may have taken. Later, we investigate the rockfall.'

'Thank you, colonel,' said Bukharin, and the thought crossed the watchmaster's mind that he seemed almost too grateful, overeager to keep them on course, keep them going where he wanted.

But then, otherworlders often wore their emotions plainly, and his focus was elsewhere at that moment. He was watching Graven. He could not fault the decision he had made, but had he hesitated for a second? Had he doubted?

Last night, standing at his lonely sentry point, the watchmaster had heard murmurs, which had seemed to emanate from the mouths of the skulls around him. Spectres? Not so, he had become aware. The acoustics of the tunnel were such that he was hearing voices from some yards away. A conversation between an inquisitor and an engineer, relayed by echoes to his ears with crystal clarity.

He had heard everything.

For months, the watchmaster had served with Colonel Graven, more closely than anybody else, but rarely had they discussed anything but immediate concerns. Graven had never shown him his face. Last night, the watchmaster had learned more about his commander than he had in all the time before, and he was troubled by it.

As the kill team moved on, he followed them in pensive silence.

He had much to think about.

X

Idelax's heart was racing.

He had slept badly in the night until he had given up trying. The medics at command headquarters had wanted him bed-ridden. The witches' abuse of him had broken him inside. They wanted further scans, but he had had work to do. He knew his heart was failing, but the Emperor would give him the time he needed.

His mind was racing too. He watched the Vostroyans, navigating the ossuary tunnels. They had kept their distance from him, which he didn't find unusual. What did feel off to him was how rarely they spoke to each other. After all they had been through, the losses they had suffered, surely they had much to process. Self-discipline was a laudable quality, but this was something else.

Perhaps they took their cues from their allies. The Krieg were not known for their small talk either. They communicated brusquely, efficiently, pragmatically. That morning, he had heard a group discussing the position of a beastman's heart, how protected it might be and whether it was best to aim for the throat.

The Krieg were different, though, force-bred by borderline abhorrent methods, intensively conditioned to the point where some considered them no longer entirely human. From birth, they were instilled with collective guilt for their world's sins, which was normally a strength but on Oleris made them vulnerable. Hence the inquisitor had been watching them, their leader in particular. Had he been looking in the wrong direction?

They came to another junction, where again there was no hesitation. The Vostroyans' acting sergeant took the left-hand tunnel without consultation, without breaking step – but the one time he had trod this ground before, hadn't he been under pursuit? He had not stopped to mark the walls, nor make a map.

If Bukharin is possessed, then so must the other three be.

Idelax's sleep had been disturbed by dreams. Dreams that worsened every night. He didn't know if spectres had been present, invisible, or if his mind had taken up their whispered taunts. It hardly made a difference. Details of the dreams had quickly faded. He only remembered the feelings evoked by them, the gnawing in his stomach that had woken him repeatedly. His stomach felt the echoes of it now. Guilt. And something even worse.

Idelax's duty was to act on his suspicions. Even if he wasn't sure. Far better that innocents die than the guilty escape judgement. But he also remembered the Krieg engineer's testimony: *'Finding no doubt in my heart, the spectre tried to place it there.'*

Might they have done the same to me? How many times had he employed similar techniques? Told someone he could sense their guilt to make them paranoid, questioning themselves? He had sworn not to be blind again, but was it really any better to see daemons in every shadow?

He suspected the Vostroyans. He suspected Colonel Graven and the Krieg. He was starting to suspect that his true problem lay closer than either.

He took another stimulant tablet from his cloak. He had procured a good supply from the compound, but already it was running low. Still, he had to clear his head, sharpen his thoughts. He was a witch hunter, after all. The last thing he could afford to feel was doubt.

The beastman made up Idelax's mind.

He didn't know what it was meant to be: some manner of red-haired rodent with a flat, twitching snout. It had lain up on a natural shelf near the roof, possibly in ambush but possibly – as it was alone – just sleeping.

The engineer's auspex detected its bodily emissions, but couldn't pinpoint its location. Only when Graven was almost underneath the shelf did he notice a webbed toe protruding over its edge.

The beastman pounced on Bukharin, who dodged it thanks to the colonel's warning. It scrabbled at his greatcoat as it fell past him, landing deftly on its feet. It was short and slight, only reaching the Vostroyan's chest. He kicked it away from him, but it quickly caught itself – and froze in fear.

Perhaps it hadn't understood how many soldiers it was facing. Perhaps the view down fourteen gun barrels gave it pause. Perhaps not.

The beastman bolted, pursued by las beams, which failed to strike it. Idelax's own sights had been blocked by allies' heads. To most of the Krieg, the same applied. The four Firstborn were near the front of the procession, however, and his eagle eyes saw that two had also held their fire.

The creature's paralysed stare had been fixed on Bukharin. On him, not on his weapon. Its mouth had twitched as if to ask a question in whatever crude language it might speak. Had it seen something in his face – which had been turned away from Idelax – to change its mind? Bukharin had had the cleanest shot at the beastman as it fled. Had he missed by chance or by design?

The female Vostroyan turned to Colonel Graven. 'Sir, that thing will warn the witches we are coming.'

'Only if they don't already know.' Idelax shouldered his way through the Krieg, his plasma pistol levelled at Bukharin's head. 'I think they do.'

'Inquisitor?' Graven queried.

'Drop your weapons,' he commanded the Vostroyans. 'All of you. Drop them. On your knees. Hands on your heads.' The look in Bukharin's eyes confirmed it. A look not of fear or confusion, as an ordinary Guardsman might feel upon being accused, but of pure loathing.

The others were waiting on their acting sergeant's lead, clinging to their pretence. Bukharin gripped the stock of his lasgun two-handed, stooping to set it down, but his eyes remained fixed on Idelax.

The witch hunter ducked, too late, as the gun butt lashed at him, cracked his temple. The flash behind his eyes mirrored that of his weapon as his plasma burst went wild. He stumbled backwards into Graven, who stood firm, his las beam flashing past Idelax's ear to punch Bukharin in the shoulder.

Barely reacting, the Vostroyan sprang forwards, swinging his gun again. Idelax blocked the blow, meant for his head, with a leather-armoured forearm but was driven back into the throng of Korpsmen, overbalanced. Bearing down on him, Bukharin pressed his weapon's stock across the inquisitor's throat, threatening to crush his windpipe.

He was snarling and frothing like a madman, like a man

possessed – which, Idelax realised, had been his mistake, expecting the incorporeal being attached to him to fear death. The Krieg, as many as could, were piling on the Vostroyan, bayoneting him, but he battled on with crazed strength. Idelax's gun was pinned against his chest. His head was growing light, his vision tunnelling, but finally the pressure on him ceased as his attacker succumbed to his mounting wounds.

Bukharin's bloody corpse slid to the ground, between his killers, but Idelax knew, as did the Krieg, that his threat was not yet ended.

A spectre was ejected from his shadow, like the one he had driven from Djallon. The same one, for all he knew. The Krieg's readied bayonets passed through it, but at least it was deterred from solidifying to attack. Idelax felt cold in its presence, but he drew himself to his full height, squaring up to it. He wanted it to sense what he was feeling, his confidence restored by the knowledge that his instincts had been accurate. The time for doubt was over.

The other three Vostroyans were escaping. The spectre lingered in the tunnel, as if to bar pursuit. Four Korpsmen, ignoring it, fired through it. Their las beams raked the back of the rearmost Guardsman, bringing him crashing down, but the others disappeared around a bend.

'Get after them!' roared Graven, and his Korpsmen started forward, apparently intent upon barrelling through the apparition too.

Idelax's voice halted them: 'No! They were leading us into a trap, and still are.'

'Yes,' agreed Graven. 'Evidently.'

Idelax stared at him and then nodded.

The spectre had vanished while his eyes had not been on it.

Idelax prodded the second dead Vostroyan with his foot, but

roused nothing. His spectre too must have slipped from his shadow unobserved. It could have seeped into the ground.

The Krieg followed the two that had fled, but Graven assigned a spotter to scout the way ahead of them. It wasn't long before they heard a brief las fire exchange and running footsteps. The spotter called back to them, 'All clear!'

They found her at the next junction. 'That way, sir,' she said, pointing. 'One of them was down there. He took a pot-shot at me, but ran when I returned fire.'

'Making sure we don't lose them,' said Graven.

The pattern was repeated at the next two junctions, supporting his theory. They caught up with their spotter once more at the entrance to a small, low-ceilinged cave, from which three other tunnels led.

'I wonder,' said the watchmaster, 'what our enemies would do if, this time, we chose not to follow them.'

'I wonder too,' said Graven. 'In the tunnels, our numbers work against us. Here, we would have room to fight.'

They crouched around the edges of the cave and in the tunnel mouths. They placed a lumen cube in its centre, to give them light without betraying their positions. They waited.

After several minutes, Idelax heard movement from along the centremost tunnel. A shadow crept closer but stopped short of the light's edge. Straining, he thought he discerned the silhouette of a tall Vostroyan fur hat. Another minute passed before, quietly, the figure withdrew, but it was not long gone.

It returned, lugging something mechanical. 'Grenade launcher!' yelled the closest Korpsman, over the pop of the weapon firing.

A projectile streaked through lumen light and struck a wall, bursting open and spewing out black smoke. The enemy was using the Krieg's own tactics against them, but they still had their gas masks' filters.

'Hold your positions,' the watchmaster yelled, 'and fire at will!'

Idelax heard ringing hoofbeats, followed by las fire. Smoke billowing around them, the Krieg were shooting blindly, but having set their sights upon the centre tunnel, they were able to fill it with a lethal las beam gauntlet. Bestial throats released pained squeals and bleats as hoofbeats stumbled.

The smoke had filled the small cave quickly. Now it rolled along the entrance tunnel, where Idelax crouched alongside Graven and another Korpsman.

'Inquisitor,' the colonel suggested, 'you may wish to step back.' Then they heard a noise behind them, from along the entrance tunnel. 'Belay that, get behind me!'

The two Krieg pushed past Idelax, shielding him with their bodies as they fired along the tunnel. He heard an angry roar and bullets rattled from the darkness, pinging off the wall beside him and off Graven's helmet.

Idelax saw no other option. Drawing his cloak around his nose and mouth, he backed up into the cave. By now beastmen were pouring into it in droves, closing to hand-to-hand combat, gunfire barks giving way to clashing blades. He felt for the cave wall as smoke engulfed him. He pressed himself against it, its embedded bones jabbing into his back. He missed his whip. His plasma pistol was powerful, but he had learned to use it sparingly.

Smoke shifted, allowing him to glimpse Vostroyan red, lost before he could aim at it. Mostly, he saw black Krieg coats. He realised that they were protecting him as Graven had, as they had in the Devourer's lair. Despite himself, he felt mildly affronted. *Had they ever seen me in full health…* They had no idea of his true power. Emperor willing, never would they.

Graven was holding his tunnel mouth. On Idelax's other side, a goat-headed beastman swiped a Korpsman to the ground. It lunged at the inquisitor, who took great satisfaction in pumping white-hot plasma into its face. 'We fight for the Emperor of Mankind,' he bellowed as the beastman toppled, burning, 'and I know we will not let Him down!'

'But you already failed him.'

His heart froze at the whispered words. 'Show yourself,' he tried to demand, but his voice was a whisper too. Despite his cloak, the smoke was in his throat.

'Spectres!' somebody cried. 'There are spectres in here with us.'

Idelax's eyes were watering. Smoke wreathed about him, forming nightmare shapes – leering, taunting daemonic faces – everywhere he looked, so he couldn't tell which of them, if any, were real.

He heard Graven: 'Everyone make sure you have eyes on two comrades.' When the spectres attacked, they were vulnerable, but only if they could be seen. Only if their foes were free to take advantage of their weakness.

So, this was the trap, and despite our precautions, we are caught in it! A shape solidified in front of Idelax: the remaining male Vostroyan, slashing at him with an elegant but no less deadly shashka. He twisted away from the sharp blade, which sliced through his cloak and was immediately, deftly, brought round in an arc, its tip scoring his breastplate.

His gun was still recharging but his opponent didn't know this, so he aimed it and the Guardsman broke off his attack to evade the anticipated shot. He was fooled for less than a second. Long enough. Two bayonets, one to each side, skewered him. Though bleeding and probably dying, the Guardsman elbowed a Korpsman in the jaw while thrusting his blade into the other's stomach.

He came at Idelax again, the shashka whirling, the spectre clinging to him intent on taking down the biggest threat before its enslaved body failed it. *It knows!* Bracing himself against the wall, the inquisitor planted his foot in the Guardsman's stomach, pushing him back onto bayonets behind him, and even still, he fought with undiminished Firstborn skill.

Backing away from the melee, Idelax collided with somebody. He spun around, snapping up his useless weapon, as did the Korpsman behind him. They locked stares. Idelax wished he could see through the dark lenses of the Krieg gas mask, see into his eyes.

The Korpsman was likely having similar thoughts about him. *If he were possessed, he – or she – would have struck me by now.* They came to the same conclusion simultaneously, turning away from each other. The Korpsman spied another beastman and made for it.

'What good is a witch hunter who can no longer recognise a witch?' Shadows coalesced three feet above Idelax's head, and this time he was certain. His weapon's light snapped on at that moment, and he fired into the heart of the malignant shape and through it, the shadows dissipating in a bright plasma burst against the roof. Had he done it? Had he just destroyed a spectre?

'Never will you truly know. Doubt will forever haunt you, until the day you come to us.' Another shape – the same shape? – was forming in the same spot as the first. A skeleton, cloaked, pointed a bony finger at him, and Idelax thought he recognised it, thought it looked somewhat like Djallon, his old acolyte. His dead and desecrated acolyte.

His gaze was trapped in the bottomless shadows of its eyes, and try as he might, he couldn't tear it free. *'You were tainted long ago and have known ever since that you were damned. Why fight it any longer?'*

Idelax's vision tunnelled and he saw himself assailed by daemons, unable to resist them. Their claws, their teeth, their horns rent his flesh, shredded his soul. Barely could he hear the whispered voice above his own heart's hammering, but he realised that it was not Djallon's voice but his own.

With a whimper, he sank to his knees. He felt the gun in his hand but let it go as it was useless to him now. Oddly, he felt no pain, just fear, fear like he had never known before, reducing him to helplessness. *Almost.* Surrender was the only way to end that fear. *Not quite.*

The spectre was doing this to him. Fear was its greatest weapon. Graven had warned of it. Graven had, in fact, resisted it – and was Idelax not an inquisitor of the Ordo Hereticus? Fear was his weapon too. Even now, it was building in his chest, flowing along his every nerve. All he had to do was accept it, seize it, turn it outwards. Three times he had done so in the past, most recently chained to a black altar underground, when the power unleashed by his fear had repelled a daemon.

Accept it!

The power flooded from him, feeling wrong but at the same time very right. All Idelax could see was blazing green, although his eyes were closed; all he could hear was screaming, possibly his own, and when it was all over, once his fear had been released, he felt empty, drained of life.

He couldn't lift his head. He needed a stimm, but couldn't lift his arm to find one. Green faded to black. He couldn't lift his eyelids either.

He sank into a deep and mercifully dreamless sleep.

He came round briefly as a boot stamped down beside his head.

The smoke in the small cave had cleared and he saw Korpsmen fighting beastmen and no sign of spectres. There were bodies strewn about him, mutant bodies. One more added to the total as it fell beside him, dead eyes staring into his. He saw a beastman making a run for a tunnel, being slashed down from behind.

Relieved that things appeared to be in hand, he slept again.

* * *

When next he woke, it was to voices. The clamour of battle had ceased, and only one side remained standing.

The last surviving Vostroyan knelt with head bowed, hat in her hands. Colonel Graven and two Korpsmen stood around her. She had been disarmed. The other Krieg watched the tunnel mouths as they patched up their wounds.

'I could see what I was doing,' said the Guardsman in subdued tones, 'but it felt right. It all made sense at the time. I... couldn't reach myself to stop it.'

'How did it happen?' barked Graven. 'How did the spectre take you?'

'The same way they tried to take you, by waiting until we were distracted and then striking. I think now we were meant to find their temple.'

'That much, at least, was true?'

The Vostroyan nodded. 'We couldn't defend against both witches and spectres together. I didn't even see mine coming. When Sergeant Vanko fell as we were trying to retreat, I... Emperor forgive me, for a second I lost hope, and that was when it swooped upon me. It felt so cold as... as it forced its way into... I felt helpless.'

'How long have you served, Guardsman?' Graven asked.

'Six months, four days,' she said.

'On how many battlefields?'

'Oleris is my fourth.'

'You have slain heretics and mutants for the Emperor?'

She raised her head, fear flickering across her face. 'Colonel, the spectre is gone, completely gone. When the inquisitor... did what he did, unleashed his power, I heard it shrieking in my mind as it was destroyed with the others.'

'I believe you,' said Graven.

'I feel no different than I did before.' The Guardsman's shoulders sagged in resignation. 'I know what you have to do.'

'The touch of Chaos leaves a mark that cannot be erased.'

'I ought to have been stronger.'

'Your life,' said Graven, 'was well spent.' He put his laspistol to the Vostroyan's temple. She closed her eyes and muttered a prayer to herself. He allowed her to finish it before he executed her.

'Sir,' a Korpsman said as her body crumpled, 'the inquisitor.'

He had noticed Idelax's open eyes, and now nine Krieg heads turned the inquisitor's way. With an effort that made him perspire, he levered his head and shoulders up to rest against the wall. With two strides, Graven reached him, looming over him. His Korpsmen flanked him, lasguns readied. Graven noticed the dropped plasma pistol and his boot sent it skittering away.

'So now you know my shame,' said Idelax weakly, 'but I saved all our lives.'

'Yes,' said Graven flatly. 'Yes, you did, but you are still a witch.'

He winced at the descriptor. 'Colonel, I have faced down daemons. I have looked into the warp itself. Of course I have been touched by Chaos.'

'And it left its mark upon you.'

Idelax could not deny the charge. 'The use of these… abilities exhausts me and threatens to one day overwhelm me. I keep them suppressed, keep my mind closed and shuttered, but for in desperate need.'

'You were afflicted with this curse before Oleris?'

'Some four years since now, and I have it under control.'

'Sanctioned?'

'I reported my symptoms when they first manifested, and of course I have been sanctioned. Had the witches not taken my rosette, I could have shown you the brand of the Adeptus Astra Telepathica.'

Graven glared down at him a minute longer, doubtless deciding whether or not to believe him. In other circumstances, Idelax might even have smiled at the irony of their role reversal.

'Then,' said the Krieg colonel finally, 'it is none of my concern.' He lowered his pistol and his comrades followed suit. 'Can you stand unaided, inquisitor?'

Idelax thought he detected some disdain in his voice, but it was difficult to tell. It might have been his own projection.

He could not stand unaided, not for long. When he tried, his chest felt tight and his head spun. He sank back to the ground, needing to catch his breath.

'We must get you to a medicae,' said Graven.

'No,' gasped Idelax, 'I only need a moment.'

But Graven had already turned his back to issue orders to his Korpsmen. He sent six out in teams of two to find an exit to the surface. He warned them that should they detect more foes, they should avoid them if they could.

It seemed to Idelax that they returned quickly, but then, he had rested his eyes and more time might have passed than he had felt. An exit had been found. In the meantime, the Krieg in the cave had improvised a stretcher using tent poles, ropes, and a red greatcoat still wet with blood.

That spurred him to try standing again. Halfway to his feet, a skull in the wall cracked under the pressure of his hand. He waved away the Krieg who rushed to help him. His head throbbed where Bukharin's gun had struck it.

He reached inside his cloak for his bottle. 'Inquisitor,' said Colonel Graven, 'I would strongly discourage–'

An explosion interrupted him, followed by a rockfall, like the one that morning but closer, close enough for them to feel it. Close enough to leave no doubt about its source. It had emanated from along the centremost tunnel in the wall across from their entry point. The one along which the possessed Vostroyans had attempted to lead them.

Graven despatched his engineer and two more to investigate. Their light soon disappeared around the tunnel's bend, their footsteps fading. Idelax and the rest of the kill team waited in tense silence. It wasn't long before first sound then light returned.

'The way is blocked, sir,' the engineer reported, 'deliberately. Whoever, whatever was waiting for us down there, they no longer wish to be pursued.'

'How far along? On what bearing?' Graven turned to his mapmaker. 'Mark the spot as precisely as you can. If the witches are bringing down tunnels in our path, there can only be one reason.'

'They're afraid of what we might find,' the watchmaster surmised.

'Their temple,' said the colonel, 'and whatever lies beyond it. Their stronghold. The seat of their dark power. That is our objective now.'

The route to the newly found exit took them back the way they had come for a few hundred yards before branching to the right. Idelax had insisted on walking, which he could just about do now, but Graven had insisted just as firmly on remaining close by him, for which he was secretly grateful.

Gravel shifted underfoot and Idelax lost his precarious balance. Graven caught him, kept him upright. 'Again, inquisitor, I suggest you allow us to carry you.'

Embarrassed, he waved the offer away. 'I've slowed you down enough. If not for me, my weakness, you might have reached the witches' temple in time.'

'Or been caught in the rockfall. You said yourself, you saved our lives.'

'Even still,' said Idelax gruffly as the pair struggled on, 'leaving me behind might have been the pragmatic option.'

'An option I considered.'

'No doubt.'

'Inquisitor... During the melee, in the cave, again a spectre chose me as its target. I knew it was behind me. I know their touch by now. That cold, which does not cool the skin but chills the soul.'

Idelax suppressed a shiver at the memory.

'A beastman was in front of me. I should have turned my back on it. Better to be gored than...' Graven left the thought unvoiced. 'My focus was divided. The next thought in my mind was that my life was undeserved. I believed another soul, its own life unjustly curtailed, could do more with it.'

Idelax looked at him in surprise.

Graven kept his gaze fixed dead ahead. 'In that moment, I knew I was lost. Then I saw flames, green flames. I feared I had been cast into the immaterium, until the flames burnt out and I...' He took a breath. 'Inquisitor, you are our best – our only – weapon against such warp-spawned horrors.'

The words gave Idelax heart, which lent him a modicum of strength. They walked on for a minute more in silence. Then, shrewdly, he guessed, 'Your engineer told you of our talk last night.'

'He did,' said Graven.

'Had you wished yourself rid of my scrutiny, I gave you a plausible excuse.'

'Pragmatism dictates keeping you alive.'

'Yes,' said the witch hunter. 'Yes, I believe it does.'

They had reached their goal: a drain cover in the tunnel roof. It was low enough to reach, but spikes had been hammered into the wall to assist. Graven's spotters had confirmed that outside was an empty barn.

'Inquisitor,' said Graven, 'I regret that I was not more open with you.'

'You answered the questions I put to you,' said Idelax.

'I could, I should have made it clearer that my nightmares – the doubts that have been plaguing me, the guilt that haunts my soul – did not begin here on Oleris III, but long before.'

Idelax waved the confession away. 'And, as I have explained to you already, Colonel Graven, such feelings are far from uncommon.'

XI

The watchmaster climbed the spikes first. He levered up the cover with his shoulders, setting it quietly aside. He listened for a moment. He could hear voices, but distant. He raised his head through the aperture.

As promised, he was in a barn. The afternoon sun streamed in between its walls' loose-fitting slats. He saw grain sacks and tools.

Climbing from the hole, he signalled the all-clear down to his comrades. He crossed the barn to check outside it, but suddenly the door in front of him flew open, revealing two middle-aged women in grave worker's smocks. One had stepped inside before she saw the watchmaster and froze. The other shrieked, 'Intruder!' and grabbed a pitchfork from beside the door.

The watchmaster snatched his bolt pistol from its holster. 'Stand down. Drop the weapon. Show me your hands.'

'Sergeant!' shrieked the armed woman. 'Sergeant, over here!'

Sergeant?

Footsteps converged upon the building and the watchmaster heard a horse's snort. A third figure appeared in the doorway, lifting his hopes. He recognised her white-scarred face and unkempt hair, but she was pointing a laspistol at him.

'What are you doing, sneaking up on us?' demanded Sergeant Batu. More Attilan Rough Riders were running up behind her. If there was a chance they might have been possessed, the watchmaster had to act before he was outgunned.

He took a chance. 'We didn't know who might be here.'

'I know that voice. Is that you, Watchmaster No-Name?' Batu didn't wait for an answer. 'Pray with me. Adore the immortal Emperor…'

The Emperor's Prayer. Slightly nonplussed, he joined in: 'For He is our protector. Admire the immortal Emperor for His sacrifice to mankind.'

Together, they completed the recital. The Attilan lowered her gun and stepped forward with a grin. The worker set down her pitchfork too, but continued to watch with wary eyes. 'Witches can't pray. Nor can the possessed,' said Batu. 'They stutter and choke on the words.'

'Is that true?' The watchmaster reholstered his own weapon.

'It's what the folk here believe. Who knows?'

The rest of Graven's kill team climbed up into the barn. Inquisitor Idelax needed some assistance, one Korpsman pulling from above, one pushing from below, and by the time he had made it he had to lie down again.

The barn stood on the edge of a hamlet, similar to all the other hamlets, only more populated than most. Workers were emerging from huts, with autoguns and forks and shovels. The Attilans called to them, telling them everything was fine, the new arrivals could be trusted.

'The spectres came here five nights ago,' said Batu, 'but the workers were ready. Refugees had come from other hamlets, bringing warnings. They posted sentries through the night, and no one slept alone.'

'We fortified our minds with prayer,' the worker with the pitchfork boasted.

'So, not all on this world are weak,' said Colonel Graven.

'A few were taken all the same, but dealt with,' Batu added, darkly.

'Where are we?' asked the watchmaster.

Batu gave him the settlement's official designation, but the same worker piped up, 'We call it Sanctuary, now.'

'Those refugees keep coming,' said Batu. 'Some find their own way, and our riders bring others as they find them.'

'No sign of witches yet?' asked Graven.

The Attilan shook her head.

'They'll come,' he said. 'They must know of this place by now and surely resent its defiance.'

'That's why we're here. Protection.'

Each hut was over-occupied already, but in deference to Idelax's exalted position, Batu cleared a downstairs room for him. Graven assigned a Korpsman to watch over him lest his condition worsen or a spectre come for him.

The inquisitor, his face drenched in sweat, slept fitfully. 'Colonel,' his guard reported, 'he seems tormented. I don't know whether I should wake him.'

'No,' said Graven. 'His overtaxed heart needs some respite.' *And hopefully, that will be enough,* he thought, but he was far from confident.

The hamlet had a vox-set, which Graven used to contact command headquarters. It was within range now, somewhat to his surprise. His squad's underground explorations had led them back towards it. He requested that Idelax be airlifted back to the compound for medical attention. A terse voice told him that no flyer was available, but one would be sent as soon as possible. He stressed the urgency of the situation, but found himself cut off abruptly.

Two Korpsmen pored over their ossuary maps. Now that they had a surface reference point, they could refine them. The colonel inspected their work, especially interested in the locations of the two rockfalls, the one they had seen and the one they had only heard that morning.

He circled his finger over a blank patch on the dataslate. 'This secret temple must be in this area. That suggests two potential routes to it – from the north-east here, or circling around to approach it from the south-east.'

The mapmakers concurred.

Graven pondered. Hours of the day remained. His squad was relatively unscathed by its battle. Thanks to Idelax. 'Some witches may remain there,' he considered, 'no longer protected by their beastman servants nor their spectres, but believing we can't reach them. If we are bold enough, and the Emperor smiles upon us, we may take them by surprise.'

So it was that, after a short break, seven Krieg descended back into the darkness.

The watchmaster and one Korpsman stayed behind – partly to reinforce the Attilan squad in case of trouble, mostly to watch over Idelax, a task with which the colonel would only trust one of his own.

Their first attempt to find the temple ended in frustration. Not through any manmade blockage, but because the tunnels' bends inexorably turned them away from where they wished to be. Glaring at a bone-embedded wall across his path, Graven felt as if its many skulls were taunting him. 'If only we could see behind them!'

They had three mining charges left between them. An explosion would signal their presence, however, and probably for nothing if it didn't make things worse. Reminding his squad that speed was of the essence, Graven turned them around to seek another route.

They passed close by the exit to the barn again, a chance to change direction. By now, they had walked almost two hours with silence deepening around them. They hadn't heard a distant scrape in all that time, nor even a beastman's snort. Were they being left alone on purpose? What if they were being steered again, by foes who remained a step ahead of them?

Either way, each second gave the witches more time to regroup.

Graven cast such doubts aside. He couldn't let them cloud his mind. The inquisitor had expressed faith in his judgement – albeit obliquely – which had always been guided by his instincts. Instinct told him to keep going, so he did.

At first, this second route appeared more promising. Though incomplete, the Krieg's maps suggested that they were closing in on their objective.

Then a faint tremor passed through the ground, through the soles of Graven's new boots, through his feet. Had another tunnel just been collapsed? Was he too late? He didn't think so. This tremor was subtler, longer-lasting, slowly building. It seemed to originate from nowhere and everywhere at once.

'An earthquake?' breathed his engineer. 'Is that even possible here?'

'No,' said Graven, though his senses told him otherwise. 'Oleris' tectonic plates are highly stable, as these catacombs attest by their endurance.' As an engineer himself, he had scrutinised the records before sending his entire regiment below ground. 'This must be something else. Unnatural.'

'How far do you think it extends?' a Korpsman asked.

'Is it centred on us?' another wondered.

If it is, thought Graven, *it portends disaster.* He made a decision. Before he could voice it, the very unnatural tremor spread to the walls around them, making them shake too. *No. No, not the walls. The bones!*

It was the bones. The bones embedded in the earth. They were vibrating, twitching, as if straining to free themselves. A thigh bone popped out of the wall beside him, landing with a thud at Graven's feet, where it continued to clatter. And alongside the tremor, he felt something worse, something in the very air, something dark and malevolent that he lacked words to describe but was almost suffocating him.

The seven Death Korpsmen had no target for their weapons. No defence apart from one, the last resort.

'Run!' Graven spluttered, and they ran, back the way they had just come.

They had covered a mere hundred yards when the tremor relented. Silence settled once more upon them. The ossuary's bones were still again. Graven stopped his squad and they exchanged uncertain glances. It was the engineer who first voiced the thoughts of them all:

'What in the Golden Throne just happened?'

The watchmaster had reopened the knife cut on his forearm. He perched on the edge of a moss-encrusted wheelbarrow, sterilising the wound again.

Evening was drawing in and some workers were warming up food, unappetising gruel, over a fire. The general mood was subdued but not despondent. Rather, it was resolute. Somewhere behind the huts, an Attilan drilled a group of volunteers in self-defence. Others patrolled the hamlet's perimeter on horseback, drawing the watchmaster's eyes whenever they passed across his field of vision.

Sergeant Batu sidled up beside him. She offered him a hot drink, which he declined. 'Do you never take off that mask?' she asked.

'Not around strangers,' he replied.

'Oh,' she said. Then, after a moment, 'Makes it hard to tell what you're thinking, but I think you wish you were down there with your people.'

The watchmaster looked into the Attilan's face. He wondered how old she was, how long she had served, how much she understood. How could he possibly explain to her? He surprised himself by making the attempt. 'I was trained to obey orders. Without question, without hesitation.'

'Sure,' said Batu with a shrug. 'Chain of command.' She didn't understand. For the Krieg, it was more than that, far more.

'What happens,' he ventured, 'if there are legitimate questions?'

'Don't trust your colonel? Think you should be watching him, yeah?'

Her incisiveness pierced his heart, making him regret his candour. He backtracked: 'On Oleris, can anyone be trusted?'

'Sure, if they can say the Emperor's Prayer.'

Could it really be so simple? Not long ago, the watchmaster would have thought so too. Had this world really changed him – without changing Batu – or was it just that he had served too long, lived too long? *If I have, is that not also the colonel's doing?* To the Krieg, such longevity itself was almost suspect.

'You've gone inside yourself again,' Batu prodded him. 'What are you thinking?'

He was spared the need to answer her. He felt a sudden tremor in the earth. He and Batu both leapt to their feet. Frightened murmurs from the hamlet's workers confirmed that they felt it too, and a couple of Attilan horses whinnied.

'What is it?' breathed Batu, but the watchmaster had no answer for her, and after a minute or so the quake subsided, leaving them none the wiser. 'All riders, saddle up,' the sergeant yelled, 'and keep your eyes open!'

'Sergeant!' The cry came from a worker by the barn. 'Come look at this.' Batu hurried over, the watchmaster on her heels. They found the worker, white-faced, voiceless, pointing out across the fields with a trembling finger.

The watchmaster saw nothing at first, only the endless headstones, but then a stone toppled, then another. *Dislodged by the tremor? No.* The ground around the fallen stones – between some others too – was churning. With horror, he realised that something – some *things* – were clawing their way up from underground, out of the rain-softened earth. *God-Emperor, fortify us!*

He told himself it wasn't possible, even as he drew his pistol and Sergeant Batu raced to her mount. If one thing was sacrosanct to the Krieg, it was the prospect of their final rest, but this...

Emaciated bodies, rotted flesh and clothing sloughing from their skeletons, were rising from their graves. They pushed themselves to their feet, standing, swaying in bewilderment, shielding lidless eyes from fading sunlight. 'The dead! The dead return to life!' a worker shrieked.

'No,' the watchmaster barked. 'Those things are not alive. They are a mockery of life and even worse, a mockery of death.'

One by one, the cadavers took notice of the nearby hamlet and its occupants and turned in their direction. With halting, jerky steps, learning how to use their limbs again, they set out across the field. There were over a dozen of them now, with more still emerging from the soil.

'No matter what they look like, these are not the people you once knew.' Batu had returned on horseback, fiercer-looking in her spiked riding helmet.

'They are abominations,' the watchmaster concurred, 'cheating your friends and neighbours of their well-earned peace.'

'And their defilement of this land will not be suffered!'

The words rallied the nearby workers somewhat, persuading them at least not to flee in terror. From the hamlet's far side, however, there came fresh cries of alarm. Batu cursed under her breath. 'Surrounded. Yeah, of course.'

Two of her Rough Riders had joined them, and Batu sent them out to meet the more visible threat. Turning towards the watchmaster, she asked him, 'Can you marshal the civilians? Hold the line here as long as you can, then into the barn.'

'Agreed,' he said, and she galloped away.

Out in the field, a horseman bore down on the foremost zombie, which plodded towards him, undeterred. The Attilan thrust his lance through the zombie's ribcage, lifting it clear off the ground. Skewered, it pedalled the air, clawing, spitting at a foe beyond its reach, until he shook it off and trampled over it.

The second rider charged a knot of zombies, hacking with his sabre as he scattered them. Slicing through an overstretched tendon, he removed a skeletal arm, which through some vile sorcery continued to flail in the dirt. Meanwhile, the trampled zombie was already climbing up again.

The watchmaster cast a doubtful eye over his ragtag civilians. What good would their implements be against creatures impervious to pain? He mustered three with autoguns. 'Aim at the one there, on your right. Wait on my mark and... fire!' He added a few bolt rounds of his own to a barrage of bullets, most of which flew considerably wide of their target, though some cracked rotting bones to no avail. The zombie's sunken eyes fixed firmly on the gunners; it kept coming.

Behind it, the Attilans came around for a second attack run. No longer did the watchmaster wish he was below with his colonel. He wished he was out there on horseback – although he almost changed his mind as a zombie leapt upon a horse itself, sinking overgrown, cracked, filthy fingernails into its flank.

The horse bucked, whinnying, and only through consummate skill did its rider remain mounted. His sabre battered his unwanted passenger, slicing off a finger, then a hand, but the zombie clambered up behind him doggedly, lunging for the back of his neck with jaws wide open. The Attilan whirled his blade, neatly lopping off the zombie's head, which flew and bounced and rolled away. Its decapitated body stayed upright for a second, then collapsed.

'The head!' the watchmaster cried. 'That is their weakness. Remove or destroy the head and they can't function!'

The closest zombie was within a hundred yards of him now. The watchmaster and his gunners focused their fire on its head, but this only increased the frequency of missed shots. The watchmaster shattered its jaw with a carefully placed bolt, which made its head snap back but didn't stop it.

His civilians were starting to back away, and he could hardly blame them. They had no armour, no defence against a creature surely riddled with disease. *Perhaps with the Chaos plague itself!* The watchmaster thought about retreating to the barn. *Not yet.* He reached for a frag grenade.

'Get down,' he growled. 'Flat on the ground.'

He dropped to one knee, pulled the pin and bowled between the zombie's legs. Its attention was taken for a moment, dipping its head to follow the pineapple-shaped projectile, though without comprehension.

The frag grenade exploded, buffeting the braced watchmaster with its concussion wave. Debris pattered off him, and a rotten hand landed with a plop beside him. It twitched as if to grab him and he blasted a hole through its palm. The zombie had been dismembered with gratifying ease. Its limbs, strewn across the field, fell still. He couldn't see its head.

But he could see more zombies like it. Four more, shambling towards him.

The Attilans had problems of their own. Though several zombies lay destroyed, more had replaced them. One rider was surrounded, zombies clawing at his horse again. Distressed, it reared up, kicking out, but though it cracked the skulls of some, they didn't fall. The other rider fought fiercely with his sabre, taking another head, but he too was hard-pressed.

The watchmaster had one more grenade. Just one. He didn't want to waste it. He turned to his civilians. 'Do you have such a thing as a flamer?' They murmured that they didn't. 'Promethium, then? In any form? Go find it, as much as you can. Bottle it and bring it back here. Rags as well, and a combustion source. Wait, give me that.'

He snatched a worker's shovel from him. Its edges had been sharpened. The watchmaster weighed it in his hands. It would make a better weapon than his sword bayonet for hacking through a neck, lending him better reach.

He instructed his gunners, 'Keep aiming for their heads. If you can only slow them, that may suffice. When your co-workers bring the promethium, you know what to do? Above all, don't let these creatures touch you. I'll draw away as many as I can. Try not to shoot me.'

With that, the watchmaster did what his people did best, what he had had few chances to do in many months. A war cry rattled from his throat as he charged onto enemy ground, his weapon raised.

* * *

Idelax was wrenched out of his nightmares.

The daemons in his mind receded, wooden walls rushing in to replace them. He lay, clothed, on a mattress on the floor. A masked Death Korpsman was urgently shaking him awake. 'Inquisitor, the hamlet is under attack!'

He felt like he had barely closed his eyes, although the nightmares had lasted an eternity. He had no idea where he was. He murmured vague questions, his voice thick in his throat.

The Korpsman asked if he could stand. 'Of course I can,' Idelax snapped, with no idea if it were true or not. He accepted assistance, all the same.

Remembering the inquisitor's plasma pistol, the Korpsman pressed it into Idelax's hand.

Short of breath, Idelax leaned on the Krieg soldier as they stumbled out of the hut. He couldn't see anyone, but could hear fighting close by. Only vaguely did he recall being brought this way before.

'Where are you taking me?' he asked.

'The barn, sir.' The Korpsman stiffened as they passed an alleyway between two rundown huts and saw a figure in it. A grey-faced cadaver, tattered scraps of skin and clothing clinging to it.

It appeared to be mooching aimlessly until it heard or sensed them, whereupon its head snapped up and around. Its dislocated jaw dropped open in a voiceless groan. The zombie slouched towards them, reaching for them.

The Korpsman snapped up his lasgun. Idelax fumbled with his own gun, but was told, 'Preserve your fuel, sir. I can deal with this.' The zombie grew closer, too close for Idelax's comfort. Close enough for its putrefying stink to turn his stomach. Then the Korpsman shot it squarely through its forehead.

It paused as if surprised. A livid las beam hole exposed brain matter. The zombie took another jerking step, only to be shot again. The Korpsman's marksmanship was flawless, the second hole widening the first. It took a third shot, all the same, before the zombie crumpled as if a light inside it had snapped off.

'They're only a threat if they can swarm you,' said the Korpsman, knowledgably, 'and get their filthy hands on you.'

Idelàx nodded, but in truth he had hardly heard the words. Even this small exertion had set his heart racing again. His head swam, his vision blurring. *I should have listened to the medicaes,* he thought. The release of his power had been the final straw. *Too late now.*

The watchmaster swung his borrowed shovel, connecting with a zombie's head, the impact reverberating along the wooden handle. Whirling round, he jabbed at another's throat, fracturing a clavicle instead.

The creatures assailed him from every direction. One scrabbled at his greatcoat's tear, threatening to shred the synthskin patch beneath it. He drove his handle into its guts, breaking its grip only for a second. The zombie came at him again. This time his shovel's leading edge sliced cleanly through its neck.

Three down! He wasn't getting through them nearly fast enough. Now three more of them were on him, threatening to bear him down with their combined mass. The zombie whose skull he had dented strained its jaws as if to swallow his entire head, and he felt teeth sinking into his left shin's greave.

Hoofbeats shook the ground beneath his feet. The watchmaster's attackers fell away as a curved Attilan blade scythed through them.

He wasted no time signalling his gratitude – in any case, his saviour was long gone. One zombie had lost its right arm and half a leg but was still limping towards him. He stepped away from it to another, its head lolling on its chest, connected to its exposed spinal column only by overstretched tendons. A shovel blow severed those connections, and suddenly the watchmaster found himself unmolested, with a moment to take stock.

Most zombies had lost interest in him, having learned his strength. They were headed for the hamlet once more, for its ill-equipped defenders. *Because they are weaker? Can these simple-minded creatures sense that somehow?* These civilians were ready, however. They were lighting cloth fuses dipped into promethium-filled bottles, hesitating to throw them only because he remained in the blast zone.

An Attilan horse had been tripped by a bony hand that, rising from a sundered grave, had seized its fetlock. Its rider was being swarmed, dragged from his saddle. His comrade tried to reach him, but two zombies, caked in fresh mud, sprang up in his path and his mount shied from them. Right now, that was where the watchmaster could be most effective.

He bowled through the zombies from behind, none turning to see him coming. He planted his feet and swung his shovel, his only goal to buy time for the rider and his horse to catch their breaths. The former tried to stand, but could not support himself. He clutched at the watchmaster's greatcoat as he fell again, almost dragging him down too.

An improvised promethium bomb exploded in midair. The watchmaster saw harsh beauty in its fiery blossom, but the zombies fighting with him hardly seemed to notice. At least some approaching the hamlet were now burning, flames catching in their ragged strands of hair and clothing.

He blinked away red blotches from his vision. He swung his sharpened shovel, felt it ringing in his hands as it stove in another skull.

Another promethium bomb burst, and another. Smoke was beginning to obscure the scene, but the watchmaster counted around thirteen zombies still standing – their numbers diminishing at last, but painfully slowly – half aflame and yet still plodding onwards, their aspects even more nightmarish than ever, looking like infernal daemons.

It was no surprise, and probably best, that the workers fled before them, heading for the shelter of their barn. Even the watchmaster wondered if he had made a mistake in not withdrawing earlier. Then a flaming zombie toppled forwards, landing on its face, the fire proving effective after all.

The Attilan horse was back on its feet. Its rider wasn't. His flak jacket had been shredded, blood seeping through its gashes. 'Sterilise your wounds,' the watchmaster ordered. 'Imbibe your strongest tonic. Sterilise your wounds again.'

Then he turned to the horse. He removed his glove and let it sniff his hand before looking it in the eye. He patted it firmly, then pushed his boot into a stirrup. The rider made a guttural protest, to which the watchmaster responded, 'Utilising all available resources, and the horse does not appear to mind.'

He hoisted himself into the saddle. The horse was smaller than he was used to, but muscular. It had a full mane, rather than the more practical bristles of its Krieg equivalent, and it wore neither respirator mask nor drug injectors, which would limit its combat effectiveness. Still, it would more than do.

He had heard Attilans commanding their mounts verbally, but such was not the Krieg way. Tugging on the reins, the watchmaster brought his horse around, then squeezed it with his calves, angling his body forward, directing it to charge. The horse submitted to him, and as it picked up speed, he felt the unparalleled rush of natural adrenaline, his pounding heart almost in synch with pounding hooves.

It had been too long.

They rode down a flaming zombie. With a splintering of bones, it fell and was crunched underfoot. A second zombie's neck was broken by the shovel. *One more blow ought to finish it!* They ploughed through the rest of the pack, shovel striking left and right. One zombie rounded on them, nails outstretched, but the horse anticipated the sharp tug on its reins that signalled it to rear up and lash out with its hooves.

Wheeling around, horse and rider – barely was there a distinction between them any longer – found themselves face to face with the other Attilan. He gaped in surprise but then, having seen them in action, gave a curt, approving nod before returning to the fray. The rider spurred his horse into their next attack run.

All worries, the frustrations of the past few months, were driven from the watchmaster's mind in that moment. He was a ride-master again. He had a mount between his legs, a weapon in his hands, a foe to crush. He was serving the Emperor in the way he had always been meant to, the way he knew best.

He was back in his element.

XII

Graven could hear it again. That infernal scratching sound above his head. An after-effect of the tremor? He thought not. Was something burrowing through the earth up there?

Again he considered turning back, but the tunnel was curving northwards as he had hoped it might. He was so close. Almost at the witches' temple, and turning back was surely what its occupants wished him to do.

So, Graven and his squad marched on. Until that scratching sound became a violent scraping, then a roar, before, ahead of them, the tunnel roof burst open and the seven Krieg recoiled as soil and rock came crashing down.

Their enemies had blocked their route again – only Graven had heard no explosion, no cause for the sudden collapse, and he could make out something... something shifting in the rubble. *Human bones!*

There were two of them. Two half-rotted corpses, but somehow animated, impossibly struggling to stand. 'Fire!' screamed Graven, but a fusillade of las beams hardly bothered them. He braced himself as the first zombie found its feet and came lurching towards him. It was practically a skeleton, time having eroded any clue to who it might have been in life.

Graven aimed for its chest, praying he might damage some still-vital organ. The zombie shrugged off his beam too and kept coming. A shotgun shell from behind him punched into its eye socket, and it flinched. 'Its brain! Whatever remains of its brain' – he grunted as the zombie lunged at him again, clawing at his masked face – 'controls it. Destroy the brain!'

Reversing his pistol, Graven lashed out with its butt. The brittle bone of the zombie's skull shattered, exposing grey matter. As more las beams struck it, its animating force fled from it in an instant. It collapsed at Graven's feet, and he turned to its fellow. The second zombie's foot had snagged in debris. With a snap, it pulled free but left the foot behind. Stumbling, it broke more bones and fell. Graven stepped to it, pumping las beams into its head until its struggles ceased. He turned back to his comrades.

'Sir,' said a Korpsman, 'your facemask.'

He raised a hand to it. He felt claw marks across his right cheek, three parallel scores in the fabric. They were shallow, but by gloved feel alone he couldn't tell if any part of his skin had been exposed to the air with all its pathogens.

Right now, there was nothing he could do about it. His attention was taken by more scratching from the roof. More long-buried corpses, digging themselves out of their graves. Digging downwards, aware of the catacombs beneath them. *Sensing our presence here too?*

He whirled as bones burst from the wall behind him, a cracked skull landing at his heel. Pushing through the dirt, another cadaver was stilled by Krieg gunfire before it could fully emerge. Its skull remained embedded in the wall, the bones of one hand straining out to reach him. *Keep moving,* thought Graven, *but which way?*

Though holed, the tunnel roof held. There remained a way past the rockfall caused by the zombies' emergence. From beyond this, he heard clinks and scrapes. *More creatures?* An emphatic gesture conveyed Graven's decision to his squad. *Forwards!* Leading the way, he squeezed past the rubble, rounded the tunnel's bend, and knew he had chosen right.

Before him, a cavern opened up, like the one they had discovered four days earlier. Green-and-yellow drapes and banners. A black altar with candles upon it. Wooden benches. Stripped of anything of value, as that other temple had been after its discovery, but not entirely empty yet.

Across the cavern, Graven saw another tunnel mouth, in which a pair of black-robed cultists crouched. They were mining the exit, he was immediately sure of it. Abandoning the temple, making sure they were not followed. He had made it here in the nick of time. *Or just seconds too late.*

He snapped up his pistol, even as four figures stepped from the shadows of the cavern's edges. Dark-clad, faceless figures, swiftly closing ranks before him to obstruct his line of fire. His trigger finger froze as he gaped at them, for the first time in his years of service paralysed by sheer incomprehension.

The four figures bearing down upon him were Death Korpsmen.

His own comrades. *My dead comrades!* Their movements betrayed them, although they – their all-concealing uniforms, at least – had not begun to rot. They were clearly more recently deceased than the zombies in the tunnel and yet they slouched like them, limbs jerking as if worked by puppet strings.

Two of the four still had their lasguns, but left them slung.

They advanced towards Graven with gloved hands outstretched towards his throat.

The barn was under siege.

By now, every worker in the hamlet – sixty to seventy in all – had been forced to take refuge within it. The remaining zombies had closed in around them, clawing, kicking, beating at the fragile walls. From every direction, Idelax heard wood splintering and cracking.

Green-hued, rotting hands pried between wall slats, tearing at smocks and skin. Some workers shrieked and sobbed, while the more courageous battered the intruding limbs with tools. Idelax saw three fingers sliced off by a hoe wriggling along the floor like worms until they were crushed by stamping boots.

He sat slumped against a support post. His assigned guard stood over him, rigidly, gripping his lasgun, the Korpsman's grim demeanour maintaining space about them despite the turmoil and the crush.

His instincts screamed at him to grab his neural whip – no, that was gone, his plasma pistol – and join the battle, but it was taking all his strength to stay awake, to think, to breathe. He hated feeling so helpless. He hated that, for his sake, a soldier was kept from the battle too.

From outside, however, he heard hooves circling the barn and intermittent las fire, and he knew other soldiers were still fighting. Fighting, it seemed, and winning, for the number of zombies hammering at the walls was surely dropping. Or was it just that his senses were fading?

Idelax blinked as, directly in his line of sight, a slat was wrenched out of place and a zombie squeezed itself through a gap too narrow for it, scraping flesh from dislocating bones. Then a blur of armoured flank behind it, a glint of curved metal, and the creature's head was parted from its shoulders. Dropping into the barn, it bounced into the lap of a cowering, horrified worker, staring sightlessly up at him.

Thank the Emperor, this time I am not needed, Idelax thought.

'Stand down!' Graven barked. 'That is a direct order from your regimental commander. Stand down!'

It was a desperate ploy. A hope that some defiant spark remained within his former Korpsmen, an instinct to obey him. A hope that seemed rewarded as the zombies hesitated – but only for a moment, before they surged forwards again. His Korpsmen no longer, if indeed they ever had been. Though they bore his regiment's number, *401*, on their shoulders, what if Graven hadn't brought them to Oleris? *What if they were not slain in these tunnels, but elsewhere, months ago?*

He couldn't let himself think about it. The four zombies were upon him, pushing him into the bottleneck of the tunnel at his back. Rather than allow that, Graven made a break to his right, along the cavern wall. One zombie turned to follow him and he snapped off two shots at it over his shoulder.

Its fellows reached the tunnel, bumping into each other in its mouth. They were greeted by las fire from the Krieg within, failing to slow them down. One jostled its way past the others to plunge into the opening. The other two remained hard on its heels, straining to reach past it.

Bracing himself, Graven fired at his zombie's head and melted through a gas mask lens, exposing an unfocused, rheumy eye. He was cut off from his comrades, but that was the risk he had taken. The zombie's fingers brushed his chest as if unaware of the gloves blunting its scratches. Falling back, he imagined its mouth similarly stretching open, its mask keeping it from biting.

Seizing his advantage, he allowed it closer than otherwise he might have done. His next shot burst its weeping eye, but his attacker would not drop. Graven let his pistol go and grabbed his sword. Activating it, he thrust it through the zombie's chest. Undeterred, it simply pulled itself along the burning blade. Its fingers found the colonel's throat and dug into it. Its weight pressed Graven up against the wall as the zombie choked the life from him.

Hearing a whisper in his mind, unsure if it was real or not, he tried to scream to blot it out: *I did not cause your death!* He had no voice.

Graven wrestled with the zombie. He found that its muscles hadn't wasted, its strength a match for his. He strained to work his sword inside it, pushing through vitreous resistance, rending nervous tissue. He managed to wrench one clinging hand from him, allowing him to suck in a shuddering breath.

Having gained space to do so, he delivered a jaw-cracking uppercut, which sent the zombie sprawling, freeing his sword in the process. Almost instantly, it came at him again, impaling itself for a second time. The fact that it flinched not at all from pain – its single-minded, fearless purpose – was throwing off his instincts. *Even the most stoic of us, in life, would have flinched!*

Once more, Graven was driven back into the wall. Once more, bones broke behind him, splinters jabbing his back. The zombie was clawing at the tears in Graven's mask, seeking out the flesh beneath.

And then it fell away from him. His sword had done its worst, at last. Bisected through its torso, the zombie's two parts hit the floor, its legs still kicking blindly. Head and chest strained back towards Graven on their elbows. He had dislodged the zombie's plasteel helmet, knocked its mask askew. He averted his eyes from the half-exposed, rotting face of a former comrade. *As if I might have known it,* he remonstrated with himself, but still he didn't look.

Graven's power sword flashed blue as it swiped through the zombie's neck. He looked for his pistol on the ground, but stepping to it, he came under autogun fire. He dived for the only cover he could see, behind the black stone altar. He felt a bullet punching into his backpack and prayed it hadn't damaged his rebreather unit.

The shots had come from the exit tunnel. Cautiously, Graven raised his head and the two cultists fired at him again. He was pinned down. Behind him, he could hear his Korpsmen fighting, but he couldn't reach them.

His hand went to a frag grenade, clipped to his belt, but he was loath to use it, to collapse the tunnel as the cultists wanted. He reached up instead and grabbed a lit candle from the altar, lobbing it in their direction. Alarmed cries told him that the cultists were scrambling for cover from what they presumed to be a bomb with fuse wire burning. Graven took his opportunity to race across the cavern and snatch up his gun. Whirling around, he strafed the tunnel mouth.

He waited for the dust to settle. He saw and heard no cultists. Had they fled? Could he have killed them? Were they waiting silently in ambush? Had they set their charges? He edged forwards, laspistol levelled in one hand, sword clutched in the other, straining for a better angle down the tunnel.

From deep within its gloom, a stentorian voice intoned a single word: *'One!'*

A bright flash dazzled Graven as a burst of plasma streamed towards his head. He felt its searing heat as he threw himself away from it – had it been a better shot, he would have stood no chance.

Now he heard footsteps – clanking, metallic footsteps – stomping up the tunnel towards him. A shape gained definition in the shadows – not a spectre, but something more massive and solid – and that voice rang out again: *'Two!'*

This time he was ready for the blast, diving back towards the altar as it struck the wall behind him, melting skulls. Another followed, then another, just missing Graven's trailing feet. *'Three! Four!'*

The shooter was counting his shots.

'Five!'

The next bolt pounded into the altar itself, taking a sizeable chunk out of it, and Graven could see his foe now, clearly, in the tunnel mouth. He saw his – *its* – unwieldy suit of power armour, looking like the corroded scraps of other suits. He saw the many skulls with which the creature was festooned, the yellow-and-green banner mounted on its back. *A Traitor Marine!* His throat dried. The whole of his kill team was hardly a match for such a monster, and he was facing it alone.

'Six! Seven!'

Two more blasts rocked the altar, and Graven thought the next one might go through it. Nor was the traitor waiting for its weapon to recharge, which meant it was supercharging it, risking that it might blow up in its hands. *I might have a fighting chance if it did!*

If he stayed where he was, he was dead. Try to run and he was dead. The output of his single pistol would hardly graze that armour, so he holstered it. The colonel had his sword, although its light was dimming. His final act would be a desperate charge while praying for a miracle. At last, he would rejoin his fallen comrades. Abstractly, he wondered if they would welcome him, if he had done enough.

As soon as the next shot comes, I make my move.

The next shot didn't come.

After several seconds, Graven risked raising his head again – and locked glares with the traitor, still blocking the tunnel entrance, through the recessed eyepieces of a bone-white, skull-shaped visor. Incongruously, tucked into the crook of its left elbow, he saw a large, ivory-framed abacus. Perplexingly, the traitor continued to hold its fire. *Its pistol charge finally exhausted? Or might it have malfunctioned? Is this my chance to make a break for it? Or a trap?*

Crouching between its armoured boots, trembling in its foreboding presence, the black-robed cultists had resumed their work, and now it seemed completed, because they scuttled off into the darkness. The Traitor Marine remained a moment longer. Then, unhurriedly, it turned its back on Graven as if judging him insignificant, and it too stomped away.

The explosion came before it had even left his sight. The tunnel roof collapsed, throwing up a cloud of dust that billowed out into the cavern. Graven didn't wait for it to settle. He couldn't reach the witches' temple now. His comrades were another matter. Blinded, he followed his ears back to the entrance tunnel. His squad had withdrawn some way along it, but they were still fighting.

His toe nudged a body, slumped against the tunnel wall. A masked Death Korpsman. *One of them, or…?* Without stopping to examine it, wasting time, he couldn't tell. Its skull had been staved in, however, with a marked lack of blood. *A zombie. It must have been a zombie! Which leaves two.*

He came up behind them, in the light of lumen cubes. They were clawing, snapping at the Krieg engineer, who had resorted to fending them off with his shotgun butt, just trying to slow them down. His comrades fired past him when they could. The rearmost zombie must have heard Graven's approach, because it spun towards him. Its gloves were shredded, exposing gnarled fingernails.

It swiped at him, missing. He drove the point of his sword up through its respirator tube and mask, through the roof of its presumably gaping mouth, into its brain. It slumped against him, dead. *Again.* As he pushed it aside and turned his attention to the lone remaining zombie, it succumbed to its injuries too.

It landed on its back at Graven's feet, staring up at him almost plaintively through its gas mask lenses. Stooping beside it, he reached for its dog tags, bracing himself to read them. He recognised the numbers stamped into the tarnished metal. A Korpsman from one of his other squads. *Why did I ever think it might be otherwise?* Deep down, he knew the answer to that question.

He felt relief, which rapidly turned to guilt. The ghosts of Maximus Arkanos were not haunting him as he had feared. But four more members of his regiment were dead, which brought its end a little closer.

They didn't stop to bury the four bodies. They laid them out side by side in the cavern, watched over by its silent skulls. Graven led a short prayer for them: that, despite the desecration of their material remains, these soldiers might find their deserved rest.

Gruesome though the task was, he had their brain stems severed by shovels, ensuring that they would not rise again. He resolved to do the same for any Korpsman falling on Oleris in the future, if the corpse could not be burnt.

He could do nothing more, then, but turn back. His engineer had inspected the demolished exit tunnel, agreeing with Graven's own assessment that there was no way through without heavy machinery. 'We could get a Termite down here,' he suggested.

The colonel shook his head. 'Unnecessary.'

Above ground, the fighting had ended too.

The watchmaster made one final circuit of the hamlet, ensuring that no zombies were left standing and no more incoming from the fields. Finding one crawling on broken arms and legs, he had his horse stamp on its head until it stopped. He saw Attilan riders taking similar precautions.

Workers emerged from the barn, blinking in the evening light, grateful if shell-shocked to be alive. They looked at the decomposing bodies piled up around the building with trepidation and disgust. Some still had arms or even heads stuck between the wall slats.

Trotting up beside the watchmaster, Sergeant Batu muttered, 'All need examining for bites and scratches.'

He nodded. 'And those who have them quarantined.'

Another two Attilans were approaching him on foot. One was clearly wounded, supported by the other. With a pang in his stomach, the watchmaster recognised the one he had left bleeding, the one whose horse he rode. *It is good that he is walking,* he had to tell himself. Having seen him, the Attilan was all but dragging his ostensible escort towards him.

Reluctantly, the watchmaster relinquished his saddle. Once more, his feet were dragged down by Oleris' mud. He handed the reins back to their rightful holder, who snatched them from him, scowling. Muttering something darkly under his breath, the Attilan led his horse away.

The watchmaster turned to see that Batu had dismounted alongside him. She regarded him with something like pity in her eyes. Brusquely, he said, 'We must contact command headquarters.'

'Already in hand,' she assured him. Then, disarmingly, she asked, 'Glad you stayed with us now?'

'Thankful that I was where the Emperor needed me to be.'

'Must've felt good to ride again,' she pressed him, 'feeling the wind in your... um, feeling the wind. No shame in admitting it, you know. Trouble with you Krieg is that you're uptight. So rigid you could break at any moment.'

Bristling, the watchmaster drew breath to respond. *The Death Korps,* he would have pointed out, *has the lowest desertion rate in the Astra Militarum. Nothing breaks us.* But what, he asked himself, would have been the point?

'It felt good,' he conceded.

Batu grinned her toothy grin again. 'Good for you, Watchmaster No-Name.'

A worker emerged from a nearby hut, at that moment, calling for her.

'Sounds like they've got through on the vox,' she said, all businesslike again. She tethered her horse to a hitching post and rushed away.

The watchmaster considered whether to follow her or not.

Then, from inside the barn, he heard a shriek.

Colonel Graven had returned.

His Korpsmen looked weary and, though an outsider couldn't have told, dejected. Six more emerged from the drain, however – the same number as had gone down there – so, whatever their setbacks, they had their lives to give yet.

Their appearance had startled the few workers left in the barn, who still regarded them with trepidation. One had a shovel ready to defend himself, much good it would have done him. *They have been underground for hours,* the watchmaster thought. *Anything could have happened in that time.*

Graven took in the damage to the barn, the dismembered limbs, the sallow heads poking through its walls. 'Zombies?' he asked, his unsurprised tone telling its own story. 'Any casualties?'

'None apparent yet, sir.'

Graven understood. His gaze turned to Idelax, still slumped against his pillar with his Krieg guard at his side. The inquisitor made no attempt to stand. 'Any word on that flyer yet, watchmaster?' the colonel asked.

'Sergeant Batu is on the vox to headquarters as we speak.'

'What... happened?' It was an effort for Idelax to speak, but his blue eyes blazed with determination. 'The witches?'

Graven stood his kill team down and they dispersed in silence. Looming over the witch hunter, he began his report. The watch-master's moment had passed. He could have had his colonel – the other Korpsmen too – recite the Emperor's Prayer. If nothing else, it would have eased the workers' fears. Some had already slipped out of the barn, uncomfortable with the Krieg's presence, but then that was hardly unusual.

Graven would have understood. Approved, even.

It would have been an accusation. It would have felt disloyal. The idea that one could have fallen to a spectre without the others knowing... Less still, that all could have been so defeated. Colonel Graven least of all of them. Watching him now, so self-assured, regretful that his foes had escaped him, sure that they would not get far, the watchmaster saw no reason to doubt his commander.

No reason whatsoever.

Idelax listened to Graven's report in grim silence.

He became more troubled as the story neared its end, as the colonel related his encounter with a Chaos Space Marine. 'A Tallyman!' he hissed.

Graven cocked his head. 'Inquisitor?'

Before he could muster the breath for explanations, an Attilan sergeant – he had seen her before but hadn't asked her name – appeared in Idelax's field of vision. She addressed him directly, making an effort to suppress her broad accent.

'Your transport is on its way, inquisitor. Colonel Petrakov sends apologies for the delay, but there has been trouble at the compound.' She anticipated Graven's question. 'Not zombies. I don't know details, but no zombies reported anywhere but here.'

Graven recalled, 'Just before we encountered them, we felt something. Like a physical force, a wave of evil, passing through the tunnels. It made the ossuary bones tremble. It can only have been witchcraft.'

'An incantation,' said Idelax, 'to raise... the dead, but only...'

'Only in our vicinity, because we were getting too close.'

'Even so, it shows our enemies are more... powerful than we might have... prayed. And what was wrought once can be... wrought again. How many bodies... lie in this world's... soil? They must number in the...'

'Billions,' growled Graven.

'Hundreds of... billions.'

'Each one now potentially a foe.'

'The Tallyman,' wheezed Idelax, 'accompanies the Plague Marines of the... Death Guard Legion. His creed is... numerology. He catalogues the... woes inflicted upon man by... by the followers of... Nurgle, in tallies of...'

'Seven,' finished Graven.

Idelax glared at him, but he didn't seem to know what he had said. 'Yes, always seven. If such a... demagogue has made the journey here...'

Graven spared him further effort. Unexpectedly, he squatted beside Idelax to look him in the eye. 'Down in those catacombs an hour ago,' he said, 'my worst dreams were made manifest. The dead of my regiment returned to claim my life, but I did not falter.' What would have sounded boastful from anybody else, and therefore suspect, the witch hunter accepted as plain fact.

'I care not how powerful the witches of this world have grown,' the Krieg colonel continued, 'nor how advanced their plots. I have faith that, thanks to your diligence, inquisitor, they have been discovered in time. We have these witches on the run, and forced them to act in haste.'

'I... concur with your... assessment.'

'What is more, I now know where to find them. I believe I know where the high priests of their coven must be hiding. And I no longer doubt that, with my regiment behind me, I can weather any plague of mind or body inflicted upon me, and wreak the holy vengeance of the Emperor upon them!'

A rare smile tugged at the corners of Idelax's lips. 'I believe you,' he said, and then he closed his eyes for what he knew would be the final time.

The flyer sent for Idelax was an Aquila lander.

Absent of a landing pad, it lowered itself into an already churned-up field north of the hamlet, and began sinking into the mud. Its Naval pilot was keen to load up quickly. A pair of Korpsmen stretchered the inquisitor aboard.

The passenger compartment was well appointed, for high-ranking personnel, but cramped. Graven had hoped for something large enough to accommodate his full squad. He boarded the Aquila with a single Korpsman – the rest would have to make their own way back to headquarters.

Idelax lay on his stretcher across a row of cushioned seats. He hadn't stirred since the barn, not even when manhandled. His face was pale, his breathing hoarse and shallow. Someone had crossed his hands over his chest. His overburdened heart had lost its struggle against his ailments of body and soul both. Had he been Krieg, by now Graven would have granted to him the Emperor's Mercy.

Rain pattered on the shuttle roof as rocket engines strained to extricate it from the clinging planet. Their flight time was mere minutes, still too long for the patient to endure. Graven was not surprised when Idelax drew his last, shuddering breath and then fell still.

He prayed for him, his Korpsman standing by him, both with heads bowed and hands clasped in front of them. Then the colonel leaned in closer and whispered a private thank you into Idelax's ear.

Straightening, he spoke aloud again: 'Your strength will be missed, but your example has made us all stronger. Rest easy in the Emperor's embrace, and know that your life counted.'

XIII

Two ground vehicles pulled up to the landing pad as the Aquila settled on it. One was a Krieg Centaur for Graven, the other a Samaritan medical transport.

Gruffly, the colonel informed a medicae that she was too late. He left her to deal with Idelax's body, no longer his concern.

Wrapped in thought, he rode in the Centaur's passenger compartment with his Korpsman rather than its turret. This meant he had no view of the outside world until the vehicle braked and the hatch was yanked open from without.

With night drawing in, the command compound was floodlit. Emerging, blinking, into the actinic glow, Graven found two Vostroyan lasguns trained upon him. Their wielders flanked their colonel, who ordered them tartly, 'Disarm him!'

A Guardsman approached him, keeping his weapon trained. He reached for Graven's power sword. Instinctively, Graven blocked him with his elbow.

'Shoot him in the leg if he resists,' snapped the glowering Petrakov.

He cursed himself for a novice. *Trouble at the compound.* He had assumed it dealt with. He had assumed an Imperial victory.

If spectres possessed them, he told himself, *I would be dead already.* Nor did he read malice in Petrakov's expression, only tired apprehension.

There had been fighting here. He saw the bodies – Vostroyans and Attilans, all fresh as far as he could tell – along with walking wounded, applying salves and bandages. An overturned Samaritan lay by the burnt remains of what had been the medicae hut. It wasn't hard to guess what must have happened.

He snapped to attention. 'Adore the immortal Emperor, for He is our protector.'

'What are you doing?'

Graven continued to recite the Emperor's Prayer, until first the Guardsmen and then the reluctant Petrakov joined in. When they were done, the Vostroyan colonel scowled. 'What does that prove?'

'I understand your caution,' said Graven. 'My own kill team encountered spectres attached to three of your Firstborn.'

'There were six of them,' said Petrakov, 'their mission evidently to assassinate me. They arrived on the pretext of requiring medical care. Just as you have.'

'Were any of them Krieg?' asked Graven, mildly.

Petrakov's lip curled. 'Not this time. Nor had I prior cause to doubt their faith.' Graven caught the implication, but deemed it unworthy of response. *Let him say what he means.* He met Petrakov's glare with his own blank-eyed gaze, knowing its unsettling effect.

'Inquisitor Idelax,' said Petrakov, at length. 'You know our medicaes advised him against returning to duty?' Graven had not known, but he was unsurprised. Clearly, Petrakov had learned of the witch hunter's passing. His Samaritan crew would have voxed him straight away. Clearly, too, he had much more to say on the subject, but he took a breath and held his tongue.

With a gesture, Petrakov dismissed his Guardsmen, who seemed relieved to escape that situation. Graven's Korpsman too relaxed somewhat, stepping from the Chimera behind him. 'We need to talk,' the Krieg colonel said.

'My office.' Petrakov pivoted on his heel and led the way.

Graven lingered, having instructions for his Korpsman. By the time he had outlined them, Petrakov had disappeared inside, having not looked back to see if he was accompanied. Graven supposed he ought not to keep him waiting. His sword still slung at his hip, he followed the commander-in-chief of Oleris' forces, rehearsing an argument in his head that he knew would most likely fall on deaf ears.

The engineer had managed to get an old farm vehicle running.

It was an open-topped truck with space for eight Korpsmen on its cargo bed. A residue of fuel sloshed in its tank, which he topped up by draining the few unused promethium bombs, even wringing their cloth fuses. At last, he proclaimed that it should – just – make it as far as the command compound.

The watchmaster had considered riding with an Attilan to recover their Chimera from the hamlet where they had left it. This way, to his chagrin, would be quicker. He loaded his squad onto the truck. He took the passenger seat in the cabin beside the engineer at the control wheel.

They left the residents of Sanctuary in moderate spirits. The horrors of the zombie attack behind them, most felt proud to have survived it. It helped that a second Attilan squad had arrived to bolster their defences. They were building a pyre for the corpses and pieces thereof, wearing – at the watchmaster's suggestion – gas masks so as not to inhale lingering spores.

Sergeant Batu had addressed the workers. 'You've all seen the Death Korps of Krieg and their Colonel Graven. Who'd want to be a witch today and have to face their fury?' They only had to hold out a little longer, she had insisted. Colonel Graven would deal with the witches.

Her motive, of course, was to raise morale, but still it made the watchmaster all the more determined to justify her faith in his people.

The truck's exhaust coughed up smoke as they set off from the hamlet. Its suspension was shot, and the watchmaster's bones felt every pothole in the boggy tracks. Through a cracked windscreen, in the glow of a single working headlight, suddenly he saw something strewn across their path. Another ragged corpse, and it was stirring. *Not again,* he prayed.

'Watchmaster?' the engineer queried.

'Keep driving!' he said grimly, and the engineer stamped on his accelerator pedal.

The zombie was struggling to stand. It lacked its lower left leg, which was probably the reason it had never reached the hamlet. *The witches haven't cast their spell again, I would have felt it. This is a remnant from their previous effort.*

Surging forwards, the truck crashed into the zombie and through it, demolishing its brittle skeleton – but the watchmaster saw more dark shapes rising from the fields about them. From behind his head, through a thin partition, he heard las fire cracks. His comrades back there had seen them too. He drew his own weapon. He looked for a way of opening the window in his door.

A broken body sprang out of the dirt, as if from nowhere. It leapt at the speeding truck, and though the watchmaster was already past it, he felt its impact with the rear fender. In a cobwebbed mirror, he saw the zombie clawing its way up and over the sideboards of the cargo bed.

Another creature loomed ahead of them. It was on the track's edge, at a sharp bend for which the engineer had to slow down. Tyres spinning in mud, the truck just clipped the zombie, apparently dislocating its right shoulder – in the same moment that it jumped and spread-eagled itself across the windscreen.

Its pale eyes fixed upon the watchmaster through the glass. Ordinary glass, not armaglass as any Krieg vehicle would have had. Cracked glass. The zombie drew back its good arm.

The watchmaster realised that the green scraps clinging to it had been an Imperial uniform, though he couldn't identify the regiment. Sergeant's stripes decorated a fluttering, torn epaulette. He spared a thought for a fallen comrade, brought here from his last battlefield to rest.

The zombie's fist punched through the windscreen.

The engineer threw up an arm to fend off flying glass, which caused the truck to veer. The watchmaster pumped three bolts into the zombie's head. Its flesh melted, sloughing from its skull as, straddling the dashboard, it clawed at his throat. The engineer wrestled the truck back under his control and picked up speed. Wrenching his wheel around, he slammed the watchmaster hard against the door but also tore the zombie's grip from him.

The watchmaster glimpsed a body falling from the cargo bed, reflected in his mirror. He couldn't think about that now.

His rotting foe came at him again, met by his drawn bayonet, which he thrust into its throat and out through the back of its neck. Continuing the motion, he pushed the zombie through the shattered windscreen. Vainly, it scrabbled for purchase on the truck's front end. As the watchmaster withdrew his blade, it fell headfirst beneath the wheels.

He found the handle to wind down his window. The truck

was running straight again and he could no longer hear fighting. 'What's your status back there?' he yelled out into the night.

'All good, watchmaster,' came the reply. 'No casualties.'

'No more hostiles in sight,' another Korpsman added, confirming the evidence of the watchmaster's eyes. The road ahead, as far as he could see, was clear. They must have crossed the boundary of the witches' spell by now. They had also left a handful of zombies behind them, crippled but still animated.

Our orders are to make haste to command headquarters. Once there, the watchmaster could vox Sanctuary and warn Batu of the threat. Her Attilans were more than capable of dealing with it. He turned to the engineer beside him.

'Keep driving,' he repeated.

'You do know what you're asking is impossible.'

Colonel Petrakov's face was rigid. His moustache was a straight line across his tightened lips. Sitting stiffly in his chair behind his desk, he glared across at Graven, who had declined a seat.

'I have made no formal request as yet.'

Petrakov cut across him. 'The Sisters would never allow it.'

'Certainly, they would raise a protest,' agreed Graven, 'but were I to speak to the Sister Superior, I might persuade her to–'

'I will not allow it,' stated Petrakov.

'Colonel, I have shown you the maps that–'

For the third time, Graven was interrupted. He reined in his irritation. 'You have outlined a theory to me – and yes, on the surface, I see the logic of it – but where is your proof?'

'The evidence, I grant, is circumstantial.'

'And nowhere near sufficient to justify such drastic action.'

'The situation,' said Graven doggedly, 'demands that we consider it.'

Petrakov pushed himself to his feet, bringing their eyelines level. 'I spoke with the witch hunter. Before he left here to join you and never returned. He shared certain suspicions with me. Suspicions about you, Colonel Graven.'

Now they were getting to it. 'He feared me susceptible to the spectres' whispers.'

Wrong-footed by the frank acknowledgement, Petrakov faltered.

Graven continued, 'For that reason, I was instrumental in his death, if that suspicion drove him into battle alongside me against medical advice.'

'You must see how that looks to me.'

'On his deathbed, Idelax expressed his confidence in me, but I cannot prove that to you either. All I can do is add him to my tally, and fulfil the vow I swore to him, to see his work on Oleris III through to its conclusion.'

'That is my purpose too,' said Petrakov through gritted teeth.

'Then understand that we must change our tactics,' Graven urged him. 'The witches are poised to unleash horrors upon this world that can scarcely be imagined. They have the advantage of home ground in the ossuary and can frustrate our progress almost endlessly. We must locate their coven's heart.'

'And strike at it. I agree.'

'I believe that heart lies beneath the mausoleum. Or inside it.'

'The Grand Mausoleum. Of the sainted Josefina.'

Petrakov turned his back pointedly on Graven. He stared out through his window for a minute. Rain pattered on the pane. Graven stood and waited patiently, knowing there was no more he could say at this juncture. The Vostroyan turned back to him, at last, his face overcast.

'Impossible!' he snapped.

They almost made it, but not quite.

The farm truck sputtered to a halt, still in sight of the Grand

Mausoleum's spires. The Krieg watchmaster and engineer climbed out. 'I was afraid of this,' the latter muttered. By the vehicle's yellow light, he twisted off the fuel cap and poked a lasgun's cleaning rod into the tank.

'Out of promethium already?' asked the watchmaster.

'Barely had enough to start with, and we used it inefficiently. Too many sharp accelerations, shaking off those zombies. I might coax another mile out of it on fumes, if I can unclog the filter.'

The watchmaster nodded as if he understood, and left him to it. He turned to check on the rest of his squad on the cargo bed. He found himself looking up into a zombie's dead white eyes.

Its head was mounted like a trophy on the spike of an entrenching shovel. The watchmaster made no comment.

Returning to the driver's seat, the engineer attempted to restart the engine, but this time had no luck. With an asthmatic sigh of machine spirits, the truck seemed to sag in resignation. The watchmaster considered. 'We can only be two and a half to three miles out of the compound. At quick time, we can make it in an hour. We're unlikely to encounter more foes in this region.'

'If we do,' said a Korpsman, jumping down beside him, 'we can add them to our collection, maybe hang them from the compound gates.'

The watchmaster looked up at the zombie's head. 'Get rid of that thing before we reach headquarters,' he instructed. 'It may be diseased.'

The Korpsman sounded disappointed. 'Yes, watchmaster.'

They formed up in ranks of two and, beneath the glowering light of Oleris' red moon rising, resumed their journey.

Artificial light seeped into Petrakov's office, round the edges of bolted window shutters. His ceiling lumen-globe remained shut off. He sat in the deepening gloom with elbows on his desk and head in hands.

'What is it the rumours say?' His own words echoed in his memory. *'That the veil between life and death is thin here?'*

Graven, before leaving, had urged him to think about all he had said. Though making no such assurance, Petrakov found he could do little else. The Krieg colonel had been right before. That was the thought he couldn't shake. *What if he is right again?* But this was not Graven's decision. Petrakov would have to give the order, and its consequences would be on his head.

One of Graven's assertions, at least, could hardly be denied. Oleris' witches were growing in both power and audacity. Petrakov shuddered at the memory of spectres infiltrating his own compound, lurking in his soldiers' shadows.

His presence had been requested in the medicae hut, on the promise that its newly arrived patients had brought vital information. With eerie synchronicity, they had risen from their beds, closing around him. Only quick thinking, and the sacrifice of two of the colonel's aides, had got him out unscathed.

He had faced death before and was unafraid of it, but this – what the spectres had presumably planned for him – was unthinkable.

He had raised the alarm, and all soldiers in the compound had come running. The infiltrators had been besieged in the medicae hut, but when the structure had been stormed, they had set off prepared charges. Though their usurped bodies had been immolated, Petrakov had been chilled by the sight of ghostly shadows writhing in the smoke.

Could they be in here with him now?

The thought jolted him to his feet. He ought to have been more careful: spectres could have crept into the corners of the darkening room. Petrakov snapped on the light, relieved to find himself alone. He called for a scribe, who rushed in with dataslate and stylus. The colonel dictated a new standing order. Going forward, any person entering this compound, regardless of standing, would first be required to recite the Emperor's Prayer and would be executed if unable to comply.

Petrakov dismissed the scribe, then called him back.

The thought occurred to him, *A spectre in here with me would have explained my doubts. Knowing from where they arose, I might even have dispelled them!* He wished he could seek Inquisitor Idelax's counsel, but that was impossible now.

'Take an instruction to the vox-operator,' he said, 'to contact the Grand Mausoleum and ask for the Sister Superior in person. Relay my apologies to her for the presumption, but assure her that the matter is most urgent.'

Spectres, he thought, *now zombies too. The dead returned in body as in soul. No longer is that veil just thin, it must be positively fraying.*

It had been a long day, and even the Krieg were weary as at last they tramped up to the command compound.

The last thing they needed was to be denied entry by a pair of Vostroyan sentries, who questioned them relentlessly. 'Yours is the second Krieg squad to return here in an hour,' one of them said, accusingly.

'I can't speak for any other,' the watchmaster explained patiently, 'but we are here on Colonel Graven's orders.'

'For what reason? Why are you not out fighting?'

'We are here,' the watchmaster repeated, 'on Colonel Graven's orders.'

They were made to say the Emperor's Prayer, each of them in turn. When a Korpsman, throat dry because his water supply was exhausted, made a minor stumble over the word 'venerate', two lasguns snapped towards him.

'Enough!' the watchmaster bellowed.

Other Korpsmen had been reaching for their weapons, but now froze. To the wavering Vostroyans, the watchmaster said, 'I passed your test.' He had been the first to do so. 'I vouch for the rest of my squad. So, take your fingers off those triggers, else I'll see you court-martialled.'

'With respect, watchmaster, we have our orders too.'

'Caution is justified, but do not let it blossom into paranoia. Our enemies win when we mistrust each other. My Korpsman will say the prayer again.'

The sentries exchanged glances and agreed.

The Korpsman in question pulled himself to attention. He launched into a fresh recital, his scratchy voice the only sound in a world that otherwise stood still. Ten lines of prayer had never seemed so long before. As he intoned the final words – 'for without Him we are nothing' – the watchmaster was not the only soldier present to breathe a sigh of relief.

The ordeal was not yet over. Three more had to pass the test.

The tension further dissipated as each did so in turn, and the gates were opened for the Krieg, at last. The watchmaster ensured that they marched proudly through with heads held high.

They were greeted in the compound, not by Graven as expected, but by a Krieg commissar. She checked the watchmaster's shoulder flashes. 'Command squad?' He confirmed this. He recognised this commissar, though masked, as his regiment had so few remaining. Her name was Skarangard.

As soon as the watchmaster had stood his Korpsmen down, she drew him to one side. 'What is Graven planning?' she demanded in her distinctive husky voice.

'As yet, the colonel has not seen fit to brief me. I can only inform you of what we discovered underground.'

She waved aside the explanation. 'I read the reports. I know about the zombies – and the Tallyman, though only one man has seen that.'

'That is my understanding too.'

'What I need to know is why Graven instructed all Krieg squads to pull out of the ossuary tunnels and regroup around the mausoleum.'

'You know more than I do, sir.' The farm truck had had no vox-unit.

'We were close by and heard the order first-hand as we set up camp for the night. I chose to come here straight away. Colonel Graven has spoken to no commissar in weeks.'

'You suspect he's hiding something?' the watchmaster asked sharply.

'Do you?' Skarangard asked, equally so.

'Where is he?'

'Bedded down in the mess hall, having deferred my request to meet. Watchmaster, I've served for over three years with this regiment. I'm resigned to the fact that my primary role is to represent the Krieg to otherworlders. To do that, I must know what you – and your commander in particular – are thinking.'

'Surely he has earned our trust?' the watchmaster prevaricated.

'My trust,' said Skarangard, 'is not the issue, as you must realise by now. I am waiting for a chance to speak with Colonel Petrakov. I had hoped you might give me something to say to him.'

'Commissar, please, delay that meeting. I will speak to the colonel, as soon as he awakes, and apprise him of your concerns.'

Skarangard considered, then nodded. Marching away, she barked over her shoulder, 'As soon as he awakes!'

In the mess hall, the new arrivals laid out bedrolls alongside those of Skarangard's squad, two of whom stood on watch. The Korpsman who had travelled on the flyer was present, asleep.

The door to the next room was ajar, and while only darkness could be seen within, deep, steady breathing could be heard.

The watchmaster couldn't be sure, but it sounded to him like Graven was very much awake.

Sister Superior Serafina's boots rang off the mausoleum's tiled floor.

She was in a foul mood, having been disturbed at prayer, which meant she would have to begin her litanies again. *For Colonel Petrakov's sake, he had better have good cause.*

The ever-scowling Sister Elvana marched two steps behind her. Both were decorated veterans of the Second Tyrannic War. They had fought in defence of the cathedral on Okassis, witnessed the heroic last stand of Canoness Praxades. Serafina felt affronted that so many of their Order had since perished on the blighted world of Armageddon, and that she had not been with them.

Her squad had not seen battle in what felt like an age. Their tour of duty on Oleris was to have lasted three years, but they had been here twice that long. Of course, their presence served a holy purpose. Still, sometimes she felt they had been forgotten. *Until now, when we might be called to battle after all.* The thought was easily dismissed. Three Astra Militarum regiments had to be sufficient to deal with a ragtag band of heretics.

This late, the mausoleum's main chamber was unoccupied. As Serafina and Elvana crossed it, the prayers of the Sisters left in the chapel followed them. Their susurrations echoed from the vaulted ceiling, around the high galleries, calming the Sister Superior's ire.

Saint Josefina bathed her in her ever-benevolent gaze.

The saint's marble statue crowned her sealed stone crypt. The rougher-hewn effigies of plague victims clustered about her, prostrated on the stepped sides of the edifice, reaching up to her in supplication. Josefina, on one knee, reached down, ministering to them. Candles had been hung behind her so that, when viewed from ahead, soft golden light outlined her.

An honour guard of ten Sisters served here, along with sundry aides and servitors who maintained the mausoleum, keeping its candles lit and its surfaces dust-free. One such aide Serafina found in the small comms room, little more than a cubicle in truth. She leapt to her feet as the Battle Sisters entered, bowing her head in reverence. Dismissing her, the Sister Superior took her place at the vox-caster, Elvana looming over her.

'What is it, Colonel Petrakov?' she asked crisply.

He made the usual apologies for taking up her time, which only wasted more of it. He spoke of grave developments since last they had conversed. He read to her reports of bodies rising from the earth and Traitor Space Marines, and this was where he earned her full attention. She was mollified to learn that the threat had been contained – if only, Petrakov warned, for the present.

Then he made a suggestion. He ensured that Serafina knew it did not come from him and had not his approval. When first he mentioned Colonel Graven's name, she felt quite well disposed towards it. That soon changed.

'I will not allow it!' the Sister Superior roared.

'I expected that would be your decision,' Petrakov said, *'but you understand I had to ask.'*

'You "had to ask" if you might desecrate a holy shrine?'

'Only under the suspicion that such may already have occurred.'

'You ask my leave to sunder Saint Josefina's crypt, which for five hundred years has stood inviolate? To disturb her sacred remains?'

For a short time, the only sound was a static crackle over the vox-link.

Then Petrakov ventured, *'Sister Superior.'* Had he seen Elvana's face, like thunder, he would have held his tongue. *'Forgive me, but did you not yourself speak of a "nocturnal presence"?'*

She shook herself. 'Phantasms, that is all.'

'I assume, by that, you mean the things we have been calling spectres.'

'Some may have crept in through the shadows in the mausoleum's corners. Finding no purchase in the minds of any here, they slunk away. None have been detected in days. Increasing the frequency and volume of our prayers has warded us against them. And let me assure you, Colonel Petrakov, that had any tried to violate the crypt itself, whatever blackened tatters of their souls they still possess would have burnt in its consecrated soil.'

Accepting her emphatic proclamation, the Vostroyan apologised again and broke off the connection. Serafina remained seated, brooding, long enough that Sister Elvana felt compelled to prompt her: 'Sister Superior?'

'I am disturbed by these developments,' she confessed.

'You don't imagine there is truth in Petrakov's suspicions?'

'God-Emperor, no! As if the crypt, our sacred charge, could be so violated and not one of us aware of it.'

'As if.'

'Still, I wonder if it may be time to apprise the Palatine of our situation.' Serafina shook her head. 'No. No, Petrakov can send for reinforcements if needs be. It is his responsibility to keep spectres, zombies, Tallymen and witches from our doors, and even should he fail–'

'God-Emperor forbid it,' Elvana interjected.

'–then the worshippers of Chaos, usurpers of death itself, will find that, with our saint to guide us, we are more than ready for them!'

Decisively, she pushed herself to her feet and stomped out of the room. She spared not a glance for the vox-operator, who scurried back to her post.

As she crossed the main chamber again, her last doubts drained away. Saint Josefina watched over all her supplicants, and the echoing whispers from the chapel enwrapped her like a blanket. In a corner of Serafina's mind arose the fleeting thought that evening prayer was surely over, but this was soon forgotten. She felt as if the saint herself spoke to her. She commended her for standing strong against those weak and fearful men who knew not the power of her faith.

Serafina basked in that approval. Her momentary doubt had been a weakness to be overcome. No witch had any power in this sacred place, only what she ceded to them by such suspicions. The mausoleum was protected. Serafina had no cause to feel concerned. She would stand firm.

XIV

Graven found his watchmaster rather than the other way around. As the latter emerged from the Krieg stores with fresh nutrient and power packs – the quartermaster had no frag grenades to spare – his colonel was waiting for him.

The compound bustled with activity as Vostroyan staff and servitors erected a new medicae hut and dug a mass grave beyond the chain-link fence. The watchmaster noticed an Attilan tending to a horse whose rider had been lost.

Graven was pensive as he led the way to the office allocated to him, rarely used. At the door, the watchmaster cleared his throat. 'Colonel, you should know that last night Commissar Skarangard approached me. Anything you say to me, I am under orders to share with her.'

Graven said nothing. He opened the door and ushered the watchmaster past him into the office. The watchmaster was surprised to find Skarangard waiting inside. They acknowledged each other with stiff nods.

The colonel took a seat behind his desk and motioned to the others to sit too. Unsettled, the watchmaster did so. Graven hesitated for a second before speaking, which was another ominous sign.

'Last night,' he said at length, 'another spectre paid me a visit.'

The watchmaster stiffened. 'How did I not know this?' Reacting exactly as Graven had known he would.

'It came and went unseen,' he explained brusquely, such details beside his point. 'Perhaps it whispered to me through the wall. Whatever. By now, I know their voices, even in my dreams.'

He had lain on his bedroll, brain full of thoughts, accepting he would not find sleep tonight. The next he knew, he was waking in a sweat, a fresh nightmare fading from his memory. He must have made a noise, as a sentry had looked in on him. Graven had dismissed her. The spectre was already gone, he had been sure of that.

'You should know this,' he continued, 'because the spectres turn guilt into doubt, and I… I have been wrestling with both.'

He let the words hang in the air. He expected a reaction, but the masked faces of the watchmaster and commissar both betrayed nothing of their thoughts. 'On Maximus Arkanos,' he expounded, 'I made a decision that still haunts me.'

Skarangard spoke up, then. 'I am aware of what happened on Maximus Arkanos and the part you played in it.' Graven looked at her, surprised. 'I requested a transcript of the subsequent tribunal. It was my job to know.'

He turned to his watchmaster, who, with more reticence, admitted, 'I overheard the details from Inquisitor Idelax.'

'I see,' said Graven, wrong-footed.

'Sir, Krieg high command judged that you acted properly.'

'The fact remains that had I only followed orders, a thousand

Death Korpsmen might still be alive, striving for our world's atonement. I chose a different path – and with good reason, I do not say otherwise – but equally it cannot be denied that I chose wrong.'

Skarangard cut to the heart of the matter. 'Why tell us this now?'

'Because,' said Graven, 'through some ironic twist of fate, or because I am being tested, I now face a similar decision.'

'And you doubt your own judgement?'

Nightmare fragments flashed behind his eyes. The images were horribly familiar. His comrades writhed and screamed in a nuclear inferno, blaming him. They swore that they would never cease tormenting him, and they had a new charge to level against him.

'Bad enough our lives were expended so cheaply.'

'Now you risk our regiment's honour.'

'You disgrace the only name we could ever lay claim to.'

Why me? he had asked himself in anguish. *Why do they still target me, when I thought my guilt laid to rest?* He had only been able to think of one possible reason.

The commissar awaited an answer to her question. Clearly and firmly, Graven stated it. 'No. This time, I have no doubts.'

'This is the situation.'

Graven thrust himself to his feet to pace the narrow space behind his desk. As if, by releasing his confession, he had energised himself. The watchmaster hadn't seen him like this before.

'Beneath our feet, beneath the surface of Oleris III, heretics have spent centuries in hiding, scheming, plotting, growing stronger. Witches have refined their necromantic arts. Bestial foot-soldiers have been bred, vile apparitions conjured. Even Traitor Space Marines have swelled their ranks.'

'We know this, Colonel Graven,' said Skarangard, impatiently.

'And now they have revealed to us their ultimate ambition.'

'Which is?'

'To raise this planet's dead, as they did outside Sanctuary two nights ago. I believe that was merely a test run.'

'Or maybe, that night, they showed us the limits of their power.'

The watchmaster said, 'Sir, what of the incident that brought an inquisitor here? What of the lord and lady and their son?'

'We know that not only spectres have been freed from the immaterium,' said the colonel.

'One tried to usurp Idelax's very soul,' the watchmaster recalled, 'but was resisted by him at dreadful expense. Who knows how many other such attempts have been successful?'

'I believe these beings – let us name them truly, daemons – give the witches all the power they need to raise a zombie army, numbering in the hundreds of billions, carrying the Chaos plague beneath their fingernails.' Graven pre-empted the commissar's next objection. 'Why else would a Tallyman come here, but to catalogue the spread of the infection?'

For a moment, there was silence as the trio considered that scenario.

The watchmaster thought about his battles with a mere few dozen zombies. The numbers advanced by Graven were unthinkable. Oleris would be swiftly overrun, that much was certain, but then what? To other worlds, their numbers swelled by fallen foes on this one? The watchmaster himself now an unthinking soldier in their army? He protested, 'We cannot allow it.'

'On that, of course we are agreed,' said Skarangard.

'I believe there is but one way to stop it,' declared Graven.

Graven ceased his pacing, standing straight-backed, fixing his commissar and watchmaster in turn with his gaze. They must have known, at least suspected, what he would ask of them.

He was giving them time to process the magnitude of it before he said the words.

'How many squads do we have in the catacombs?' he asked. 'Krieg and Vostroyans together?'

'Something in the region of one hundred and ten,' Skarangard guessed.

'How many witches have been discovered?'

'Not every squad has been able to report in yet.'

'Either there are far fewer than we thought – which, given all they've done, I find unlikely – or they are still hiding from us. In which case, the question arises, where is left for them to hide?'

'Sir,' the watchmaster offered, 'the influenced Vostroyan squad may have come close to their sanctum.'

Graven agreed: 'As must we when we followed in their footsteps.'

'What are you suggesting?' asked Skarangard, in a tone that made him picture her eyes narrowing.

'Let me reframe my question. Where in those catacombs are we not looking? Where do we dare not tread?'

She leapt to her feet. 'You don't mean…?' she spluttered, scandalised. Clearly, she had not foreseen this detail.

'Commissar,' said Graven firmly, 'as I told you, I have no doubt about this, none at all, and the reason is that, last night, a spectre whispered to me in my dreams and tried to make me doubt.'

Skarangard was forced to consider that point.

Graven pressed his advantage. 'Oleris' witches hide in the crypt of Saint Josefina, beneath her Grand Mausoleum.'

He glanced at his watchmaster, who sat in rigid silence.

'I imagine they tunnelled up inside it decades ago, and if any scrap of bone escaped destruction' – he caught the commissar's intake of breath – 'then the consecrated earth in which they lie is by now thoroughly despoiled.'

* * *

'You outlined this theory to Colonel Petrakov?' asked Skarangard. She sounded as disturbed as the Krieg watchmaster felt.

'As far as he was willing to listen.'

'You suggested that he...' Words failed the commissar.

Graven had no such problem. 'Break open Saint Josefina's crypt.'

'And his reaction?'

'Much the same as yours.'

'Then that is an end to it. Petrakov is commander-in-chief here, he makes the decisions. To say nothing of the Adepta Sororitas.'

Graven asked bluntly, 'What if Petrakov is wrong?'

Skarangard countered, 'What if he is right and you are wrong?'

'Then I will face the consequences of my actions.'

'But,' the watchmaster interjected, 'no lives will have been lost.'

The commissar turned to glare at him.

'And I have no doubt,' said Graven, 'while Petrakov does. Tell me you haven't seen it. Doubt that holds us back when logic tells us what must be.'

The watchmaster frowned. 'Might spectres have whispered to him too? Or worse?'

'We can't know that,' said Graven.

'And yet you know better than he does,' said Skarangard, accusingly, 'because of your own spectre? A spectre unseen by you or by anybody else?'

'I understand your reservations,' said Graven.

'I should hope so.'

The watchmaster looked at his colonel, really looked at him. He saw the almost imperceptible stoop in his shoulders as if a great weight lay upon them. His nervous energy of earlier had ebbed, and he seemed tired. His rebreather mask still bore its zombie scars, as if he had lacked time – or not cared – to replace it.

'Sir,' he said directly, 'what are you asking of us?'

'On this world of doubt,' said Colonel Graven, 'I want, I need, you both to trust me.'

Graven remembered:

Standing in the dock before a panel of one general and two marshals. As a captain, never had he been addressed by such high-ranking officers before. Never had he even seen a Krieg-born general.

He remembered the thrum of deck plates through his feet, reminding him that he stood aboard an orbiting grand cruiser, despite the cathedral-like opulence of the tribunal chamber. He had wondered how any Krieg could thrive in such surroundings without becoming soft.

He had delivered his solemn testimony to a row of blank, masked faces. Whatever judgement they pronounced upon him, it would be the Emperor's will and he was ready to accept it.

So he had told himself. Now, as he faced judgement once again, he knew that to have been a lie.

'What if I speak with Colonel Petrakov?' Skarangard suggested. 'He might be more amenable to me.' *To someone non-Krieg-born, who shows her face,* she did not have to say.

'To what end?' Graven asked.

'To satisfy myself that he has given your proposal due consideration.'

'And how about you, commissar?'

She hesitated. 'I... accept its logic.'

'Then I have your full support?'

Still, she prevaricated. 'I will put your case to Petrakov, and look for any sign that he is influenced.'

'Whether he is influenced or not is immaterial. What if his decision stands? If he wavers, but the Sisters overrule him?'

'Let's not cross that bridge too soon.'

The watchmaster felt he would have left the matter there. The commissar had listened, offered hope. Graven had the bit between his teeth, however. 'What will you do if Petrakov condemns this world, condemns us all, by stubbornly refusing to accept what any eye can see?'

'More pertinently, colonel,' Skarangard bit back, 'what will you do?'

'I think you know the answer to that question,' said Graven.

The watchmaster's chest tightened. He edged forward in his seat. 'You already gave the word. To surround the mausoleum.'

Graven nodded. 'Regardless of Petrakov, Serafina or anybody else, I have my duty. I will fight to save Oleris III.'

'Even if you must disobey orders?' asked Skarangard.

'As I did once before.'

'That time, you were cut off from Colonel Kleber. You had discretion to adapt to a changing situation. No court-martial would acquit you this time.'

'Not if I am wrong.'

'You might be repeating the greatest mistake of your career.'

'Hence I needed you to know about Maximus Arkanos. I needed you to have the full facts at your disposal before you made your own decisions.'

'To follow you,' said Skarangard, 'or not.'

He was at their mercy now.

Either one of them had the authority, if they suspected his motives or his sanity, to relieve Graven of his command. He prayed it would not come to that, but if it did there would be no point in resisting.

'I can't do this alone,' he said. 'I need my officers' support and my watchmaster's most of all. I need the commissars attached to my regiment to fulfil their traditional role, to ensure that my orders are obeyed even when my Korpsmen find themselves opposed by those who also serve the Emperor.'

'Even if they doubt you,' muttered Skarangard.

'I know I am not mistaken.'

'This time.'

They would chain him in the dungeons beneath the Ecclesiarchal Tower. He was fully aware that he was asking these two comrades to risk being chained alongside him. Waiting for a ship to take them to meet their judgement. *No, waiting for the world to end.*

'Many squads will not have checked in yet,' said the commissar. 'They won't have their new instructions, while others will already be en route. Petrakov will soon see what you're planning, before you are ready to act.'

'I am aware of that.'

Skarangard thought a while longer. Then she reiterated, 'I will speak to him. That has to be the first step.'

This time, Graven nodded and let her go. He sensed that he had pushed her as far as he could, for the present. She had listened, understood and not condemned him out of hand, for which he felt grateful. It meant that, despite what she knew about him, what she had always known, she had at least a measure of trust in him.

With Skarangard gone, the watchmaster felt the full force of the colonel's attention turned upon him. It was his turn to decide.

'Sir, I disagree with you on one point,' he said.

'Oh?'

'The Krieg will follow you, regardless of the view of any commissar.'

'Even those who know my... history?'

'Other regiments have been compromised. Even those who haven't seen it will have heard of Vostroyans and Attilans succumbing to the spectres. Given conflicting orders, we will obey none but yours.'

'Did you never doubt me?' Graven asked him.

He answered frankly. 'For a time, I did. Until I realised – until an ally made me realise – that doubt plays into our enemies' hands. On Krieg, we were trained not to doubt, and now more than ever I see why. Doubt makes me weak, and I reject it.' It really was that simple, after all.

The watchmaster stood and pulled himself to attention. 'Colonel Graven,' he said, 'what are your orders?'

Petrakov consulted with one of his own commissars. The commissar deputised two Vostroyan Guardsmen. The four-strong squad set off across the compound towards the Krieg command centre. To Colonel Graven's office.

Petrakov had received a vox-call from Serafina. Once again, he had found their conversation quite uncomfortable. She had asked why his forces were mustering in her vicinity, and he had been unable to tell her.

The forces in question, he had ascertained, were Krieg Death Korpsmen – which had only inflamed his suspicions.

Earlier that afternoon, he had accepted a meeting with the husky-voiced Krieg commissar. She had tried to persuade him that Graven's insane plan, to launch an assault upon the Grand Mausoleum, was not so insane. Though he would never have admitted to it, he had struggled to refute her points.

He had fallen back on the same argument, repeatedly. 'The Adepta Sororitas simply won't allow it.'

'You have the authority to overrule them,' Skarangard had insisted.

'The Sister Superior is intractable on this point.'

'As is Colonel Graven.' It had sounded like a threat.

Petrakov had told himself not to worry. He felt that, lately, he had worried overmuch. His first command of an Imperial army. Of course he would second-guess himself, especially when undermined by officers from other regiments. *Officers with more experience than I.*

He couldn't help but worry now.

'I am not accusing,' he had stressed to his own commissar. 'I simply have questions to put to Colonel Graven, and I – especially in light of the inquisitor's concerns about him and subsequent death in Graven's presence – would like you to hear his answers.' *And then the decision will be yours.*

He was to be disappointed. Graven wasn't in his office, nor in the mess hall where he and his command squad had been sleeping. In fact, there was no sign of his squad at all. Nor of the other that had arrived last night. No Krieg Death Korpsmen anywhere. No Skarangard. Petrakov collared a few aides and a stores quartermaster, but none could – or would – tell him where their commander might be.

His gate guards reported that a pair of Krieg Chimeras had rolled out of the compound an hour ago. With turret hatches closed, the guards had not identified their occupants, nor thought to question them. The only surprise was that they had headed north, not east towards the mausoleum. What was Graven playing at?

I should have acted earlier, Petrakov chided himself. *I should never have doubted myself.*

He sent out a general vox-message. Any soldier who laid eyes upon Graven was to report his whereabouts at once. He had half-hoped his commissar might step in and issue a warrant for

Graven's arrest. Instead, he advised prudence, while agreeing that there was cause for concern.

Serafina was less circumspect. *'Is it not abundantly clear to you by now,'* she raged over a vox-channel, *'that Graven has become possessed?'*

Petrakov gave an honest answer. 'I don't know that he is. Opinionated he may be, but he was always so.'

'The witches control Graven and, through him, an army of unquestioning drones. They will lay waste to our sacred shrine.' The Sister Superior was starting to sound hysterical. *'I hold you responsible for this, Colonel Petrakov. You allowed things to escalate this far.'*

'Sister Superior, I assure you–'

'I expect you to do your duty, colonel. Honour your vows to the Emperor, and the promise you made to me too. Protect Saint Josefina.'

Rain pattered on the wooden roof of another hut.

Colonel Graven lay awake on his back, on his bedroll again.

Once out of sight of the command compound, his Chimeras had changed course. Skarangard's squad had headed west, to find a fellow commissar whose support she judged might prove decisive. Graven's vehicle, under the Ecclesiarchal Tower's glare, had crawled towards a hamlet north-east of the mausoleum. Not the closest, for that could have been predicted.

He had hoped to find the settlement abandoned. An Attilan squad had visited here, but neglected to file a report yet. To his disappointment, from his turret, he had seen figures gathering to meet him. Another battle was the last thing he had needed, but he had been ready for it.

There had been no battle. Half a dozen older workers were holed up here, in hiding, so they claimed. Faced with the grim visages of nine Death Korpsmen, they had been apprehensive – one had even dared suggest that their arrival would draw trouble, pleading with them to move on. As one elder had succinctly put it, however, 'By now, we know our tormentors' aspects. They look like us.'

Graven had had the six workers clapped in chains.

They had protested bitterly. He had sworn to release them when his kill team left the hamlet, which would be in mere days. He had no reason to suspect them, nor to trust them either. Free, they would have been a distraction.

'Any of those workers could have slipped away into the catacombs,' he explained out loud, 'and reported our location to the witches.'

Any of those workers could have reached a vox-caster, he kept to himself, *and reported our location to command headquarters.* For as long as Petrakov couldn't find Graven, he couldn't question him. For as long as Graven could avoid Petrakov's questions, he didn't have to lie to him.

Lie to my commanding officer. When put in such stark terms, it felt unreal. That his path could have led him here. *'On Krieg, we were trained not to doubt.'* His watchmaster's words. Graven had been taught to follow orders. He had not been taught to give them, but like any Krieg who lived too long, he found himself in that position.

'Doubt makes us weak and I reject it.' Easy for the watchmaster to say. He only had to remember his training. Put his faith in the chain of command. Obey. Much harder for Graven, who had to find faith in himself.

As a young Korpsman, he had heard the story of Veteran Colonel Tyborc, who had led a Krieg regiment during the Siege of Vraks. Perhaps the most infamous engagement in the Death Korps' history, the siege had lasted seventeen years and claimed some fourteen million Korpsmen's lives before ending in glorious victory, cementing his people's reputation for single-minded perseverance.

At the height of the fighting, as the sky was torn asunder and daemons had poured from it, Colonel Tyborc had ordered his soldiers to turn back. Against orders. Orders given by a non-Krieg commander. A decision that had kept their lives from being expended futilely.

Graven had learned this story not from propaganda vids but from comrades in the trenches, where the consensus had been that Tyborc was a hero. Never had he heard mention of him from a more official source. Never had he met an officer called Tyborc, honouring this hero's name. He had come to understand that Tyborc had done what he had had to do, but in a way officially discouraged.

He was said to have served out his time in attendance to an inquisitor lord, and that Krieg high command had been glad of the opportunity to forget the whole difficult business.

Graven knew it was hubristic to compare himself to Veteran Colonel Tyborc. Still, he wondered if, two hundred years from now, his name too might be whispered in Krieg trenches. *Not that it matters.*

What mattered was that he did what was right, what he knew to be right. He had not lied to his watchmaster and commissar. He had no doubt any longer. *Not really.* The spectres wanted him to take the easy way, to not think but to follow, to plough through the ossuary tunnels inch by inch. To give them time. So, that was the last thing he ought to do.

This is why the Emperor brought me here, he thought, *after testing me on Maximus Arkanos.* Finally, he understood.

From the darkness around him, he heard the soft breaths of sleeping Korpsmen. One was awake, keeping a watch for spectres, listening for movement from the six prisoners upstairs.

Two more patrolled outside, their footsteps regularly passing by the window. Graven had taken his watch as the sun set. Though he had been, and still was, deeply tired, he felt sleep beyond him.

Suddenly, sunlight streamed through window shutters and a Korpsman was prodding him awake. He sat bolt upright, snatching up his pistol. 'What is it?'

'It is past dawn, sir,' came the calm reply.

Graven blinked, absorbing this information. He couldn't remember the last time he had slept so deeply for so long. *The night before the bomb,* his mind unhelpfully prompted him. More to the point, the last time he had slept in peace. Six hours of blissful oblivion, such as he had never thought to feel again.

There had been no bad dreams.

Centaurs and Chimeras had been pulling up all day, disgorging quiet, faceless soldiers. A dozen or more Krieg squads pitched their tents in narrow byways between the well-appointed tombs of wealthy pilgrims.

Having sprung up over centuries, these tombs formed an inward-looking circle around Saint Josefina's Grand Mausoleum. Newer tombs were squeezed between the old ones, jostling with them for a view of the hallowed structure.

Shortly after noon, Serafina had marched out to remonstrate with the new arrivals. She had taken with her a full squad of Battle Sisters.

A lieutenant and a watchmaster had met her. The Sister Superior had to allow that they had been perfectly respectful. She couldn't have said that either plotted treachery, but still their conversation hadn't dampened her exasperation.

The Krieg didn't know why they were here. They were awaiting further orders. Serafina had implied, not caring to be tactful, that their orders were senseless when their foes were known to be elsewhere. Colonel Graven, they had stated, had his reasons, but upon these they refused to speculate.

'Swear,' she had demanded, 'to protect this sacred place from any threat, no matter from where it arises.'

'With our lives,' the Krieg lieutenant had answered without hesitation, 'for as long as the Emperor requires it.'

Serafina had been far from reassured. She had voxed Petrakov repeatedly, but he had no more information. Colonel Graven's intentions were unknown, as were his whereabouts. In the meantime, the Krieg had kept on coming.

Petrakov had spoken with his Attilan counterpart, who had redirected ten Rough Rider squads to the mausoleum area. Under pressure, he had further agreed to pull two dozen of his own Vostroyan squads out of the ossuary. *'Possessed or not,'* he had asserted, *'Graven would be mad to make a move against us with his forces so outnumbered and, if I may say so, outclassed.'*

The Sisters of Battle were also more than ready to defend their faith.

Serafina slept on a basic cot in her monastic cell. She woke a short time after midnight, not knowing why – until she felt vibrations in her bed's metal frame. Placing a bare foot on the cold stone floor, she felt a tremble running through it too. Though still faint, it was inexorably building. It rattled her black power armour on its nearby stand.

The guns of the Krieg, she thought. But no, her sentries would have seen their Earthshakers brought up in the night and would have roused her. Besides which, a feeling accompanied this tremor: a sense of something evil thickening the air. She could almost taste it, feeling it might even choke her, and as the quake built, the evil taint grew stronger.

Serafina screamed for servitors to assist her in donning her armour. From somewhere close outside, too close, she heard the first crack of las fire.

The witches and their weak-minded thralls had begun their attack.

XV

The horses sensed the tremor first.

Sergeant Batu heard their consternation and, an instant later, knew its cause. She leapt to her feet, beside her campfire, raising the alarm. Around her, ten Attilans stirred. Half, her own squad, knew what the quake portended, having felt its like three nights before. They were pulling on helmets and gloves, racing for their mounts. They were tired, but that didn't slow them.

They had ridden through the evening, into the night, to be here, close to the mausoleum. Sanctuary's refugees had been left to defend themselves, until another squad could reach them two days hence. The order had come directly from Colonel Tegana. Uncharacteristically, he had been circumspect about his reasons. Clearly, trouble was anticipated. Ominously, he had reminded Batu that not even allies could be trusted.

She had known that some Krieg were stationed here. Still, the number of Korpsmen had surprised her. She had wondered if Colonel Graven's squad was among them, but evidently not.

Their ranking officer was a masked lieutenant who had not offered her a name. He had made his command post in a disused tomb – according to a grave worker, bust open a century ago, its lordly occupant violently disinterred once a scandal in his past had come to light.

Batu had asked, boldly, why so many Krieg were present. Like her, the lieutenant had said, they had their orders – only theirs had been issued two days earlier. The Attilan's eyes had narrowed in suspicion. Unable to see the lieutenant's eyes, still she had felt his mistrust in return.

Saint Josefina's Grand Mausoleum towered over the jumbled tombs around it. From its forecourt, surrounded by a railed wall, broad steps swept up to a tall portico, topped by a marble pediment inlaid with gilded fleurs-de-lys. Above this sat a more compact third storey, from which three spires reached for the clouds, the centremost and tallest crowned by the 'I' of the Adeptus Ministorum.

Batu had had no time to appreciate its grandeur. Venturing close, she had been met by hostile glares from two Battle Sisters at the wrought iron gates atop the steps. Withdrawing, she had set up a campsite within the necropolis, from which she had to crane her neck to see the spires' tips. The Attilans slept out in the open, against the leeward sides of a pair of marble tombs, which kept them mostly dry. She had placed herself on first watch, wanting time to think.

All signs had pointed to a most disagreeable conclusion. She was here to watch the Krieg. Perhaps to fight them, if given a reason?

'Never trusted them,' one of her Guardsmen, sharing the watch with her, had grumbled. 'Hiding their faces like they do, barely talking, and have you seen the bones they carry with them? Morbid.'

'Ah, they ain't so bad,' Batu had said. 'Not so different from us, once you get to know them.' She prayed that she was right. The Krieg lieutenant could have lied to her face – how would she have known? – but surely not her 'Watchmaster No-Name'. Not him too. She would have felt more confident had he been here. Her stomach might not have turned so at the thought that her ten Rough Riders were so badly outnumbered and surrounded.

If the Krieg plan treachery and know they are suspected, they will strike tonight. Deal with the enemy in their midst before more of us arrive. Is that why we were sent here? To test them? To reveal their intentions by our deaths?

She had told herself that she was being paranoid. Something about this place. The night had crawled past its midway point and nothing bad had happened. The watch had changed, but Batu had remained awake. The Krieg, most of them, had been sleeping. She had begun to relax.

Now, she swung herself into her saddle. Warning cries came from all directions, echoing between the stone walls of the tombs. It didn't sound at all as if the Krieg had expected this. She heard a lasgun crack. She hadn't seen a zombie yet, but her every nerve told her they were close. It occurred to her that many would find themselves sealed inside their own memorials.

She spurred her horse along the shortest route to the necropolis' edge. Behind the barred gate of a squat white tomb, she saw a cadaver in lords' robes straining to reach her with its nails. Contained, it could be dealt with later.

Zombies were rising in the surrounding fields, spying living flesh and drawn towards it as in Sanctuary. Death Korpsmen massed along the edges of the tombs, fixing their bayonets. Ten Attilan Rough Riders thundered past them. Batu charged a knot of zombies, scattering them, her lance's frag tip bursting as it struck one's head. Attilans considered it an honour to be painted by enemy blood, but these things didn't bleed like living creatures.

The earth tremor wasn't subsiding. Already it had lasted twice as long as the previous one. It seemed more widespread too. Batu saw disjointed figures hauling themselves to their feet as far as the moonlit horizon.

She came around for another attack run. Hers had not been the only mount to plough through zombies like a battering ram – still adjusting to their newly gained ambulatory state, they were reeling and some broken. 'Keep it up,' she bellowed, 'keep them disorientated!' They had to press their advantage of numbers while they had it, but she feared it would not last very long.

The Krieg, however, mostly held their fire.

They know lasguns don't hurt these things, thought Batu. *They're conserving ammunition, waiting for a chance to get in close and use their blades.* By drawing the zombies away from the Krieg, the Attilans had robbed them of that chance. *That's all it is. Unless…*

She never completed the thought. Her horse was swarmed, zombies clawing and biting at its barding's seams. A hoof lashed out, staving in a brittle skull, but that did not dissuade the rest.

Then, out of the corner of one eye, she saw that two Korpsmen by the tombs had assembled a large, heavy weapon, which looked like – yes, it was – a flamer. One braced the other as he hefted it and aimed, and first one group of zombies, then another close beside it, were engulfed by cleansing fire.

The flames licked the backs of several of Batu's attackers, and though they hardly seemed to care, two crumpled as their clothes caught fire and their bones weakened. That gave her an opening, through which she spurred her horse. A single zombie clung to its flank, but was dislodged by a lance swipe.

Batu yelled directions to her riders. She had them clear a quadrant of the battlefield, to give the Krieg flamer a clear shot.

A pair of flame-wreathed skeletons lumbered after her. Her horse wheeled around and shattered both with a double hoof strike. 'Nice work, Hunor,' Batu whispered in its ear, using the secret name known only to her.

The flamer roared again, and more zombies were unceremoniously cremated. No longer did she doubt the Death Korps' loyalties. She wondered why she ever had, why her colonel – *More likely,* thought Batu, *that Vostroyan colonel speaking through him* – ever had.

'Aim for their heads! Cut their throats!' the Krieg lieutenant yelled.

He matched his actions to his words, stepping forwards and slashing at the leading zombie. His sword bayonet cut deep but didn't slow the creature, which was suddenly upon him. It clawed at his greatcoat, at his mask.

Stepping up behind it, a Korpsman landed a resounding shovel blow, snapping the zombie's weakened neck. It lost neither strength nor focus. It tried to wrestle the lieutenant to the ground, but, emaciated, it lacked his flak-armoured weight. He slammed the zombie onto its back, stamped on its chest. He thrust his blade into its throat again, working it from side to side until its last tendon was severed.

It continued to glare up at him, taunting him. Its tenacity had delayed him longer than he could afford. Others had closed in, and before he could turn, one leapt on the lieutenant's back. It clamped his ribs between its knees, attempting to pry off his gorget.

He threw himself back into a tomb wall, feeling the zombies' bones breaking, but still it clung on. The Korpsmen around him were fending off similar threats. *Where are my flamer teams?* He only had two, and with foes to all sides of them, doubtless they were busy elsewhere along the perimeter.

None of which helped him. The lieutenant had sight of four squads, his own included, along the necropolis' eastern edge, and they were being overwhelmed. The influx of zombies had been manageable at first – frag grenades had proven somewhat effective against them – but more were rising from their muddy graves each second. Where at first they had numbered in the dozens, now there were hundreds of them – and the grenades were running out.

'Pull... pull back,' he spluttered, 'back between the tombs.' *If only I am able to myself!* He battered his attacker against the hard stone wall. He must have reduced it to a pulp, yet still he couldn't shake it. Cracked fingernails dug into the nape of the lieutenant's neck, into his flesh.

Blindly, he fired his bolt pistol over his shoulder and, Emperor be praised, struck true. The zombie disintegrated into carrion fragments, but two more were already coming at him. Dropping his shoulder, he charged through them, bowling them out of his way.

He joined with three comrades, backing into an alleyway between tombs. The lieutenant and a single Korpsman filled its width between them, so that only two zombies could reach them. More were squeezing up behind them. This evened the odds, as he had planned, allowing him to concentrate on one foe at a time.

As one zombie slumped, neck severed by his bayonet, another trampled over its remains to continue the assault. Step by hard-fought step, the Krieg gave ground, but with a lengthening trail of bones and viscera before them. The Korpsmen in the rear could do little but prepare to take a comrade's position should one fall – until they reached the corner of a tomb, another narrow passage running alongside it, into which they stepped.

Now, as the zombies strained forward, they were cornered, two enemies striking at them from ahead, two from their left.

'Stand your ground here,' the lieutenant ordered, and the Krieg did. They hacked and battered at one zombie after another for uncounted minutes, each absorbing incalculable punishment before it fell at last, each relentlessly replaced by one more like it.

The lieutenant's muscles ached and his scratched neck felt hot and stiff. He wondered how his other squads were faring. He only knew that none had come to his assistance. *What if some have been overrun, allowing these horrors a route to the Grand Mausoleum?*

How many more? he asked himself. *How many buried in those fields?* The tremor, he realised, had ceased, its damage done. He was horribly aware of noises from the tombs around him. Bare fists hammering on solid gates, which for now were holding. Until, suddenly, that changed.

A crash came from behind him, from the shadows, as a heavy gate was flung from its hinges. A zombie staggered out of a red-brick tomb, another close behind it, and one more. From what remained of their clothes, apparently a lord and lady and an attendant buried alongside them.

He reached for a frag grenade, remembered that he had used his last. 'Can't let them surround us,' he grunted to the Korpsman at his side. 'On my mark, make for the–' A zombie lunged at him, and his gloved fist broke its jaw. 'Make for the passageway behind us, to our left. Go! Go!'

With a final burst of bolt rounds – meant to give his zombie pause, which it did not – the lieutenant turned and ran. He felt hands clutching his greatcoat's scruff, pulling him back, but he tore free of them. He outpaced the zombies behind him, closing on those ahead, turning before he reached them. The closest Korpsman, he was pleased to see, remained beside him. The other two, he didn't know about. Hopefully, they still held their side passageway, though harder-pressed now.

The passageway ahead of him, past six more tombs, was empty. He made a decision: 'Keep going. Best thing now is to find another squad and–'

A patch of earth in front of him erupted. A gloved fist burst through the soil, its fingers clutching at the air.

'Keep going!' the lieutenant yelled again, and he and his Korpsmen cleared the flailing limb with a prodigious running jump. *They're tunnelling out of the tombs!* he thought.

Haring around another corner, he came upon a melee in progress, involving six Death Korpsmen and twice as many zombies. In unison, four of the latter turned, sensing fresh prey behind them, easier reached than those in the crush ahead. The best he could do for his comrades, the lieutenant judged, was allow these four as close as he dared, before drawing them away.

At the critical moment, to his horror, bony fingers clapped around his ankle.

A second hand dug into his calf. A zombie was pulling itself out of the earth at his feet, using him as a support pole. Its head surfaced, near-fleshless, pearly teeth set in a rictus grin. He and his Korpsman battered it with weapon butts, but the zombie kept gripping, kept rising. It took hold of his greatcoat's hem. The zombies before and behind them were closing in.

'Leave me,' the lieutenant barked, and when his Korpsman hesitated, yelled, 'That's an order!' *No point in risking a second life!*

The Korpsman ran. To the lieutenant's surprise, the zombies behind them, all of them, turned to follow him. The four ahead kept coming, but he had a second's reprieve. He didn't stop to question it. Three more blows splintered an eye socket, and the zombie clinging to him collapsed. Too late.

The four were upon him. He didn't have time to turn his bolt pistol upon them. *At least,* he thought, *I had the chance to add one more to my balance.* Perhaps he could slit another throat or break another skull against a wall before he was dragged down. He braced himself.

The zombies lumbered past him. Dumbstruck, the lieutenant gaped after them. It was as if he had been invisible to them. As if… *God-Emperor, no!*

In that moment's stillness, he realised that his muscles weren't just tired but cramping, and the burning sensation in his neck was spreading up and down his spinal column, into his brain, making his vision blur.

Infected! A mere scratch had sealed his fate. *The zombies are ignoring me because they sense that they have done their work. I am already dead!*

No, worse than dead.

How long did he have left? From the speed with which symptoms had taken hold, he suspected only minutes. His rebreather unit was already lacing his air with antibiotic agents, in vain. *How may I best serve in my time remaining?* He realised that his random travels through the necropolis had brought him almost back to where he had started.

His command post. With its vox-caster unit. Upon realising the scale of the zombie threat, the lieutenant had sent two Korpsmen back to warn command headquarters. To call for reinforcements. He could not know if they had made it, if the message had been sent, but now he could ensure it.

He proceeded at a measured pace towards his destination. His heartbeat, elevated by exertion, wouldn't settle. Given a chance to listen, he heard fighting from every direction and glimpsed some between the tombs. He saw the remnants of it everywhere he stepped. He encountered crippled zombies, left behind, which turned their heads to glare at him but made no attempt to approach him on their broken legs. He saw few fallen Krieg. *Does that mean few have fallen or…?*

He saw the command post, the sundered tomb. It seemed the fighting had not reached here yet. A lumen-globe blazed inside. The lieutenant stepped through a broken gate, out of the night into the cold white light. His desk was as he had left it, with dataslates awaiting his attention. He would never read them now.

He didn't fear death. None of his people did. Death was a fact of life, its most fundamental fact, and he had served longer than many, served his purpose. One of those dataslates, however, one he had had time to peruse, had told of another battle, fought by Graven underground. Another battle with the walking dead, including four clad in Krieg colours.

Stiffly, the lieutenant stooped over the old vox-set. Command headquarters not being far away, he quickly raised an operator. In a studied monotone, he laid out his situation.

'A Korpsman already reported in, lieutenant,' he was told. *'A general order has been sent to all units in range to make haste to your position.'*

So, that was that.

He slumped into the seat behind his desk. His heart still pounded as he sweated into his mask. His muscles were starting to lock and his head felt fuzzy. He drew his pistol, checked it was still loaded. He prayed a single bolt would be damaging enough. He believed it would be.

Across the stone chamber, a receiver flared again. He recognised Colonel Graven's voice. *'Kill Team Alpha approaching mausoleum, two more squads behind us. Estimated arrival, twelve to fourteen minutes.'*

The Krieg lieutenant felt contented as he raised his pistol to his temple.

Graven had hoped for more time. Time to get his forces into position before he had to join them. He had known he would likely not get it.

Once the witches saw the Krieg gathering, realised that he had found them, a pre-emptive strike had felt certain. He had kept Korpsmen close by his Chimera overnight to monitor vox-chatter. He had been woken by the unsurprising news that the Grand Mausoleum had been attacked. *Untrue,* he had thought. *It is not being attacked, but defended. Defended against us.*

The mausoleum's spires were lit by night, a beacon for his driver. Attendant tombs lay huddled in its shadows. Approaching from the east, he expected to see Death Korpsmen holding the perimeter. Their absence augured badly. Even so, the last stretch of the way was strewn with broken zombies. Some perked up at the approaching sound of engines, scrabbling to reach them. Graven kept his driver on a direct course, crushing bones beneath caterpillar tracks.

Two more Chimeras followed, one Krieg, one Vostroyan. The latter's commander had voxed Graven as their paths converged, and had doubtless immediately reported in to Petrakov.

The Vostroyans peeled off to the north, where fighting was still fierce and Graven made out the shapes of wheeling horses. His own Chimera, maintaining its heading, probed into a gap between two tombs, scraping their walls. A hundred yards along, a T-junction loomed. He saw for himself, before his driver yelled up to him, that they lacked space to make the turn.

They ground to a halt, Graven ordering his squad to disembark. The other Krieg Chimera braked behind them. Poking his head up through its turret hatch, a lieutenant called, 'Colonel, should we back up and seek a way around?'

'No. From here on, we proceed on foot.'

'Yes, sir.'

The junior officer didn't question his orders, simply relayed them to his own squad inside the vehicle. Nineteen Death Korpsmen poured from the two Chimeras. Graven led them through the dense necropolis, the watchmaster by his side. Of course, the lieutenant's suggestion had made tactical sense. Useless in these confines, the Chimeras with their armoured hulls and heavy bolters could have been effective in the fields. *Effective in the short term.*

The only way to stem the tide of zombies was to cut off the source of their blight. Graven considered explaining this – perhaps preparing the lieutenant for the shock to come – but there was no time and he would have seemed uncertain, raising greater doubts than he assuaged.

The staggered passageways between the tombs took them on a meandering path towards the mausoleum's lights. Where Graven heard fighting ahead of him, he turned to avoid it, much as it pained him to do so. He thought about the Korpsmen who might die when he could have saved them. He thought about the many more lives, not only Krieg, that might be lost if he delayed.

Then, suddenly, he had no choice. Barely had he registered another tomb gate as he passed it when, with a high-pitched screech, something sprang out through its bars. Another cadaver, but the smallest he had seen – that of an animal. It landed on the shoulder of a Korpsman behind him, clawing, spitting. *A feline pet,* thought Graven, *interred with its master for irrational sentimental reasons.*

The Korpsman, with help from her nearest comrade, tore the creature off herself. She made to batter it against a wall, but it wriggled out of her grip. Dropping to the ground between their feet, it scratched and nipped at Korpsmen's shins. They stabbed at it with bayonets, but it was fast and nimble, darting between their stamping boots, and they were getting in each other's way.

An observer might have seen the black humour of the situation, that such an inconsequential pest could so impede two elite Astra Militarum squads, let alone two made up of Death Korpsmen.

Graven felt only frustration, boiling over into anger, at the feeling that some dark god was mocking him.

He stepped back from the melee, dropping to his haunches. He snatched the glove off his left hand. The cat zombie was a blur of matted fur and jutting ribs, glimpsed through his comrades' legs. He showed it his palm, baiting it with exposed flesh. Stiffening, it spun its head to fix Graven with a cloudy-eyed glare, and then came at him like a rocket.

The colonel held his stance, levelling his pistol. He would only get one shot. He waited until the creature was inches from his face. Then he put a las beam through its eye. He was gambling that one would suffice to destroy its smaller brain. Momentum kept it coming. At least, he hoped that was the only reason. He snatched his bare hand away and the creature smacked into his chest. It burst open like a ripe fruit, entrails spilling out onto the ground.

Graven stood and was about to give the order to proceed when several Korpsmen in unison warned him, 'Behind you, sir!'

Whirling around, he saw that three zombies had appeared at the far end of the passageway. They had seen him and were lumbering towards him. He took a second to replace his glove as he weighed up his options. *Easy enough,* he thought, *to find a way around them, but what if we run into others?* And he was so close to his goal, only these three standing in his way.

'Fix bayonets,' said Graven, 'and charge!'

The sight of nineteen Death Korpsmen thundering towards them would have shattered the morale of most living things. The zombies did not baulk, but nor could they withstand such a powerful advance. Graven felt their brittle bodies breaking as he and his watchmaster hit them like Earthshaker shells. Scattered like skittles, the zombies swiped at their prey but couldn't slow them down. One was skewered by the watchmaster's blade and driven back before him, until it too lost its footing and slid into the mud, and Graven found himself clear of them.

Behind him, his Korpsmen lashed out at the flailing zombies as they trampled over them, ensuring that if not destroyed they would be crippled. Before him, the lights of the Grand Mausoleum beckoned.

The sounds of violent clashes rose from among the tombs.

No combatant had yet been seen, but the sounds were demonstrative enough. Serafina itched to join the fighting, but she knew her duty. Her ten-strong honour guard ringed its sacred charge. The Sister Superior herself blocked the mausoleum's entranceway. Behind her, across the small forecourt, up the steps, the great gates had been bolted from within.

She rested her hand on her Godwyn-De'az-pattern boltgun, entrusted to her at the conclusion of her training, blessed by the Canoness of her new Order. The single chainsword available she had allocated to her most stalwart Sister, an obdurate presence at her elbow. Elvana's muscular frame – enhanced, as were they all, by power armour – made her best suited for the heavy weapon. The wirier Serafina preferred to rely on her bolter, and to employ her martial arts skills unencumbered.

Of course, these Battle Sisters had no weapon stronger than their faith.

When first Serafina had met the Krieg Colonel Graven, she had thought this an attribute they shared. Having heard his people called fanatics, she had wished that more deserved such praise. Like Petrakov. How disappointing, then – if not entirely a surprise – to learn that Graven was a weak man after all.

She sensed him out there somewhere, in the night. She sensed that he was close. At first, the motive for the zombie attack had puzzled her. If the witches, through their spectres, controlled

Graven, who controlled the Krieg, then why was there fighting at all? The witches must know that, no matter what their orders, no soldier of the Emperor could suffer such aberrations as they had unleashed here to exist.

The lieutenant yesterday spoke true, she had concluded. *The Krieg don't have their orders yet – meaning that this is but a distraction!*

Time and patience proved her right.

Serafina heard the scattered battles edging closer, then, detaching from the tumult, a purposeful tramp of boots. Shadows parted to disgorge two columns of black-clad, masked Death Korpsmen. She recognised their commander's crested helmet as he marched before them. Since last she had seen him, Colonel Graven had also acquired a set of tears across his facemask.

Around her, Serafina felt her Sisters tensing, drawing weapons. Graven's own power sword and pistol remained holstered – an obvious deception – as he halted ten feet before her with a dozen or more Korpsmen at his back.

The Sister Superior addressed her own smaller but assuredly greater force. 'So, now,' her voice rang out, 'the time has come. The Emperor reveals to us our purpose on Oleris III. *A spiritu dominatus, Domine, libra nos.* Prepare for battle, sisters. Our enemy shows us his face, at last.'

XVI

'In the name of the Emperor–' Graven began.

'Dare not invoke His name!' Sister Superior Serafina spat.

'–and by my authority as an officer in His Astra Militarum–'

'You have no right!'

'–I require that you let us pass.' He had no expectation that she would accede to the demand, having already signalled her intent to fight, but he had to say the words, had to try. More for his Korpsmen than himself.

Ten Battle Sisters stood in the harsh white glare of the mausoleum's light. Those who had watched the building's rear were edging up along its sides. Never had Graven faced a more intimidating sight, the worst of it being the fleurs-de-lys on the Sisters' crimson robes, symbolising his own faith.

Doubt makes me weak and I reject it!

'Check your orders,' said Serafina icily, 'with Colonel Petrakov. He carries the Emperor's authority on this world.'

'I no longer recognise Petrakov's orders as lawful. I find his judgement suspect.'

'On what basis? Merely that he disagrees with you? You are the one whose judgement is impaired. Perhaps you have become possessed.'

In response, Graven voiced the Emperor's Prayer. Serafina looked perplexed at first, then angry. As he reached the part about the begetting of daemons, she screamed at him, 'Be silent!' Ignoring her, he continued to the end.

'It proves nothing,' grumbled the scowling, brawny Sister who stood, brandishing a chainsword, by the Sister Superior's side.

'I have evidence and reason,' said Graven, 'to believe that witches hide within this structure.'

'Impossible!' Serafina spat. 'I reject your "evidence and reason". What is either, compared to our faith?'

'Sister Superior, I would not take these steps if my faith weren't equally strong. I believe the threat, if not soon obviated, may reach beyond Oleris.'

'Precisely why the Emperor requires you, Colonel Graven, to hunt these witches down through the ossuary tunnels and break them on the anvil of His vengeance. Repledge yourself to this duty, turn around, and your transgression here tonight may be forgotten.'

'Then we have a difference of opinion, simply settled by a search of the mausoleum.' Graven drew in a breath before adding, 'And the crypt beneath it.'

From the Battle Sisters' scandalised reactions, he may as well have cursed the Emperor Himself. The chainsword-wielder started up her weapon and, pumping its throttle, made it roar. The Sister Superior's raised hand stayed her. She warned Graven, 'One step forward and you prove yourself a traitor.'

Implacably, he stated, 'No Krieg will raise arms against the Adepta Sororitas – but in self-defence.'

The time for words was all but done. He wished he knew how the Korpsmen at his back were reacting to all they had heard. Unlike the Sisters, they kept their feelings cloaked. *They will follow me,* he told himself. *I have faith in them.*

He continued, 'I intend to make that search.'

'One. Step. Forward,' Serafina hissed, drawing her boltgun.

'On my mark,' he commanded, 'we break down the mausoleum gates. Allow no one to obstruct you. That said, harm the Sisters of Battle only as much as you must. They remain faithful servants of the Emperor, who have merely lost sight of His way.'

Serafina's nostrils flared. She raised her gun.

'Sister Superior,' said Graven, 'out of respect for you and your exalted position, I must ask you a final time to step aside.'

'My position has been stated clearly,' she said, 'as has yours. Your orders have been given. Why hesitate to put them into practice? Unless, deep in your heart, you doubt yourself?'

Her question could hardly have been more ironically timed. From around the back of the mausoleum came the distinctive *whoomph* of a krak grenade implosion and a shattering of stone. The Sisters meant to be on guard there, who had turned their backs, whirled, horror-struck, and raced towards the sound.

Graven responded as quickly, if not more so, to a cue he had expected. Engaging an instant before his throat, his feet propelled him forwards, his fingers flying to his sword hilt.

'Charge!' he yelled.

The krak grenade had blasted through the mausoleum wall.

Before the dust had settled, the building's vengeful-looking guardians appeared, two from one side, one from the other. They would certainly have captured any would-be intruder attempting to squeeze through the hole – which was why none had tried.

Krieg Korpsman 319-938-25549-04 – the former engineer – had

attached the explosive and primed it, before racing its fuse back to cover.

'Defilers! Cowards! Show yourselves!' a Battle Sister screamed.

The engineer peered around a corner of an ostentatious tomb. By chance he caught a Sister's eye, and with lightning reflexes she unloaded her weapon in his direction. Her bolts blew a chunk out of the tomb's elaborate stonework as the engineer hurriedly withdrew.

So, it's true, he thought. *The Sisters of Battle stand against us.* He hadn't quite been able to believe it until now, but hearing the bark of his watchmaster's bolt pistol and the answering fire of larger boltguns made it certain.

The engineer shouldered his own weapon, palms sweating into his gloves. He edged back up to the corner. The three Sisters had converged to barricade the mausoleum's breach with their own bodies. Their black power armour would easily shrug off shotgun shells. Their raised bolters likewise protected their faces. Just as well he had no wish to hurt them.

Colonel Graven had sent three members of his squad to circle the Grand Mausoleum, threading their way between the tombs to approach it from the rear. He had briefed them out of earshot of the rest – and with good reason, as the engineer had realised.

Never had he questioned orders, even privately, but these orders had unsettled him. He was thankful for his watchmaster's reassurance. *'Do either of you have a problem with our mission?'* he had asked, as the trio had parted from their colonel. *'Speak now if you do.'* The engineer had answered that as long as the watchmaster didn't, then why would he?

Now, however, with a Sister in his sights, his trigger finger froze.

He gritted his teeth, reminding himself that doubt only served the spectres. It was almost inconceivable that these holy warriors worked against the Emperor, but his colonel? Even more so. Still, the engineer adjusted his aim a fraction. When he fired, it wasn't at black armour, rather at the wall behind it.

His slugs were joined by las beams from two more directions. The Sisters weathered the assault, unflinching, and their bolters barked again, forcing him back into cover. He heard a short, muttered conversation, and when he looked again, one Sister had planted her feet in the mud, the others striding out towards the tombs – one of them heading straight towards him.

The engineer ran, but not far. He waited at the back corner of another tomb. The Sister rounded his old corner without pretence of caution. Her fearsome visage bearing down on him, this time he aimed for the chest, but his shotgun failed to fire. *Guns often jam,* he told himself. *It isn't – it can't be – a sign.*

He ran again, ahead of the inevitable bolts. He took three turns at random, at full pelt. His pursuer could easily outrun him, unless he used these narrow thoroughfares to his advantage. Earning a moment's respite, he rattled his shotgun's magazine and worked its action. In desperation, he slammed its butt into the ground, risking its detonation in his face.

The live round popped out of his barrel, to the engineer's relief – even as the Sister reappeared behind him.

'You will beg for the Emperor's forgiveness before He lets you die!' she roared.

Don't let her feed your doubts!

He plunged into a dark passageway, not very long. He wished he'd had time to check it first, because he found its far end blocked. A zombie in front of him, a vengeful Battle Sister to the rear. His eyes lit upon a rotten wooden door, which he shouldered off its hinges. It led into a maintenance shed, about six feet across. The engineer stumbled over buckets and shovels. He had taken the only chance he had, but now was well and truly cornered.

He could only pray that – *Yes!* – the zombie and the Sister had clapped eyes on each other. The latter was shooting at the former, screaming at it, 'Fall, you abomination, the Emperor commands it!'

The engineer hid behind the door as the zombie shambled past the shed, jerking as each bolt round ripped through its body. He waited two more seconds before leaping out behind it and resuming his headlong run. At the passageway's end, he stopped and turned in case the Sister required his assistance.

She didn't, of course. The zombie, having almost closed with her, collapsed spitting at her feet. Recoiling in disgust, still she maintained the presence of mind to loose off a shot past it. A bolt grazed the engineer's left shoulder, tearing armour, and he ran again.

Long campaigns underground having honed his directional sense, he knew he was heading back towards the mausoleum. As planned. That would give the Battle Sister little option but to keep after him. He didn't know how long he could elude her grasp, but for as long as he did – one Korpsman tying up one Battle Sister, and hopefully his two comrades doing likewise – he could make a difference.

The watchmaster's team had served its purpose, luring three guards away from the mausoleum gates. The odds were now sixteen to seven in the Krieg's favour. Two Korpsmen to each Sister – two to spare.

Graven had made straight for the Sister Superior. He had never reached her, nor had he expected to. The krak grenade's detonation had provided a distraction, but it was one from which the Sisters had swiftly recovered. As the leader, most deadly and foremost of their foes, he had naturally drawn their fire.

He had thrown himself onto his stomach in the mud, bolts

whistling over his head. Fifteen pairs of boots had thundered past his ears. For a second, despite himself, he had thought they might not.

He sprang back to his feet, advanced again. His Korpsmen had closed with the Sisters, silencing their guns. In fact, the Sisters had turned their guns around to use as cudgels, with which they were brutally effective. The Krieg, as instructed, fought defensively but were outclassed by their power-armoured foes. Two lay unmoving in the mud, shot down on their approach. The rest were being beaten like sandbags in training, their opponents' frustration growing as they weathered rains of blows with stubborn pride. Still, the battle wouldn't last long at this rate. It was up to Graven to see that it too served its purpose.

He set his sights on the gates.

A cloaked figure reared up in his path. One with a chainsword. Serafina's constant companion had kept herself clear of the melee – waiting for him. Mechanical teeth gnashed at and barely missed his stomach.

Graven swiped back with his sword, trailing blue light in its wake. The Sister had been overconfident and he sliced into her breastplate. She swung for his neck, the blow deflected by his shoulder plate. *My weapon is superior – and lighter, offsetting her greater strength – but Emperor, she's fast!*

Her next attack, he parried. He felt its force jolting through his bones, but struck sparks off her blade, which shrieked indignantly. A second such clash made it sputter, spitting oil. Ducking under it, Graven tackled his opponent round the midriff. She gave two steps but braced herself.

She drove her pommel, two-handed, down into his helmet, making his head ring, loosening his grip on her. He reeled back, trying not to fall, as she thrust for his heart, her chainsword chewing at carapace armour but choking. Smoke spewed from its motor. In the second it took to cast aside the useless weapon and draw a bolter, Graven's sword cut through his foe's gauntlet, into flesh. The pain made even this stalwart Sister gasp, her gun dropping from numbed fingers.

He feinted, and, dodging his anticipated blow, she provided him an opening. He took it, but was thwarted by her speed again. The Sister leapt on his back, hooking his throat with a brawny arm and choking him. He couldn't shake her off. His eyes teared, and through a misty veil the Grand Mausoleum filled his vision, its gilded holy symbols scornful of him.

Suddenly, Emperor be praised, a wiry black figure mounted the steps beneath those very symbols. Graven heard an anguished cry – Serafina? – as a Korpsman clamped a magnetic krak grenade to wrought iron. He was cut down by a fusillade of bolt rounds, but he had done enough.

Dealing with him had split the Battle Sisters' focus, and the previously under-pressure Krieg were able to regroup and gain ground. Meanwhile, a pair of Sisters detached themselves from the melee altogether. Racing across the forecourt, up the steps, they trampled the triumphant Korpsman's bloodied corpse.

The first to reach the gates tried to pry the grenade from them, but it blew as her fingers brushed it. Its shaped charge hurled her into her sister behind her, but shattered the great gates' bolts and hinges.

One of us still must make it through them!

Graven stabbed blindly over his shoulder with his sword, praying that he could discourage the Sister on his back without killing her. *Better one life lost than many. Any Korpsman would make that calculation.* But this life would weigh especially heavy on his conscience. *One more for my nightmares.* He heard his attacker's grunt of pain, smelled burning flesh, felt her grip on him loosening. Managing to shrug her off, at last, he didn't pause to look back.

A running jump carried him over the low, railed wall into the mausoleum's forecourt, which already heaved with combatants. Under Serafina's barked orders, Battle Sisters were trying to regroup on the steps, obstructed by their remorseless opponents. Spying a Sister duelling with a losing Korpsman, Graven struck her from behind, slicing through robes and armour, withdrawing as she rounded on him, allowing his comrade to recover his footing and his breath.

He focused on the gates again, the sundered gates, but could see no way to them. 'Squad Delta Four,' he commanded, 'remember, the rear wall is also breached, and only three Battle Sisters guard it.'

That caused an immediate disruption to the melee's ebbs and flows. Several Sisters backed up to the building's corners. 'No traitor must pass you!' Serafina bellowed, fending off three opponents simultaneously.

They had fallen for the feint. The Krieg surged into the spaces thus abandoned, continuing their press forwards. Now there were Korpsmen on the steps themselves, with only the Sister Superior and one other in their way.

There was no Squad Delta Four.

Graven hung back, awaiting his moment, which came soon enough. Serafina stumbled under the weight of increasing opponents – one the lieutenant commanding the other Krieg squad. A Sister came at Graven from his left, but a swipe of his energy-wreathed blade fended her off.

And he was running. Taking the broad stone steps three at a time. Sparing not a glance for the fighting, the carnage around him. Dimly aware of warning shrieks and a single hand clutching at his greatcoat, quickly wrenched from him. He only had eyes for his goal, the broken gates and the aperture between them.

His last, his only chance to save a world.

* * *

'Faster!' yelled Petrakov, fully aware that his driver was giving him all the speed he could.

His Salamander bounced over rough tracks towards the mausoleum's shining spires. He had been woken by news of the zombie outbreak there. He had thought he had more time. *My Firstborn are controlling the situation,* he insisted to himself. *For now, at least, the Krieg are fighting with them.* Still, he couldn't calm the grumbling dread in the pit of his stomach.

The Salamander's vox-set flared to life, its incoming message relayed to the micro-bead cradling his cheek beneath his fur hat's earflaps. A nervous-sounding aide to the Adepta Sororitas announced the very news that the colonel had prayed not to hear. The news he had expected since Graven had been sighted en route to the mausoleum too.

Operating the micro-bead with his tongue, he addressed every Vostroyan soldier within range. 'The Krieg have been corrupted and lay siege to the sacred shrine. Its defence is your highest priority. Any Korpsman standing in your way is now your foe. Their commander, Colonel Graven, is a traitor to be shot on sight.'

Sergeant Batu heard the news from a Vostroyan captain – one already training his laspistol upon a Krieg watchmaster.

The watchmaster's squad had also snapped up their weapons, aimed at the captain. His Guardsmen's finely crafted lasguns were trained on them in turn. The standoff was one nervous twitch away from escalating into slaughter.

'I repeat,' intoned the officer as Batu and her mounted squad arrived on the scene, 'by order of Colonel Petrakov, commander-in-chief of this world's Imperial forces, lay down your arms.'

'Sir, what is going on here?'

'Mutiny, sergeant! This soldier refuses to obey a lawfully given order.'

'Captain, I have cause to suspect you may be under the influence of spectres,' said the Krieg watchmaster. 'Therefore, your orders are invalid.'

'Sergeant,' the Vostroyan captain snapped, 'you know your duty.'

'This Vostroyan pulled his weapon on an ally.'

'Sergeant, execute this traitor!'

Uncertainly, Batu drew her lasgun from its sling beside her saddle.

The watchmaster challenged the captain: 'Pray with me. Adore the immortal Emperor...' His Korpsmen joined in the recitation. The captain's nostrils flared, but first he and then the rest of his squad joined in too.

Just minutes ago, they had been fighting together. The Attilans had ridden down dozens of zombies in the fields, while the Krieg with their flamer had held the necropolis' northern perimeter against them. Just as the flamer had run dry, the arrival of a Vostroyan Chimera with its bolters and in-built lasgun arrays had been extremely welcome.

At some point, mercifully, the earth's trembling had ceased. The waves of zombies had stopped coming. The other Attilan squad was still out there, dealing with their remnants. Most of the Krieg, Batu only now realised, had melted away between the tombs, only this squad remaining. *No cause for suspicion if they calculated that they could be more use elsewhere.*

Ten Vostroyans had leapt from their transport – to help with the mop-up, she had assumed at first, but they had had something else in mind, surrounding their supposed allies.

The prayer was almost done, and no one had stumbled. Batu wasn't sure if she ought to be relieved. The captain's eyes told her he wouldn't back down. She had a decision to make. Which of these allies did she trust?

She had heard of Vostroyans possessed, but not of Krieg – which didn't mean it couldn't happen. *'Not so different from us, once you get to know them,'* she had said herself, mere hours ago, and hadn't her colonel sent her here to watch the Krieg, or so she had inferred? Not to mention the Vostroyan captain's rank and the fact that he had given her an order.

Batu's lasgun felt as heavy as her heart as she levelled it at the watchmaster. She prayed he might see sense, do as he had been instructed, that this would satisfy the captain so she needn't pull the trigger.

She looked into the blank eye-lenses of his gas mask.

'Sergeant!' one of her riders shouted.

So focused had Batu been on her dilemma that she had missed more zombies, slouching out of the shadows of the nearby tombs. They must have breached another section of the perimeter and, meandering through the necropolis, scented flesh and blood beyond it. Eight or nine of them.

The Krieg watchmaster was first to bark orders to his squad. Forgetting all else, they charged the zombies with bayonets fixed. Hesitating for only half a second, the Vostroyan captain despatched his Guardsmen to join them. He addressed Sergeant Batu before she could do likewise: 'We can handle this. Colonel Graven has launched an assault on the Grand Mausoleum. Take your riders, both squads, directly there and support the Sisters of Battle as they direct you.'

'Yessir,' said Batu, concealing her relief at escaping that situation.

Calling all nine riders to her, she led the way between the tombs. They left Krieg and Vostroyans fighting a common foe, as if nothing had occurred between them. Would that convince each faction of the other's loyalty? *Depends,* she thought, *if it's true about Graven.*

She found more running battles throughout the necropolis:

Krieg versus zombies, reassuring her that if any of the former had turned traitor, then they must be few in number. She kept clear of them, needing not to be slowed down. She would know more once she reached the mausoleum. She could hope, at least.

Detouring to avoid another melee, she approached the sacred shrine from the rear. Steering around a tight junction, she saw a Death Korpsman crouching ahead of her. He was firing around the corner of another tomb, at a target Batu couldn't see. Hearing hooves behind him, he leapt to his feet, whirling to train his bolt pistol on her. She snapped up her own gun, but then recognised this black-clad figure.

Another watchmaster – once she would have said indistinguishable from any other, but this one she knew. Pulling on her reins, Batu cantered to a halt. Her two squads stretched out in a column behind her. About to lower her lasgun, she felt a niggling doubt. *He is Graven's watchmaster.*

'What's the situation?' she asked. 'What are you doing here?'

The Krieg watchmaster shot her.

His bolt punched into Batu's right forearm, through her light flak jacket, wrenching a cry from her throat, and even her mount spluttered in indignation. Her fellow Rough Riders, hearing the shot, strained forward, but her horse still blocked the junction. By the time she could aim her lasgun again, the watchmaster had run for it. She fired at him, missing wildly, as he disappeared into another passageway.

At the corner around which he had fired now appeared an angry-looking figure. Still recovering her breath, as much from shock as from the physical pain of her injury, Batu gaped at her. 'Sister?'

'You saw him? The traitor?'

Batu nodded, swallowed. Though she didn't want to believe it, what choice did she have now? 'I saw him.'

'Which way did he go?'

Pain lanced through her arm as she gripped her reins again. Gritting her teeth, she spurred her mount forwards. These narrow confines benefitted a lone fugitive on foot, but speed and numbers would still win the day. This watchmaster, her former ally – even, she had thought, a friend – would pay for his betrayal.

'Follow me.'

Crossing the Grand Mausoleum's threshold was like stepping out of the world.

Suddenly the air felt stale but with a sharp, cold edge. Despite the broken gates, the sounds of combat from outside were immediately deadened. Barging through a short narthex, Graven burst into a vaulted chamber. His ringing footsteps echoed around galleries above him.

The light in here was gentler. Candlelight. Before him were the stepped sides of Saint Josefina's crypt and, atop this, looming over him, the statue of the saint herself, ringed by a golden halo.

Graven thought he could have found peace here, had he allowed himself. He focused on what was important. Back at command headquarters, he had sought out a Vostroyan officer who had been allowed in here to pray. He had questioned him subtly about the mausoleum's layout. Saint Josefina's gaze upon him might have given him pause for a second, had he not known to expect it.

Avoiding her marble eyes, he didn't break his step.

He reached the crypt and planted a krak grenade on it, between the carved effigies of two beseeching wretches. He activated its fuse, set to its shortest length. He stepped back and only then allowed himself a moment's contemplation. His mistake. He became aware of ringing footsteps charging up behind him. A screamed curse on his name. Graven couldn't turn in time. He felt a cold blade pushed through his back with enraged force. He tasted blood.

Then the krak grenade exploded, blowing him backwards off his feet.

He landed in a storm of stone dust, tangled up with his attacker. The Sister pushed him off her, yanking a punch dagger with a fleur-de-lys handle from his body. He recognised her as his erstwhile opponent with the chainsword. The livid, weeping burn in which her right eye had been swallowed was his own work. She must have remained on his heels ever since.

She scrambled away from Graven, leaving him for dead. Not without cause. He couldn't move. Lying on his side, he couldn't even lift his head. Oddly numb, he watched his life's blood pooling underneath him, soaking into his greatcoat, draining away into the seams between floor tiles.

On her knees, the Sister squinted through the settling cloud. What she saw dragged from her lungs a reverberating howl of grief.

Colonel Graven welcomed death. It felt right, even fitting. His eyelids were growing heavy, but before he let them close there was one thing he had to know. *One final shred of doubt.*

A hole gaped in the crypt's side. Most of the rubble had fallen inward, into the chamber beyond, which extended underground. Enough of the edifice remained to support Saint Josefina's statue, albeit with a pronounced list. One of the plague-ridden supplicants had crumbled into marble chunks.

For a breathless moment, Graven heard no sound but the settling of debris. Then, from below came desperate movement, panicked voices, and all he had risked, the lives expended for his cause, was justified. He had done what the Emperor had brought him here to do: exposed a threat to which others had been blind. He could rest now, his purpose served. Almost.

Beneath his cheek, the floor trembled to the beat of stomping metal footsteps. He heard rubble dashed aside and pulverised beneath the surface as something forced a route towards the exit hole and up through it.

A monster bashed its way out of the partially demolished crypt, a monster Graven knew too well. Corroded power armour with a bone-white, skull-shaped visor. An abacus tucked under one huge arm. The face of the kneeling Battle Sister turned ashen at the sight of such an abomination in this sacred space.

The Tallyman!

XVII

Sister Superior Serafina heard the blast from inside the Grand Mausoleum and knew exactly what it meant.

She had failed her beloved saint, failed the Emperor Himself, and she could feel their disappointment in her. It stoked a white-hot rage in her breast.

Seeing Graven headed for the gates, she had tried to intercept him, but turning her back on his masked thralls, she had been borne to the ground by four of them. With a series of screamed invectives, she shook the last one from her.

Her sin had been overconfidence. She had underestimated Krieg resolve. No matter the wounds inflicted upon them, they fought to their last breaths. *And so they shall!* She swore that every one of them, every Death Korpsman on this planet, would die for what they had wrought today.

They were already on the ropes. Now, a Vostroyan Firstborn squad raced onto the scene and, sizing up the situation, laid into the Krieg from behind. Their fates were sealed. *But Petrakov acted too late, as I knew he would.* They would go to their graves well satisfied with today's ill deeds.

Another Korpsman came at Serafina, and she put a bolt round in his head. Her righteous vengeance tasted like ash on her tongue.

'S-sister… Superior…'

She recognised Elvana's voice, but cracked and feeble. Her sister had stumbled through the broken gates, teetering on the mausoleum steps. She was bloodied and battered, had lost her chainsword, and – *Emperor!* – what had happened to her eye?

'The… crypt,' she wheezed. 'The crypt is…'

A figure appeared in the gateway behind her, and Serafina's breath caught in her throat. A Traitor Space Marine. One whose presence on Oleris III she had been informed of but had scoffed at, distrusting the source of the report. *Where did it come from? How could it possibly be here?*

She saw a plasma pistol raised, its muzzle pressed to the back of Elvana's head. A gauntleted finger tightened on a trigger. Cruelly, time slowed for Serafina, allowing the full horror of what she was seeing to sink in, and yet she had no time to move a muscle. Flames engulfed her sister's ruined face. Her headless body toppled down the steps.

Serafina heard the Tallyman's booming proclamation: *'One!'*

Now, through the gates, between its feet, streamed dozens of diminutive horned creatures, their clammy flesh a sickly green in colour, rotted entrails spilling from ruptures in distended stomachs.

Nurglings! Daemonic harbingers of the Great Unclean Ones. Graven had been right all along, but she had been too blind to see it.

Around her, Battle Sisters and Death Korpsmen saw it too, disengaging from one another, bracing themselves as Nurglings swept towards them. One came at Serafina, its pinpoint eyes gleaming with malevolence, a mouth full of razor-sharp teeth twisted into a sneer. She sidestepped it, setting her sights on the creatures' master.

Her rage had a new focus now. She released it in a scream as she mounted the mausoleum steps. She thumbed her bolter to full-auto, sending out a deadly spray ahead of her. The Tally-man shuddered as bolt rounds pinged off its armour, drawing its attention to her.

Its plasma pistol turned in her direction.

The Attilans had split up. The watchmaster heard their hoof-beats from every direction, closing in around him. Too many of them. Running for his life, he had thrown off his pursuing Battle Sister some time ago. Or else she had given up the hunt to return to her post, believing his execution assured.

Might that buy him time to explain himself to Sergeant Batu?

He doubted she would listen. In her eyes, he had betrayed her. Her angry voice echoed around the tombs: 'Nowhere to run, Watchmaster No-Name. The longer it takes to ride you down, the more you suffer!'

He had seen Batu's suspicions in her eyes when she had cornered him. There hadn't been time to talk to her. Had he tried to run, she would have caught him and held him for the Sister on his heels. Once she calmed down, she might see that he had aimed to wound, not kill. Perhaps when – if – he too had time to think, then he might understand why he had taken such a risk.

He was almost back at the mausoleum. He heard the battle still in progress there. Suddenly, a figure came hurtling around a nearby corner, almost colliding with him. His squad's former engineer. For just half a second, they looked at each other uncertainly.

Chances were, the engineer still had a Sister tailing him. The watchmaster weighed up their options. His ears discerned no safe direction for them.

'This way,' he decided, and they turned and raced towards the battle.

In front of the mausoleum, spilling out of its forecourt to the walls of the tombs around it, Krieg and Vostroyans were fighting. Not each other, as the watchmaster had expected, but… He couldn't tell. Until, setting his sights lower, he saw daemons scampering between the soldiers' feet, snapping at their thighs and calves.

On the mausoleum steps, he saw a quartet of Battle Sisters, the Sister Superior among them, battering at the obdurate form of a Traitor Marine, one he recognised at once from his colonel's description.

He felt a rush of relief, then one of guilt. His faith in Graven had not been misplaced. *Better for this world if it had been.* Still, his duty was now crystal clear. He needed to say nothing to the engineer beside him. In unison, they drew their bayonets and plunged into the fray.

The watchmaster joined a trio of Vostroyans, stabbing at a snarling, spitting, foot-high daemon. It writhed and twisted away from their blows, but they kept it hemmed between them, and a few palpable hits tore its flesh. The watchmaster punctured a pulsating pustule on the daemon's neck, which erupted with malodorous green pus. It flew at him, razor teeth bared.

Stepping out of its way, he collided with someone behind him – who, whirling, snapped up her lasgun. Krieg and Vostroyan locked mistrustful gazes, then the latter nodded and, lowering her weapon, turned away.

The daemon, in the meantime, had been dealt with, toppled

onto its back and shredded. The watchmaster sought another target. He found one, just a step away. It had sunk its teeth into a Korpsman's leg and, no matter how he stabbed and clubbed at it, wasn't letting go. The watchmaster's bayonet skewered it. He wrenched it off its victim, unleashing a welter of his blood. He dashed the squirming creature to the ground, repeatedly, until it was a bloody pulp.

These things were neither durable nor strong. At a glance, the wound inflicted by the daemon's bite seemed neither large nor deep. The problem was that, like the zombies, they were certainly diseased. The toll taken by them would increase in the days to come, by drawn-out, painful deaths.

Right now, the Krieg and their allies were still fighting, getting the measure of their slippery opponents. They were teaming up in threes and fours, methodically despatching one daemon at a time. Two more Krieg squads emerged from the surrounding tombs, while a thunder of hooves heralded the reappearance of Batu's Attilan Rough Riders.

The daemons were all but beaten now, but the watchmaster feared they had only been meant to distract. The critical battle still raged at the mausoleum gates. The Sisters of Battle were trying to wrest the Tallyman's pistol from it – without success, but at least they were keeping it from shooting into the melee. Three plasma bolts burst from its muzzle, the first streaking skyward, the other two harmlessly over the combatants' heads.

The Sisters scattered at their leader's warning shout. The pistol glowed white-hot, shedding waves of electricity, which swarmed up the Tallyman's arm. It made as if to cast away the weapon, but found its gauntlet locked to it.

The pistol exploded: a gun butt must have cracked it, or its wielder had pushed it past the point of overload. The Tallyman, thrown backwards, collided with a mangled iron gate, wrenching it from its remaining hinge. Failing to arrest its fall, it crashed down in a metal heap.

The Sisters, having dived for cover, mounted the steps again. Their foe was hauling itself back to its feet, but surely they would be upon it first.

The watchmaster missed what happened next, having his own concerns. A daemon had slipped through a knot of Guardsmen, and he stepped forward to intercept it. He snatched away his foot as the pustulant creature lunged at it, and it floundered on its distended stomach in the mud.

As soon as it was dealt with, two comrades having speeded its demise, he glanced back at the mausoleum steps and was dismayed to find the situation there changed for the worse.

Now there were beastmen present, a heaving black mass of them, pouring from the mausoleum. Forced to fall back again, the Sisters formed a defensive line at the bottom of the steps. It was no use. The creatures bulled, gored, trampled their way through it, adding to the unruly scrum in the forecourt and beyond.

Nor were they alone. In the gateway behind them appeared more human-seeming figures. One was a withered crone, leaning on a walking stick, but when she spread her fingers she summoned lightning to them from the sky and moulded it into a ball, which she flung like a grenade. Idelax had described such a witch. The lightning struck a Sister in the chest and, despite her power armour, felled her.

A second and third witch wielded fire and force, like the ones he had encountered days before. The latter came marching down the steps, with the fire and lightning witches on his heels. Two Sisters standing in his path were sent sprawling by a mere sweep of his arm.

Remaining above, a nervous-looking boy wrapped a cloak

about himself and closed his eyes, or rather, just his human eyes. A clutch of additional, green-glowing orbs opened on his forehead, on his cheeks, as he began to mutter to himself. Beside him, an alabaster-skinned, ebony-haired woman looked out with disdain on her lips. Her eyes locked briefly with the watchmaster's gaze across the intervening throng, and an instant later she was gone. Like a trick of the light.

The Imperial forces now had a real fight on their hands.

The Tallyman was also back up, armour scorched black by the plasma explosion, dripping rivulets of molten metal, but standing just as tall as ever. Bereft of its weapon, it seemed content to stand atop the steps and watch the mayhem playing out before it, recording each Imperial death on its abacus' beads. Its voice sounded clear above the tumult: *'Five! Six!'*

Then, with malicious satisfaction as it slid the final bead across the first rod, *'Seven!'*

Graven descended into darkness.

He made no effort to resist it. It was his time. He was at peace.

His peace was shattered. Roars of triumph filled his ears. He plummeted towards a seething mass of zombies – dead comrades in the tatters of their uniforms – and he remembered being here before, this nightmare pit.

He fell into their clutches, borne on a heaving raft of bony shoulders. Emperor, but there were so many! They jostled each other in their eagerness to reach him. They pulled and clawed at him. He thought they might tear his limbs from their sockets. They divested Graven of his weapons, his helmet, his badges of rank, reducing him to one of them again.

He glimpsed bodies fresher than the rest, having not begun to rot. The dead as yet uncounted, whose sacrifices had paved his way to the mausoleum. He heard their voices louder than the others. They didn't understand what they had done to earn such ignominious fates. They blamed him too.

Like a scrumball, Graven was tossed from one part of the crowd to another. It felt like every zombie took a turn inflicting its revenge upon him. Then, just as he felt the torture might never end, the crowd parted and he fell through them, to land like a wet sack in mud.

Squelching footsteps approached him. Graven raised himself onto his hands and knees. He forced himself to do the last thing he wished to do: look up.

He already knew who he would see.

The watchmaster couldn't find a target.

The mausoleum's forecourt and the space around it were crammed with thrusting bodies. A deer-headed beastman, lowering its antlers, had ploughed into the crush. Death Korpsmen and Vostroyans, scrambling away from it, stumbled into each other. A comrade collided with the watchmaster, and he fought to keep them both standing.

He saw a little daemon, but red greatcoats closed about it. Bright bursts of fire and lightning told him the positions of two witches, but Krieg helmets blocked his bolt pistol's sights. Attilan horses wheeled about the edges of the melee, their riders seeking sightlines too. He had no overview of the situation, couldn't issue orders and knew few would hear him anyway.

He kept himself alert, bided his time, until a gap opened through which he saw the crazed eyes of a goat-like beastman. Gladly he closed with it, his bayonet ringing off its combat knife. He used the crush to his advantage, as the physically weaker but more skilled combatant. Feinting, the watchmaster drew the maddened creature after him. A hoof snagged on a daemon's body that it hadn't seen, stealing its balance for a crucial instant, during which he shot it point-blank in the face.

Howling, the beastman fell and was trampled underfoot. Hearing another cry, more human, alongside him, the watchmaster spun around. A Vostroyan sergeant clutched her throat, blood welling over her gorget, through her fingers. She crumpled, but the watchmaster could see no attacker. *Sorcery!*

The crowd shifted, more confused than ever, and suddenly a Korpsman yelled, 'There's something here, something we can't–' The warning was choked off – he was thrashing as if beset by unseen daemons. The watchmaster fought to make it to him, as blood spilled from the Korpsman's throat too.

He recalled the testimony of Vostroyan Guardsman Bukharin, possessed but lacing his lies with truth. *'Without us seeing their approach, there were three of them among us.'* An invisible enemy. *The witch I saw vanish from the steps!*

Others had worked it out too. 'I felt it! It went that way! There!' Blades jabbed, hands snatched at empty air, and suddenly, between them, appeared not the witch as the watchmaster had expected, but something even more disturbing: a shapeless, glistening, blood-red mound of eyes and mouths and thrashing tentacles.

The soldiers closest to it reacted with horror, but then, as their training kicked in, being trapped with it anyway, determinedly set about it.

Something held the watchmaster back, but he couldn't quite grasp what it was. Looking at the monster made his brain itch. It didn't react to the blows rained down upon it. Nor did it try to fight back. His every sense warned him of its dark presence, its palpable threat, but blades drew no blood from the monster, meeting no resistance as they plunged into its quivering form.

He wrenched his gaze from it. *From what is it meant to distract me?*

The attack came from behind him: a slender arm thrown about his neck, a small, sharp knife pressed to his throat. The witch must have seen his stripes and chosen him as her next victim. Anticipating her – if only by a fraction of a second – the watchmaster reacted to her touch, throwing off her hold before it could be tightened, rounding on her, lashing out. His elbow struck flesh, followed by his bayonet, which elicited a disembodied shriek.

His next thrust missed its mark. The witch was running, panicking, attempting to barge rather than wend through the melee, thus marking her path by the disturbance she created. The watchmaster waded after her, shouting for attention. Enough of his comrades, hearing, braced themselves against her, and now he knew her position from the ring of Death Korpsmen penning her in.

From the corner of his eye, he saw that the tentacled monster had vanished. The witch appeared, where he had known she was. Her once-pale skin was flushed. She held her slashed right arm against her chest. Scowling in concentration, the witch took a long, deep breath. A breath that didn't seem to end.

'Kill her,' the watchmaster bellowed, 'before she can...' *Do what?* The air felt charged, as though she was sucking something from it. Her chest continued to swell. Despite the close quarters, he risked a shot at her, which struck her in the stomach. Grunting, the witch stumbled back into his comrades, who gleefully bayoneted her.

She emptied her lungs in a scream that tore the world open.

Warp horrors tumbled through the rifts into the watchmaster's mind. With ease, they smashed through his too-flimsy psychic defences. Throwing his hands to his ears – he must have dropped his weapons without knowing it – couldn't blunt the dreadful sound. Resistance was futile. *As futile as life itself.* The scream grew louder, shriller. He was blind, his brain throbbing fit to explode.

Then the sound ceased and the pressure behind his eyes relented.

The witch's scream had been choked off by a death rattle. Blood poured from every orifice in her head as she fell to her knees. They had hurt her enough, thank the Emperor, so the effort of the scream had killed her before it could kill them. Her limbs still twitched and her lips mouthed meaningless words, but her staring eyes were dead.

A slavering, lupine beastman lunged at Serafina's face.

She chided herself as she threw up an arm to block it. Distracted, she had let it get too close. The creature howled as its teeth broke on her vambrace. She pushed it away, into a pair of Krieg Death Korpsmen, who gladly set about it.

Her attention had already returned to the Tallyman. It stood atop the steps, sliding beads across its abacus with every Imperial death it witnessed. Lesser foes had kept her from it, until now. Having cursed the Krieg's tenacity minutes ago, now she was grateful for it. She realised that, even after all, they were closing ranks to keep the beastmen from her ordained Sisters.

They had bought her the respite she had been craving.

'Sisters, to me!' she commanded. As many as could strove to reach her across the heaving forecourt. Three made it. It would have to be enough.

Mounting the mausoleum steps, they strafed the Traitor Marine with their bolters. The Sister Superior prayed that, damaged as its power armour was, a few rounds might get through. She was disappointed. Another bead was slid, another number intoned in a voice like a rasp across her nerves.

'We need to get in closer,' she fumed, 'pry it out of that shell with our blades.'

Their barrage had had one effect. Startled, the multi-eyed boy-witch in the gateway jerked out of his mysterious trance and shrank behind his armoured ally for protection. The Tallyman gripped him by the scruff of his hessian cloak and hurled him down the steps towards the oncoming foes.

Equally disdainfully, Serafina batted him aside. *Let the Krieg have him!* Her sights remained fixed on a bone skull visor, through which green eyes returned her glare with apparent indifference. A chance to atone for her mistakes. *As if I ever could.* A chance to avenge her closest sister's death, at least.

She might have screamed something to that effect as she crashed into the Traitor Marine. It felt like colliding with a tank. Despite her own armour, she feared her shoulder had been dislocated. Her three Battle Sisters were right with her. Last time, they had deprived the Tallyman of its most powerful weapon. This time, they had to do much worse.

Serafina snatched at the monster's wrist but couldn't hold it as it punched a Sister's head and snapped her neck. On impulse, she lunged for its abacus and shuffled its beads, which had the desired effect. The Tallyman roared with indignation and focused on dislodging her. It winced as another Sister found a weak spot in its armour, sliding a dagger into its side.

The Tallyman shook Serafina off. She landed in an undignified heap on her rump. Though she leapt straight back to her feet, she saw that her Sisters too were disarrayed, while their foe appeared to have shrugged off its wound. Four Sisters – three already – weren't enough to take it down.

She was not strong enough.

Little remained of Colonel Kleber, Graven's old commanding officer.

Burnt cloth and burnt flesh clung to his half-melted bones. His crested helmet balanced on a leering skull, the right side of which had drooped, elongating its eye socket. The cadaver's right foot dragged as it lurched up to the prone Graven, glared down at him.

Graven's voice rasped from a dry throat. 'Sir, forgive me, please. I know I disobeyed your orders.'

A swell of noise threatened to drown out his plea. It was a sound he hadn't heard before. A harsh, staccato sound. A cruel sound. The sound of hundreds of Death Korpsmen of Krieg laughing at him. He tried to ignore them, to continue, 'I believed I acted for the greater good.'

Kleber dropped to his haunches, fixing Graven with his damaged stare and rictus grin. His voice was cold like death itself. *'Captain Graven, I forgive you.'*

Graven blinked at him, nonplussed.

'I forgive you – for all but your insufferable naivety.' The laughter around him grew in volume. *'For believing that life matters.'*

'Colonel, what are you saying?'

'You shortened our lives by an eye-blink. We'd have thrown them away for as little, soon enough. What is life, after all, but a journey back to death, a brief respite from never-ending torment?'

'No. No, death is peace. Death is atonement.'

'A lie we were told to preserve our sanity and ensure compliance. But there is no peace here, Graven, and atonement is a dream.'

'But the Emperor!'

'Will never release Krieg from its wretched servitude. A millennium and a half after one man's original sin, surely that is evident by now?'

He was right. It did seem clear to Graven, as if a fog was lifting from his mind. Now that it was too late. Every doubt ever to cross his mind and heart, that he had pushed away. He should have listened to himself. He remembered every battle he had fought in, each victory, each loss. What peace had they ever brought? His life – the lives of generations of his people, billions upon billions of brainwashed drones – had meant nothing, had counted for nothing. They meant nothing.

'No sacrifice can ever be enough,' his old, dead colonel taunted him.

A sensation new to Graven gripped his chest, as if to crush it. He didn't have a name for it, but as it drained his scant remaining strength, as a pitiful whine escaped his throat and all he wanted was to curl up into a foetal ball and fade away, the word came to him: *Despair!*

Despair such as the Krieg looked in the eye each moment of their hopeless lives. Looked in its eye and spat in it.

With that new understanding, there came light.

Graven couldn't comprehend it, because how could there possibly be light in this ultimate darkness? The light, however, would not be denied, and the laughter of the ghosts around him petered out as they retreated with the shadows.

Ghosts! He remembered the grave worker, Rayoul, and his spectre-induced lies. Remembering how certain he had been then, Graven felt his heart stirring with an echo of that faith. *Kleber spoke the very same words to me,* he realised, *in the same voice too. A spectre's voice. How did I not see that before?*

His head had drooped, but he raised it again.

Colonel Kleber still stood over him, but somehow he seemed shorter. Golden light streamed about him, transfixing him in writhing pain. It stripped away the shadows with which he had disguised himself, and Graven saw him – saw it – as it truly was. A gaunt, daemonic figure, its skull-mouth open in a silent scream.

The light built in intensity until it blinded him, but he didn't try to close his eyes. Or were they already closed? After what seemed like minutes, the light faded, leaving nothing of the daemon. Graven felt as if a portion of its glow remained within him.

Blinking, he began to make out shapes around him. The

galleries of the mausoleum. He felt its tiled floor beneath his hands. *Alive!* He was looking up into Saint Josefina's eyes. As always, she was wreathed in golden candlelight. The same light that had saved him? Had anything – the light, even the daemon and its whispers – been real? He couldn't tell. He couldn't summon up a prayer expansive enough for what he had experienced.

Then the memory of the Tallyman rushed back to him. That horror, however, was nowhere to be seen. Hearing the battle without, its sounds muffled by thick stone walls, Graven knew why he was back here.

His back ached where the Sister's blade had pierced it, but the bleeding appeared to have been stemmed. His body, which before had felt so heavy, was reinvigorated. He picked himself up. From the chamber's edges, a couple of near-mindless servitors watched him in bewilderment.

Graven snatched up his power sword. Gripped by a fresh sense of purpose, he marched towards the narthex. His pace was unhurried. He had utter faith that however long he took would be the right amount of time. Thus had it been ordained.

The gateway loomed ahead of him, his foe's substantial form framed by it. The Tallyman made its stand on the broad stone steps, its back turned to him. Three Battle Sisters, including Serafina, stabbed and battered furiously at it. It had lost its plasma pistol. Its scarred and dented, partially melted armour leaked green pus, promethium and blood, but it endured.

It swung its abacus, caught a Sister's jaw and sent her flying down the steps. Now there were only two. Shooting out, its hand seized Serafina's throat. She gasped and spluttered as she was lifted from the ground, servo-assisted metal-encased fingers in the process of crushing her larynx.

Calmly, unhurriedly, Colonel Graven took two steps. He spied a crack between corroded plates of power armour. He thrust his burning sword up into that crack, through the Tallyman's back, and out through its chest.

XVIII

With the Tallyman's fall, the battle was all but decided.

Colonel Petrakov arrived later than he would have liked. Having had to abandon his Salamander outside the necropolis, he had rounded up four Vostroyan squads to lead through its narrow byways. Few zombies remained, but ill fortune had contrived to strew them in his path.

As far as he was able, while fighting for his life, he had parsed the curt, breathless reports in his comm-bead's earpiece. He had heard of Imperial gains and losses in, it seemed, equal measure. Back on the move, almost at his destination, he had hoped to tip the balance.

Graven! he had thought sourly, upon hearing the news – from three sources, overlapping, unable to hide the admiration in their voices. *Why did it have to be Graven?* A churlish thought, he knew. He pushed it aside as, rounding one last corner, he blinked in the mausoleum's lights.

A goat-faced beastman came barrelling towards him. Petrakov

snapped up his lasgun, but before he could fire it, two Guardsmen stepped in front of him. More joined them, piling on the bleating creature – which, he realised, was already wounded and had been attempting to flee.

He sent his soldiers forward into the scrum. Petrakov himself held back, appraising the situation, judging it too chaotic to risk firing at the few foes he could see. He clicked his fingers and an aide rushed forwards, placing in them his best weapon in the circumstances. A laud hailer.

His amplified voice impressed upon the heretics the full force of his rank, his people's noble reputation and the Emperor's authority vested in him. 'Surrender,' he enjoined them. 'Throw yourselves at His mercy.'

The beastmen fought on, not so dull-witted as to be unaware that the only mercy on the table for them was a speedy execution. The witches must have known it too, but one at least retained the naivety of youth.

The boy-witch knelt at the foot of the mausoleum steps. His extra eyes had withered, their green glows extinguished. To the nearest Battle Sister, he entreated, 'Please, the... the thing they put inside me, it fled when it foresaw that all was lost. I'm free again.' He broke down, racked with shuddering sobs.

Whether or not he spoke the truth was immaterial. A bolt round through one of those vestigial eyes cleansed the world of his infection.

Despite their continued resistance, the heretics appeared to have lost heart and, with it, strength. Or perhaps it was that the Imperial defenders had gained both. There was a moment when that could have changed. The Krieg watchmaster was one of the first to see a spectre as it sprang up through the ground between his feet. He felt its frigid presence in his bones, but it didn't attack him.

He followed its flight into the sky, where it congregated with more of its kind. Their emergence caused a stir down on the battlefield, where many had not seen their like before. A few fired up into the gathering shadows, in vain.

'They can only harm those who doubt or fear them,' the watchmaster reminded all within reach of his voice – not many, but the call was quickly taken up by others, including eventually by Petrakov on the melee's edge with his laud hailer, and the truth of it was soon evidenced to all.

A few spectres broke off from the pack and, choosing targets, swooped upon them. They found themselves resisted long enough to be assailed in turn. Blades sliced into their briefly solid forms and, as they fled, beams of light holed their tattered shadows. They had arrived too late, with too few allies surviving to distract for them. More pertinently, they had materialised after the Tallyman's fall, to face foes whose hearts held few doubts any longer.

The ghastly apparitions circled at a distance, ironically beset by doubts themselves. Then, one by one, they faded.

Sergeant Batu witnessed the fire witch's fall, one last bolt from his fingers immolating an unfortunate Death Korpsman before his flesh was shredded. She wished her own sabre could have reached him, but her mounted squads were better employed on the battle's edges. Any beastman pushed this far was liable to have its skull cracked by mauling hooves.

Just once, through the melee, did she glimpse a Krieg watchmaster. *My watchmaster,* she felt certain, whom she had pursued here. He was fighting a simian beastman. Fighting for the Emperor, as fiercely as any other soldier. She felt relieved, but still angry and confused. Conflicting emotions burnt in Batu's breast, her arm aching from his bolt. For now, they appeared to be allies again – but later?

Whatever my orders, I follow them, she swore to herself, clenching her teeth. *I don't need to know the reasons – and whoever is deemed to be my enemy, they had best beware!*

Finally, Sister Superior Serafina gained a moment to look around her. She judged that the threat out here was being handled. So, she gathered her Battle Sisters to her – four were able to answer the call – and they marched up the steps across which the hulking carcass of the Tallyman lay sprawled.

Serafina fixed her eyes ahead of her as she stepped over Elvana's body on the mausoleum's threshold. The sight of the sundered crypt within, although expected, hurt her heart. She picked her way through scattered rubble. She listened, but heard nothing from below.

With much trepidation, she clambered down into the sacred space. A broad enough route had been cleared by the Tallyman's exit. She had thought she might find witches down here yet, regrouping to conduct more profane rituals. A part of her, still itching to mete out bloody vengeance, hoped so.

She found only bodies crushed by falling stones and the rest of the witches – if indeed there had been more – fled along a hole gouged from a rockcrete wall, leading no doubt to the ossuary tunnels.

And one more thing, the very worst of all.

Colonel Graven knew nothing of any of this. Not until later, when he woke in a hospital bed.

After slaying the Tallyman, he had staggered down the mausoleum steps, but had no recollection of reaching the bottom. An overwhelming tiredness had washed over him, as if a dam holding it back had burst. He had fought it, there still being work to do, but darkness had again enshrouded him.

This time, it had felt different. This time, he had not fallen far. No pit of despair had yawned beneath him. He had been left to rest.

Three days had passed. Graven woke with stitches pulling at his skin, attached to monitors and drips. A Vostroyan chirurgeon impressed upon him the extent of his good fortune. Sister Elvana's dagger had only nicked his vital organs. The concoction of drugs with which his respirator laced his air and water had slowed his bleeding long enough for help to reach him.

He said nothing. *Let him have his rationales.*

Graven sent for his watchmaster, who was at his side in minutes, updating him on all that he had missed. 'Even the Vostroyans are calling you a hero, sir,' he said, 'for exposing the witches before they were fully prepared. That would not have been possible had we waited as Colonel Petrakov insisted.'

He waved the praise away. 'How many casualties?'

'Still being tabulated, sir, but close to forty. Including four from our own squad. A small price for what we have achieved here.'

Graven didn't disagree. In any other regiment, forty Korpsmen would be easily replaced. For his regiment, their deaths – no matter how well they had counted – were another significant stride along the path to dissolution.

The watchmaster added, 'Perhaps a handful more to come.'

The colonel's eyes narrowed behind his mask. 'The plague?'

'The victims have been quarantined in tents out in the fields, staffed by our own medics, as they are best protected. Some are recovering, others not. The good news is that the disease hasn't spread beyond those scratched by the zombies' nails.'

'Good news indeed.'

'Like the witches themselves, it cannot yet have reached full potency.'

'What of the witches now? Some must remain.'

'If so, they cower underground. Petrakov has sent squads back into the tunnels, but so far they've had little to report. In the meantime, grave workers have been returning to the hamlets. Most claim they were compelled to serve the witches, or never did but hid out from them.'

'Yes, no doubt they do.'

'The Ordo Hereticus will weed out the guilty from the innocent. They sent an astropathic message. On Inquisitor Idelax's recommendation, they will purge Oleris III once and for all, so that no trace of its blight remains.'

'Timescale?' asked Graven, warily.

'Within weeks.'

'Could anybody on this world remain untainted?' the colonel mused.

'We collected our original Chimera from the hamlet where we left it. On our way back, we called in on Sanctuary. Its refugees have not laid down their arms. Only those whose recent whereabouts are proven may rejoin them. Some, who attempted to force entrance, are now staked out in the fields.'

'They may be the only ones spared.' Graven sighed. 'Either way, I expect the work will take months or even years.'

'The Vostroyans will remain to see it through.'

'Petrakov has decreed this?'

'He disbanded his army and officially released its other regiments. Captain Graff contacted the Departmento Munitorum. We have a new assignment, and a troop ship will arrive in four days' time to take us to it.'

Graven was surprised, but pleased. *Months spent underground in a labyrinth of bones, excavating heretics from their hiding places!* Most commanders with a Death Korps regiment available to them would have considered them the perfect fit for such a task. Not this time.

Not the 401st Krieg Regiment. No longer.

* * *

The chamber lay in deathly silence.

Evening prayer was over, the chapel emptied out. The Grand Mausoleum's custodians slumbered in their cells, with only a handful of cleaning servitors awake to shuffle around the high galleries.

Sister Superior Serafina had not slept. Not tonight. Nor for any of the five nights prior, but in fitful dozes. She had not visited the temple, had not wanted to face her Sisters. She had locked herself away with her guilt and her prayers.

She had sent word of her failure to her Palatine, who would decide her punishment. This morning, the thought had occurred to her that she was being cowardly. There was someone else she had to face. She had waited until she could do so alone.

She was not happy, then, to find another person in the chamber, even less to recognise him. Graven. The Krieg colonel knelt before Saint Josefina's statue. The hole in the side of her crypt had been braced and the rubble from it shifted. The damage was still glaring. The candles behind the saint burnt, but the light with which they suffused her no longer seemed holy, but desultory.

Serafina considered turning back, but Graven had seen her.

He stood. 'Sister Superior. I feel I must apologise.'

'No,' she cut across him, harsher than intended. He had destroyed everything she ever loved. Her heart still hated him. She knew that was unjust. *Would I rather have remained in blissful ignorance?* She channelled her hate inward, upon the part of herself that would have. 'You have naught to say to me.'

Graven inclined his head and said nothing.

'Why are you here?' asked Serafina, picking at the wound.

'I was granted permission.'

'I'm sure, but for what purpose? In hope of seeing me?' *To taunt me?*

He paused as if puzzled by the question before answering, 'To commune with the sainted Josefina.'

'Then your time has been wasted, for she is not here.'

'I beg to differ.'

'Did you step into her crypt, Colonel Graven?' Serafina snapped. 'Did you see down inside it as you blasted your way through its wall?'

'No, I did not.'

'If you had, then you would know. You would have seen.' The memory of it almost choked her. The ornate casket smashed to pieces. A black altar planted in its wreckage. The rubble had been sifted since, but no fragment of bone recovered. The Sister Superior took a deep, shuddering breath. 'Nothing remains.'

'Saint Josefina saved me,' said Graven.

'She cannot have.'

'I had been dealt a mortal blow. She bathed me in her holy light. She healed me as she healed the victims of the Chaos plague.'

'Your own strength saved you, Colonel Graven. The rest was a mere trick of the mind as you lay bleeding. I feel nothing.'

But he was relentless. 'So what if the witches burnt her bones? They are only remains. Sister Superior, I feel Saint Josefina's presence. In this monument devoted to her memory, I feel sure I have her blessing. A delusion that may be, but if I draw strength from it, from the example of her life, then what matters the distinction?'

Serafina ached to believe him, but how could she? It was said that, on Oleris III, the veil between life and death was stretched thin…

'I feel nothing,' said Serafina, bluntly.

She had come here hoping for something, but she couldn't fool herself. *So, either Graven is mistaken or our saint bestows her blessing upon him and not me!* Instinctively, she knew which option she preferred, and that choice made her even more wretched.

'I feel nothing,' she repeated, and she turned and marched back to her cell with its four plain walls and holy symbols and its waiting scourge.

The Krieg prepared for their imminent departure. They pulled their artillery platforms back from disused trenches. They serviced and refuelled muddy vehicles.

Striking their storehouse, they loaded their dwindling supplies into armoured carriers. The effort of unloading them, just half a month before, seemed almost wasted. They were still getting used to these shorter engagements.

No hands were left idle, as spare Korpsmen joined work parties, repairing the Ecclesiarchal Tower for its forthcoming occupants. The skull that glared down from its side might now have approved of what it saw.

Captain Graff assumed command with Graven indisposed. The watchmaster didn't know him – such was the atomised nature of his regiment's new structure – and the officer spared no time for him. Perhaps he felt slighted that Graven had kept his plans from him but confided in his lower-ranking squadmate.

Skarangard and her fellow commissars spoke often with Graff, as they did with the Vostroyan and Attilan colonels. The watchmaster was happy not to be included in those meetings. *Let the commissars do what they do best.*

The Attilan Rough Riders shipped out just two days before the Krieg did. As they mustered in the command compound, the watchmaster spent the day indoors. He busied himself filling out reports and maintaining his personal equipment. The background whickering and snorting of warhorses reminded him of old times, but he resisted the urge to look out at them.

By morning, the Attilans, along with their horses, were gone. The compound was left looking empty, strewn with heaps of fresh manure. Too late, the watchmaster regretted his diffidence. He should have sought out the ally he had shot – *betrayed?* – and ensured there was no misunderstanding.

For what purpose? Away from the battlefield, what did it matter if Sergeant Batu trusted him or not? *She understands,* he told himself. *By now, she knows the truth and must see why I acted as I did, so what more is required?* Had she needed to discuss the matter with him – had she any wish to see him – she could easily have found him. *So, why didn't she?* He would likely never know as they would never meet again.

The watchmaster wished he had told her his name.

It was raining on Oleris III as the drop-ships descended upon it.

A column of artillery platforms and armoured vehicles ground along the muddy tracks to greet them. Inside the command compound, the final Krieg Chimera idled in the fading evening light, awaiting its final passenger.

Graven had been summoned. Colonel Petrakov wished to speak with him before he left the planet. The pair had not met in over a week. Only yesterday had Graven been discharged from the medicae hut – more accurately, discharged himself. Only his watchmaster and Commissar Skarangard had visited him there.

Petrakov stood at his desk, hands clasped behind his back. He wore his tall fur hat. His greatcoat's brass buttons gleamed.

Graven felt as apprehensive as on any battlefield. The Vostroyan had had time to stew over recent events. Technically, he was duty-bound to report Graven's flouting of his orders, regardless of later revelations, and he was nothing if not a stickler for rules. A second tribunal, whatever the outcome, would surely end Graven's career – and then what of the 401st?

'I don't believe he'll do it,' Skarangard had said. *'He knows now, everybody knows, that you were right. He'd be the one facing court-martial but for you – or dead. He is ashamed to face you, only honour demands that he does.'*

Petrakov faced Graven now, his hooded eyes offering no clue to what he might be thinking. His thin moustache twitched.

'Colonel Graven,' he said, stiffly. He leaned forward, extending his right hand across the desk. 'Thank you for your valuable service.'

Nonplussed, Graven took the hand and shook it. That appeared to be all the Vostroyan had to say. The two colonels stood until the silence between them grew awkward. Graven wondered if Petrakov knew how lucky he had been. Soldiers of three regiments had died for his misjudgement, but relatively few. His dreams, for the most part, would be haunted by the ghosts of might-have-been.

They would be haunted all the same.

It would only help a little that his reasons had been valid. Who could blame him for siding with the Adepta Sororitas over an officer with Graven's chequered history? For erring on the side of caution when all around him spectres seeded doubt?

Graven could have told him this, but he did not. Enough people had tried to tell Graven, only he had never listened. Like him, Colonel Petrakov would have to work through his issues for himself.

Without a word, he turned and left the room.

An hour later, Graven was aboard another troop ship. Assigned to a cabin like all the other cabins. Feeling the adjustments of the artificial gravity as the great vessel hauled itself out of Oleris' orbit.

He laid out his bedroll on the floor beside his bunk. In the process, he caught his own reflection in a small, cracked mirror pasted to the bulkhead above a small, cracked basin. Something about it drew his eye. Something looked wrong. *Of course!* The claw marks on the cheek of his rebreather mask, inflicted upon him by a dead man in an underground charnel house. He had forgotten about them.

His gaze lingered on the image in the glass. Graven couldn't have said why. He traced the three scars with his fingertips. *'Even the Vostroyans are calling you a hero.'* He was certainly no hero. He failed to see how any Krieg Korpsman ever could be. *Our founder, perhaps. We others only follow in his footsteps.*

Tomorrow, he would find a quartermaster, have the mask replaced. If he had time. Its scars seemed almost fitting, matching how he felt inside. His people never showed their scars, but that didn't mean they didn't have them.

Tomorrow, there would be plans to make, briefings to give, squads to reorganise, resources to reallocate. The day after that, his regiment would reach its destination, where its next test already waited.

Graven needed rest, but even as he lay and closed his eyes, he felt the troop ship's lurch into the immaterium. Warp space. The domain of the dead. He felt its horrors scratching at his mind and, wearily, resigned himself to his nightly battle. As the dreams came upon him, however, the voices of his fallen comrades, even those burnt on Maximus Arkanos, were unusually muted.

He had not been forgiven, not entirely, but no longer were they quite so angry with him. His actions on Oleris III had helped to rebalance the scales. They were optimistic now that Colonel Graven and his regiment, the Relentless Dead, could do more, so much more. They urged him to fight on, for their sake. They offered him hope that, in time, he might even gain atonement.

Graven's ghosts were giving him a second chance.

* * *

The prisoner was held deep underground.

The witch hunter made the winding descent down worn stone steps into the foetid cold. The servitor jailer unlocked a cell for him. The light of sconce-mounted torches in the passageway spilled over the crumpled form therein.

The manacled prisoner looked up at her visitors pleadingly. 'Thank you,' she croaked. 'Thank you for deigning to hear my plea.'

'Speak only when Interrogator Layne demands an answer from you!' barked Colonel Petrakov, raising his lasgun in threat. The prisoner nodded. Though dressed in a grave worker's simple smock, she had blurted out her true identity when captured.

'Lady Emelian has been here before, interrogator,' Petrakov explained to his companion. 'Inquisitor Idelax sentenced her to death five months since, but before she could be–'

'I am aware of what transpired.' Layne crouched before the chained dignitary. 'Your fellow witches freed you.'

'No,' the lady protested feebly, 'not my fellows.'

'They freed you when they stormed this tower.'

'I went with them, yes. They gave me no choice. I even... Emperor forgive me, I professed to serve them, but as soon as I saw my chance I slipped away. For months, I hid out in the ossuary tunnels until...'

'She was posing as a worker in a coastal hamlet,' Petrakov supplied, standing stiffly in the doorway, 'but was soon discovered, never having done a day's work with her hands. She surrendered to my Firstborn, offering information for her life.'

'There will be no such deal,' the interrogator snarled.

'But I can tell you where to find your foes.'

'And so you shall. You'll tell me everything you know – by choice and lighten the stains upon your soul or under torture, it is all the same to me.'

The prisoner sniffed and swallowed. 'I saw traitors in the

hamlet,' she began. 'Some nights, they'd slip away to meet their masters in the tunnels and receive instructions. I... I overheard directions to the witches' temple. North from the opening behind the food store... third turning on the right, and then...'

The lady's cracked voice faded. Interrogator Layne leaned closer to her. Thus, he didn't hear – or disregarded – the three quick footsteps coming up behind him. He felt the lasgun muzzle pressed to the back of his head, too late to react. Squeezing his trigger, Colonel Petrakov boiled the interrogator's brain. Before his body hit the floor, the Vostroyan had whirled to greet the jailer, who, alerted by the weapon's crack, rushed into the cell.

He aimed for its heart, knowing that the cybernetic systems laced through its body made its brain near redundant. He missed by half an inch. The stoic servitor grunted and returned fire with the laspistol wired to the end of its left arm. Petrakov, dodging the beam, collided with the wall. As he fumbled to take aim again, the servitor leapt on him, swiping his lasgun from his hands.

'Stand down,' he barked. 'I order you as your commander-in-chief!'

The gambit wouldn't have worked on a fully-thinking soldier. The servitor, however, programmed not to question, faltered – long enough for a bolt of electricity to strike it. Crackling tendrils enwrapped its muscular body, blowing its mechanical components. It crumpled. Petrakov's nose wrinkled as a smell of burning plastek filled the cell. Lady Emelian, still chained, sat straighter now, as green fire faded from her eyes. She looked up at the Vostroyan in hope.

His lips twisted into a smirk, and she smiled in relief. 'I had heard rumours, but I didn't know for sure.'

'Not even the most arrogant of men is immune to self-doubt.' Kneeling, Petrakov snatched the jailer's keys from its belt. There were a dozen of them, hanging from a thick metal ring. He didn't have much time. He had sent his aides on fools' errands, but they never left him alone for long.

He felt the lady seething with impatience as he tried each key in turn. She warned him, 'I cannot do that again. Not soon. I am not yet strong enough.'

The fifth key worked, unsnapping a wrist manacle. Different keys were required for the others, and tense minutes passed as Petrakov searched for them.

'Will these actions not expose you?' asked the lady.

The colonel shook his head. 'The interrogator and I arrived to find an empty cell. The jailer must have freed you. It shot Layne from behind and attempted to kill me too. I shot it in return and saw a spectre fleeing from its shadow.'

The last manacle fell away with a welcome clank. Ruefully, Lady Emelian rubbed her wrists and ankles. 'How do I get out of here?'

'A new way into the catacombs. A secret way. I'll take you to it.' From his greatcoat, Petrakov produced a dataslate, handing it to her. 'You know what to do with this? You have no doubts?'

Another flash of green. 'They took my son from me, then my husband, then they tried to take my life. They sent those masked fanatics to murder us all.'

'On Oleris, we are never truly parted. You will see them both again.'

The lady nodded tearfully as Petrakov helped her to stand. 'A lifetime of blind devotion, and how was I treated for it? Abominably, let me tell you. Never once was I allowed a taste of power. Not real power such as you have shown me. My eyes are open now. I have no doubts.'

Petrakov cautioned her, 'Even in possession of this form, I cannot slow the Inquisition, only keep a step ahead of it.'

The lady understood. 'As long as one of us eludes their grasp.'

'Then we will rise again, as we have many times before.'

'And next time, or the time after, there will be a different outcome.'

They left the dingy cell together, slipping into the cold shadows of the dungeon's furthest reaches. ***'Our ultimate triumph is inevitable,'*** bragged the entity now clad in the commander-in-chief's body, ***'so we can afford to be patient.'***

'Our numbers grow with every passing day,' agreed the lady. ***'And the dead can wait forever.'***

ABOUT THE AUTHOR

Steve Lyons' work in the Warhammer 40,000 universe includes the novellas *Iron Resolve, Engines of War* and *Angron's Monolith,* the Astra Militarum novels *Death World, Ice Guard, Dead Men Walking, Krieg, The Relentless Dead* and *Siege of Vraks,* and the audio dramas *Waiting Death* and *The Madness Within.* He has also written numerous short stories and is currently working on more tales from the grim darkness of the far future.

MORE FROM BLACK LIBRARY

MINKA LESK: THE LAST WHITESHIELD

by Justin D Hill

Cadia has stood in grim defiance against the enemies of the Imperium for ten thousand years, an indomitable bulwark against the forces of Chaos… but now, the 13th Black Crusade has come, and there will be no victory. Here, Minka Lesk will be tested in the very fires of a world's destruction.
